Too Close to the Sun

Wendy Newman

Dedication

For my mum, Trish, who is not around to see my second book published.

And, as ever, to my wonderful husband Paul.

Biography

Wendy Newman is the author of two published books and Too Close to the Sun is the continuation of Malavita, the story of the Delvecchio Family. It is also excellent as a stand alone story.

Wendy now lives in Cornwall with husband Paul and much loved dog, Ned. When not writing, Wendy loves exploring the beautiful county of Cornwall with Ned the Border Collie.

The third and final instalment of this series is being crafted...

Thursday

Marco Delvecchio drove with a steady determination down the dark street. He kept to just below the speed limit, not wanting to be the centre of any unwanted attention. It was already late and he wanted to get home after a long and crappy day, home to his wife and a hot shower, both at the same time if his luck was in. He brought his mind from the hot steamy shower scene playing through his head and instead tried to concentrate on his pending meeting. He was concerned that he would be unable to keep his temper in check but at the same time, knew he needed to avoid lashing out at all costs. His anger was already bubbling around the surface and he wasn't in the right mood for this meeting, but he had somehow convinced Gabe, his number two man to let him go out alone and he knew it had to be now or never. He had told Gabe he was meeting with Jimmy Caruso and that he would, of course be fine to meet with his old friend alone. Marco was aware that it was doubtful that he could convince his right hand man to let him meet with anyone without back up again, whether friend or foe. It went against protocol and there had been too many times of late. And, he thought, he was getting too old for all of this.

Sighing heavily in increasing agitation, he pulled up in the large, near empty parking area of the supermarket. It was near closing time and only a few hardy shoppers were still milling around and Marco found a spot with ease to wait. He could see the entrance from this spot and would know when his visitor arrived.

After ten minutes of waiting, Marco began to huff, tut and sigh in growing anger and impatience. His fingers tapped in irritation on the steering wheel and he was fidgeting in his seat. He could feel the tightness of rage building up inside him and it was something he always struggled to control, like a caged beast that would always threaten to break free and when this happened, the consequences were never good. Marco Delvecchio was not a man to be kept waiting but he knew why it was happening now. The mongrel he was meeting with would think he had gained the upper hand over Marco, some perceived psychological advantage over the king of mind games. Well, let him think that, was Marco's thought on the matter. He tried to calm himself by taking deep breaths and was just about to start the car up and go home when he watched the shiny white Honda pull in, slow down and appear to check the place out before parking up next to Marco's black Lexus. Marco waited for a moment before he opened the window to speak.

"You're late!" Marco growled. The young man he was expecting got out of his own car and slipped into the seat next to Marco's.

With no apology, the boy just turned to Marco. His smile was cold and false. "What did you want to meet me for?" His voice stayed light as he toyed with Marco. He knew how to press the older man's buttons.

"This has gone on for long enough and I'm bored with it. I need to know what you want from me and my family."

A humourless laugh erupted from beside Marco. "What can you possibly give me now? What do you have that I would want? You have already taken the most important thing from me, what else is there?"

"Looking at you, I'd say quite a lot. A job or maybe money. If I can do it, you can have it," Marco said, ignoring the implication of the boys words.

"Are you scared of me, Marco? Of what I might do to you?"

Now it was time for Marco to laugh. He was finding the whole situation quite absurd. "Me? Scared of you? Sonny boy, you clearly haven't done much homework on me and so you don't know me too well, I can tell. Just let's suppose for one minute that I am scared of you. Don't you think I would have an army of men with me and just take you out? Believe me, that would be by far the easiest thing for this now boring situation."

"So why don't you just have me killed then?"

Marco sighed. "Just tell me what you want; what I can give you to make you happy."

"I haven't quite decided yet. Maybe we should meet on Sunday night and I might have made up my mind by then."

"Maybe you shouldn't waste my time. I have better things to do than keep meeting with you."

"Sure, like tell your precious family about me? Have you done that yet?" The visitor grinned. "What will that sexy wife of yours think? Or your playboy son and heir? You know what, *Boss?* I don't think you'll tell anyone. I think that you will meet me at nine o'clock on Sunday, back at the first place we met. I don't want to keep coming all the way up here. So I guess I'll see you then, Marco!" With obvious derision, the boy got out of the car.

Marco was fuming. Maybe he should just take the little bastard out after all – just put a bullet through his head and walk away. Marco decided that he would enjoy that, enjoy seeing his blood and brains splattered all over everywhere!

He sat in the car for a short while after he'd watched the kid drive away, his tail-lights long gone and he wondered how he'd got himself into this mess. What had started out a few months back with one problem had now ended up with an entirely different one. Marco had had a chance meeting with an associate from many years ago and it had led him here, on this Thursday evening when he had better things to do and bigger problems to worry about. He decided there and then, as the rain began to drum a heavy beat on the roof of his car that Sunday night would bring an end to it, whatever else happened. He started up his engine and with the anger still raging through his veins, he headed home.

Sunday

The thick acrid blue smoke drifted with a lazy slowness on the very slight but hot breeze. As it danced around in the air and the smell of burning, charred flesh reached Marco's nostrils, it made him heave. He should have moved downwind of the smoke; it would stick to his clothes and hair and he would have to shower later, to rid his body of the stink of burnt meat. The stench made his full stomach churn and for a moment, he feared his lunch would come back up. Marco tried to wave the smoke away with his hand but it was too thick and he coughed to clear his throat as he accidentally breathed it in, swallowing a mouthful of the caliginous air. It burned his eyes, making them water and he tried to blink the ash away. Marco had always been proud of his strong constitution but today, being this close to the action was maybe not a good thing. He had left his eldest son in charge but was now beginning to regret that decision, sensing what a mess Giorgio was making of the situation. But this was Giorgio's first time and he had a lot to learn still and besides, Marco had been looking forward to this since Thursday evening. He was determined to enjoy it and stretch out the moment. Moments like this did not come around very often. It was hot, too hot really, well over 100 degrees with the humidity around seventy per cent.

It was Sunday afternoon, family barbeque day and a rare day off for him so Marco decided it was time for another beer.

However, his position on the cushioned sunbed next to the pool in his Palm Beach mansion was beyond comfortable. The Florida sun beat down on his already tanned and well looked after body. He managed to open one sleepy eye to see where his wife was just in case she was in reach of the beer cooler but she was nowhere to be seen. Then he remembered she had gone back into the house about half an hour ago with their daughter and had not yet returned.

Feeling drowsy and lethargic from his self-induced inactivity, he mustered the energy to prop himself up on one elbow. It took some considerable effort. From his now semi-elevated position, Marco could see his two sons still cooking steaks on the grill and were producing the offending smoke that made his eyes water. Giorgio and Adam were new to the whole barbecue thing and had insisted on playing chef today, a rare time that the family decided to spend precious time together. Judging by the pile of part cooked, part burnt food on the table, they would all be eating leftovers for weeks if not suffering from food poisoning.

Giorgio looked up toward his father, having had the sudden feeling that he was being watched and mistook Marco's searching gaze for the desire for more food.

"Hey Dad! Another steak?" Giorgio was always eager to impress his father.

Marco groaned to himself. He couldn't face another mouthful of food. He had eaten a mountain of steak, chicken, salad and potatoes and thought he wouldn't need to eat again until Thanksgiving. He looked over to where his son-in-law was sitting under the parasol reading the Sunday paper and trying not to be noticed. Scott had also eaten more than his fair share of Giorgio's cooking that afternoon and Grace would have him straight down the gym if he even so much as put on an pound. Scott also was lean and fit but nearing his forties and had to look after himself to keep up with a wife fourteen years younger than him.

"Scott?" Marco called out.

The younger man looked up from his paper and was worried. He knew what was coming and tried to ascertain whether it would be better to upset his wife or her father.

"Scott, I'll give you fifty bucks if you'll eat my share of whatever Gio has cooked up over there." Marco almost pleaded.

Scott knew he couldn't say no to Marco. He was both his boss and his father in law. Grace, well, he could wrap her around his finger after a fashion and she was a little more forgiving than her father. "Just the fifty, Boss?" He asked with a laugh.

"That and my gratitude, which you know is priceless. Oh, and you can grab me a cold one out of the cooler." His tone indicated that it was not a request but an order and Scott recognised this. Marco had honed this tone of voice to perfection over the years and was always in charge, even on a day off and it was in Scott's best interests to get up off his seat and do Marco's bidding. He could not be ignored so with some considerable reluctance, Scott left the shade of the parasol and walked over to where his wife's brothers were *still* putting raw slabs of meat on the red hot grill.

Marco lay back on the lounger and closed his eyes again. A Sunday off was a luxury for him but Sarah, his wife of twenty five years had been insistent of late that he should spend more time with his family. It was a rare occasion indeed when they were all home together; they were all scattered and had their own lives to follow. Even their youngest child, Adam who was nearing twenty was away at college studying to be a doctor one day. He was the most studious of the Delvecchio siblings and making Marco and Sarah very proud. He was home for the summer and had wasted the days away with his revered older brother Giorgio. Grace had recently moved out with her family and lived just a few blocks away but everyone's lives were so busy it was hard to get everyone together for a day such as this.

Marco watched Adam now as he checked his mother was not around and helped himself to another beer, handing one to Scott as he did so.

"Piccolo? How many have you had?" He used his sons detested nickname as he called out across the pool, trying to sound authoritative but knowing he never was and would never be the disciplinarian within the house. He had too much of that to deal with in his working life and on the whole, he left the children's discipline to Sarah.

"Relax Dad, it's just my third, or fourth." Adam laughed knowing his father would never be tough on him. They all knew it was Sarah that ruled the Delvecchio roost and she had a tendency to pick and choose between US law and her English heritage depending what suited her best at the time. Sarah had learned well from Marco.

Marco smiled as he watched his youngest child pop the bottle top off the beer and gulp it down.

Marco was loathe to admit that Sarah was right and he was actually enjoying himself. He lapped up the burning Florida sun knowing he should put some more sun lotion on as he felt the sweat run down behind his knees. He watched Adam hand Giorgio a cold beer and then plate up another mountain of food for Scott. The three of them shared a joke which made them roar with laughter although Marco could not hear their words. He knew Scott had instigated the joke as his boys were looking up at him in reverence.

Marco thought then about when he had first heard that his precious only daughter, Grace was in a relationship with Scott and how he had wanted to shoot him dead on the spot.

Grace had exhibited signs of what one might call an infatuation with Scott when she was just seven years old. Scott had been injured in an incident and Grace had shown unwarranted concern. She had even declared that, one day, she was going to marry Scott. Everyone believed that she would grow out of it but had harboured her feelings in secret for eleven years until her eighteenth birthday. Marco had hoped Grace would get over her crush on Scott but watched his every move regardless and if he even so much as looked in the wrong way at his daughter, Scott would be a dead man.

For Grace's eighteenth birthday, Sarah and Marco had wanted to arrange a big party for her but Grace had insisted to her parents that she didn't want a big fuss, just for a few girlfriends to go to South Beach for an all-expenses paid weekend and to hit the clubs for some good clean fun. So Sarah and Marco had relented and rented out a beach house for the weekend for her and five of her closest friends.

The morning after Grace's birthday, Sarah spent a few hours trying to call her daughter to ensure she was okay and her hangover wasn't too bad. The beach house phone rang repeatedly off the hook and Grace wasn't picking up her cellphone either so in a state of near panic, Sarah insisted Marco send one of his men to the South Beach house to check it out. Enzo was instructed to take a surreptitious look around and not to let Grace know that someone had been sent to spy on her.

A couple of hours later, Enzo was on the phone to Marco reporting that the beach house was empty and looked as though it hadn't been lived in for a while. There were no cars in the driveway and no empty drinks bottles in the bin. No evidence what so ever of a teenage party.

Marco was livid and Sarah had been terrified. It was not the first time Grace had gone missing and after a hysterical twenty minutes, Marco had promised he would send some men out to look for Grace. He felt she would turn up with some feeble excuse as to her whereabouts, perhaps a boy had been involved but Sarah would not be placated until she saw Marco's troops leave in six cars to scour the streets and put the word out.

Marco and Sarah were just about to call the police the following morning when Grace had walked in the front door singing to herself. She put her keys down on the desk in her father's office before her parents rushed out to meet her.

"Where the hell have you been?" Marco raged. "We have been worried sick and almost called the police! And why didn't you pick up your phone?" He was puce but Sarah was just hugging her daughter in relief.

"Relax Dad, I'm fine. I must have just been out of range on my phone. You know what it's like."

"So where were you? And tell us the truth; we know you weren't at the house we rented. Were you even with your friends?" Sarah asked, trying to stay calm.

Grace looked a little chastised. "No, I wasn't. I'm sorry I lied to you but I knew you'd never let me go otherwise."

"Go where?" Sarah was confused.

"Dad, don't go mad, but I have been with Scott for the last two nights, at his apartment."

Marco could say nothing. He felt his rage boil over and threaten to explode. He picked up his car keys and left without saying a word with Sarah and Grace both calling out after him, to try and placate him but he didn't hear a word through his anger. He drove to Scott's house in about ten minutes flat knowing his daughter would have called ahead and warned him. He was therefore quite surprised when Scott was still home.

"Marco, I... " Scott began.

"*Don't* you dare talk to me, you son of a bitch! How dare you treat my daughter like one of your sluts! Do you know what I should do to you?" Marco was inches from Scott's face and he was trying hard not to punch him out cold.

"Boss, it's not like that. She came to me." He regretted the words as soon as he had said them.

"So now you're saying my daughter is a slut?" He pulled his gun out of his pocket and put it to Scott's temple. "Tell me why I shouldn't kill you?"

Scott said nothing. He knew there wasn't a reason on earth why Marco shouldn't pull the trigger. Scott had been warned about messing with Grace and he would take his punishment, whatever that was. He should have thought of the consequences of sleeping with the boss's daughter before he'd crawled into bed with her. It had seemed such a good idea after taking her out to dinner on the first night they'd spent together and she was so beautiful. He couldn't have any regrets even with her angry father's gun at his head.

The fire suddenly went out of Marco and he put the safety back on. Grace would never forgive him if he hurt Scott in any way. He had a better idea. "You are going to let her down gently. You tell her what a waste of space you are and that she deserves someone better than you."

"Boss, she is eighteen now."

"Meaning?"

"Meaning that perhaps she can make her own mind up about stuff. She is an adult."

"She cannot make her own mind up about *stuff* because she is blindly in love with you and thinks you are some sort of God. Why, I haven't the faintest clue. She doesn't know that you sleep with anything female that moves and now you have added my daughter to your bedpost tally. Do you know how that makes me feel?"

Scott had looked very chastened by this. He'd had no idea of Grace's strength of feeling towards him and now he felt like a dirty hound. Grace was a good girl and beautiful with it and he should feel honoured that he had been her first. Without thinking further, he made his mind up.

"Marco, with your permission, I would like to take Grace out on a date."

"It's a bit late to be asking my permission. Besides, you are too old for her and you have too much mileage."

"Exactly. I have satisfied my need to date multiple women, now I just want to date one. Grace. I want to try and make your daughter happy. If she loves me as you says she does, I will either make her happy or she will soon realise what a worthless piece of shit I am!"

Marco had looked at Scott, trying to work out how much crap was coming out of his mouth. He knew that it would be impossible to tell Grace who she could and couldn't see as she was always so headstrong but Marco had always hoped for better for his daughter.

"It had better be the first, Scott, or so help me!" He left the unsaid threat in the air and he turned, heading for the door. "And I don't want her coming home pregnant any time soon!" Satisfied he had made his point, Marco had left Scott shaking with relief at his apparent let off.

Marco now laughed as he recalled the next few months of Scott's life and how hard he had made it for him. Scott had persevered and did not complain and after a while, Marco had to concede defeat. Despite the age difference, the couple had been very happy and Grace had only announced they were expecting a baby just about a year ago.

Marco smiled as he heard the chatter of feminine voices getting louder and closer and he opened his eyes to see the two women in his life coming down the path from the house. His beautiful wife was carrying their grandson, Connor in her arms as he wriggled to be set free. They were all dressed for the pool and both looked fabulous in their swimsuits. Marco heard Scott wolf-whistle as he saw Grace coming towards them.

"Gio, darling, can you turn the grill off now? I think we've all had enough to eat for today." Sarah requested in her still perfect English accent that she worked so hard to keep. She always said she didn't want to acquire an American twang, that her accent distinguished her from her peers although Marco knew that it was much more than her accent that made her different from the other women in this town.

Giorgio did as he was told and the blond-haired boy put the lid down on the cooker, sealing off the air so the fire would die out. He put his empty beer bottle in the trash can and helped himself to another. Marco watched Giorgio walk casually towards Adam and Scott with an innocent look in his dark brown eyes and chuckled as Giorgio pushed his brother into the cool blue water of the pool.

Adam resurfaced and gasped for air after the unexpected dunking and laughing, he swore revenge on his brother. Marco often marvelled at how the two Delvecchio boys were different in so many ways and yet both wanted to be like the other. Giorgio was blond-haired and brown eyed, the perennial wanna-be playboy and bad student. He had just about accrued his high school diploma and if the truth were known, had graduated thanks to a fat donation to the new school gymnasium fund from his father. Giorgio did not want to study or go to college. He wanted to party and meet as may girls as possible. His life plan was to be like his father and the only thing he wanted to learn was the Family business despite protestations from his mother. Sarah had wanted her eldest son to have qualifications and be somebody, like a doctor or a lawyer but Giorgio had absolutely and resolutely refused. Marco often wondered how much Sarah knew about what Giorgio did for him, and how deep he was in already. He figured she turned a blind eye to most of it, for she must be aware Giorgio was being mentored by Gabe. Marco knew Sarah was putting all of her hopes on Adam.

Dark-haired, dark-eyed Adam, or Piccolo, as he was known to his family, had found school easy and had never got so much as a detention. He was a straight A student and had his pick of colleges to go to but chose Alabama so he could still be quite close to his family. Despite his aversions to where and how his family made their money, he hated the idea of being on the other side of the country to them. Apart from which, he was close to his elder brother and enjoyed every opportunity of coming home for the weekend so he could party with Giorgio. When Adam didn't make it home for the weekend, Giorgio would catch a plane to see his brother and between them, they were merciless to the girls on campus and in Palm Beach County. Marco smiled his approval to himself as he saw the resemblance between his two sons, and himself and Joe when they had been around the same age. Just like Joe and Marco, Giorgio and Adam left many a broken heart on a Monday morning and it had taken a special someone to tame Marco, much like he knew it would with Giorgio and Adam.

As Marco relaxed in the laughter of his family, he thought again about how lucky he was. Everything he had worked so hard for was all around him. The hard decisions he had had to make over time and losing some people that he cared about, it all seemed worth it to him just then, surrounded by the people he loved most in the world. In recent weeks, he'd had a troubling issue rear its ugly head but he hoped that would be resolved tonight. Tomorrow, he could go back to his near perfect life. Hell! He might even think about retiring! Sarah had been nagging him for a while for the two of them to take a long holiday, and see some of the world so maybe now was the time. Giorgio and Gabe could cover it for a while.

Just had tonight to sort out.

He smiled and his heart lit up as Sarah came over and sat next to him on the sun lounger. She had Connor in her arms, who was smiling and gurgling in delight. Sarah was a wonderful mother and grandmother, even though she refused to be called a Grandmother at the tender age of fifty-four. Marco thought she was still stunning and he desired her almost every minute of every day and always would do. He hoped they might have some alone time later, before he went out. That was another reason why he should make this his last beer – he would hate to disappoint her in the bedroom and any more beer might have the wrong effect.

They both heard a high pitched squeal followed by a loud splash and both Marco and Sarah's attention was diverted. As they both looked up, they saw their boys and Scott had all conspired to throw Grace into the pool. Scott dived in right behind her as her brothers fell about laughing. As Grace surfaced, she pushed her husband under the water in mock punishment and Giorgio and Adam all jumped in after them, laughing as they did so.

"Why don't you go in with them darling?" Sarah asked her husband as she looked into his deep brown eyes.

"I can't." He pulled away the towel that had lain across his lap and she saw the reason why he would not be able to even stand up. "You sashaying down the path in that red two piece has had some reaction on me!" He laughed and grabbed her hand. "Can you sort me out?" He pleaded, caressing her inner thigh.

Sarah slapped his hand away, giggling girlishly. "You never change, Marco, however much love and attention I lavish on you. I had thought you would have grown out of it after this many years of marriage but you just seem to get worse as you get older!"

"Can I help it that I am married to the sexiest and most sensational woman ever?"

"Just stop!" Sarah teased. "You don't need to give me any of your flannel – you know I'm a sure thing." She leant over and kissed his lips, darting her tongue into his mouth and enjoying the further pleasurable discomfort it brought him. If she hadn't had her grandson squirming on her lap, she would have slipped her hand under Marco's towel to tease him into unbearable malaise. There was nothing in the world she liked more than to titillate her husband when he was not in a position to take her up on her offers.

"If you get in the pool, the water will cool you down." She whispered in his ear, although they were out of earshot of anyone else.

"So, what? I just get up and run?"

"We are all adults here, mostly men. Grace might be freaked out but she is a married woman. She knows how things are. Come on!" Sarah began to goad him.

Marco closed his eyes and took a deep breath. He could be in the pool in about three seconds but he would also be highly embarrassed if anyone happened to look in his direction.

Cursing Sarah, and promising her retribution, he sat up on his lounger and after taking one last look at his kids and son-in-law, who were still distracted with one another, he ran and jumped into the pool, laughing as he felt the coolness wash over him. He swam over to the little group.

Giorgio turned to him with a secret smile on his face. "You okay, Dad?" It was all he needed to say to let Marco know that he knew why he needed to cool down. Marco tried not to blush as he ducked his son under the blue water.

The family stayed poolside until a sudden wind whipped up around four-thirty. Sarah noticed it first, after chasing Connor's blanket that had been caught up on the breeze. She looked up and saw the thick black clouds boiling overhead and she called out to everyone to grab and run. Discarded magazines and towels began to blow across the deck and into the pool and sleepy heads woke up and hurried to collect items up before the rain began. Grace picked Connor up and Scott followed her back into the house, his arms laden with numerous toys and the baby bag. With no further warning, the seething sky lit up as lightening darted overhead and rain drops as big and hard as olives pelted down from above, soaking everything it touched and anyone foolish enough not to be undercover. The wind howled and the thunder crashed overhead as the torrential rain ran in rivers down the windows from the leaden skies, limiting the view to just a few feet into the garden. The expensive and expansive shrubs in the garden received a battering and the huge trees that surrounded the property for privacy bent and swayed in the wind, threatening to break in two and come crashing to the ground. It seemed they were made of elastic as they were frequently subjected to such harsh storms and never appeared to be any the worse for wear when the turmoil passed.

Grace and Scott took this opportunity to leave for home. Their sleep was still being interrupted by their infant son and they were feeling weary, despite the light hearted fun they had all been having that day. They collected up the mountain of items they had bought with them and Sarah and Marco helped them into their car under the portico as they said their goodbyes, Scott being made to promise to drive extra careful in this awful weather. The grandparents watched as the young family drove down the drive towards the electric gate that opened for them on their approach. Scott tooted the car horn which was barely audible to Sarah and Marco above the din of the storm and he turned out of the drive and disappeared into the rain.

Sarah headed into the kitchen to make some coffee and Giorgio announced that he had a party to go to that night. As he headed upstairs to get ready, Marco warned him not to bring any girls home that night. He was tired of Giorgio bringing random women home. Marco hated strangers in the house. He also shouted a warning about not driving home after drinking.

"No problems, Dad. Jesse is designated driver tonight. I can't promise about the females though. Can I help it if they find me irresistible?" he laughed as he disappeared into his bedroom, already quite drunk.

"Just like Joe," Marco muttered under his breath, but not quiet enough for it to escape Sarah's hearing.

"Leave him be, darling. He's young. Let him have his fun before you knock all traces of innocence out of him," she scolded her husband.

Marco wanted to pick her up on her comment, to find out what she knew, but he had more pressing concerns. "Where's Adam?"

"Studying. Where else? He has an essay to finish, that's why he's not going with Gio for a change."

Marco smiled. He put his arms around her waist. "So no-one would miss us for an hour or two then?" He kissed her on her collarbone, his lips brushing her skin and sending shivers of delight down her back.

She smiled seductively at him, both of their minds on the same thing. "What do you have in mind, Mr Delvecchio?"

"I need a hand to get out of these wet swim shorts... "

"I think you are old enough to get yourself out of them. You barely squeezed yourself in them – they are bordering on indecency!"

"You are to blame for that and the reason is still obvious." He pulled Sarah's hand to him and she kissed him with a hard and desperate passion.

"We'd better go upstairs then and see if we can't help you out of your predicament."

They raced upstairs laughing like a pair of kids as the thunder crashed over their heads.

At just after seven that night, they stepped out of the shower together, still dripping. Sarah put her arms around Marco's neck and kissed him, pressing her body against him, never being able to get enough of him. His dark eyes twinkled at her as he felt himself come alive again but with reluctance he walked away before it became impossible to. Sarah wrapped herself in a towel and watched her handsome, desirable husband, still not believing that he was her man and had been for many years. His dark luxuriant hair was peppered with grey now but it just added to his sexiness. He had frown lines and laughter lines, but who didn't at fifty-seven? All six foot two of him was still fit and lean, always tanned – a benefit of living in southern Florida. He had softened over the years but could still act the tyrant when it suited him and when he needed to but Sarah had learned to know when he could be wrapped around her finger, which was most of the time. He was only unbreakable in a work situation. But they all knew.

"What time will you be home tonight?" She hated asking him as he would often get cross with her checking up on him but he was in a good mood so Sarah felt sure that he would answer her.

"As soon as I can. I want to get back to you and maybe play around a little more. I'm all relaxed from my day off and don't want it to end." He walked over and kissed her.

"Well, can't you send someone else?" She was close to the line that she shouldn't cross but wanted to press it a little more. "Can't Gabe go instead?"

Marco stared at her with a sudden less than warm look. "No." He replied with a short tone bordering on anger. "I don't think I will be back til after midnight. Stay awake if you can, otherwise I'll see you in the morning." His voice had gone frosty on her; Sarah had pushed too much.

She put her arms around him. "I want you to wake me when you get back, regardless of how late it is. Promise me?"

He smiled again. "Okay." Former good mood having been somewhat restored, he went into the bedroom to get dressed.

Monday

The music was getting louder, or perhaps, Giorgio conceded, he was just getting drunker. These beach house parties were always the best, especially when he didn't know the host – he could be as wild as he chose to be when he had no apologies to make the following day.

He had just helped himself to another beer in the kitchen and some young girl who looked barely sixteen had tried to make a pass at him. She was pretty, he had to admit that but he was always worried about the younger girls in case they weren't quite the age they admitted to. He was pretty sure his surname wouldn't act as a get out of jail free card for screwing an underage girl. Besides, he liked his women to know what they were doing.

Giorgio moved through the hallway, his eyes darting all over as people said hi to him, people he didn't know but they knew of him. He sauntered out of the house to the garden where the night air was cooler. He was getting hot and took a large gulp of his beer, letting the ice cold liquid run down his throat, cooling him for just a minute. He was looking for that girl again, the one who had been at Jesse's party last week but no-one he knew seemed to know who she was or had a number for her. Not that he would have been able to call her anyway – he had spent most of the time at Jesse's party just looking at her, unable for some reason to go and talk to her. Jesse seemed to think that the girl would be at this party, it was well advertised on the social network sites and Jesse was never wrong about such things. As he kept searching the crowd, his gaze settled on Claire. She smiled at him, her eyes full of hope – Giorgio knew she had a thing for him but he wasn't interested in Claire. She was too keen and he needed a new challenge.

More people he didn't know said hello to him. He was used to it but still found it more than a little bit annoying. People wanted to be with him and Giorgio was used to weeding out the hangers-on. His inner circle of real friends was quite small. He wanted this new mystery girl in that elusive circle.

Then Giorgio saw her leaning against a table, a glass of wine in her hand, chatting and smiling with Jesse. He felt a ridiculous pang of jealousy that was alien to him so he walked up to his best friend and the girl, determined to talk to her. But his courage failed him at once and he just stood like an imbecile as though waiting for an introduction.

"Hey Jesse! Who might this be?" he managed to squawk out after a few moments, his face flushing red under his golden tan.

Jesse laughed, knowing full well his best friend of fifteen years had a crush on Katey, the girl he had been talking to. He himself did not have designs on this girl, he would never do that to Giorgio. He just found her interesting to talk to. Besides, Katey had dropped hints during their brief conversation that she was rather taken with the blond boy now in their midst.

"Hey buddy, this is Katey. Katey, this is my best friend, Gio Delvecchio."

Giorgio smiled and watched for any sign of recognition from Katey and was glad that she did not register his name. He preferred it that way.

"Nice to meet you, Gio," her crisp accent acknowledged the introduction.

Giorgio melted. "English. How perfect."

Katey smiled. She knew the American boys loved the accent. She looked at the extremely handsome, dirty blond and more than a bit drunk lad in front of her and was at a loss for words herself. His dark brown eyes, despite being drink-addled were mesmerising and Katey felt herself drowning in them. Neither spoke.

"Well, this is a great conversation," Jesse broke the sudden silence, his voice thick with sarcasm. "I'll leave you to it," and he left the two feeling just a little awkward.

Giorgio laughed. "Do you want another drink?"

Katey pointed to her wine glass which was still two thirds full. "No thanks. I'd better call it a night after this one."

"Already? It's not yet one o'clock," he was very disappointed.

"I know but I have to be up early tomorrow morning. A little thing called a job. We don't all have trust funds to keep us going," she seemed a little off with him suddenly.

Giorgio couldn't work out what he had done to offend her so soon. "How do you know I have a trust fund? I have a very demanding job, I'll have you know," he teased, trying to win her back on-side.

"Most people here have trust funds. This is Palm Beach after all. So tell me Gio, what demanding job do you have?"

"I work for my dad."

"Oh yes?" Doubt spread across her face.

"Yes and he makes me earn every penny, before you ask. So what do you do that makes you have to get up so early?"

"I'm researching for my book. I'm in Florida for three months getting to grips with life in hurricane hot zones."

"A writer?" Giorgio was impressed. "Have you been in a hurricane yet? We've been let off lightly for a couple of years now, only intense storms have come through this way."

Katey shook her head. "I've only witnessed a tropical storm. It seems wrong to wish for a hurricane when they are so destructive and have such a negative impact on people's lives but that is what I need to know about."

"I was born in a hurricane. Well, a severe storm but a hurricane sounds much more exciting. Maybe that's why I'm so tempestuous! And they say it's lucky to be born in a storm."

Katey laughed. "You? Lucky and tempestuous? I don't believe it. You can barely stand!"

Giorgio nodded. "Yes, I am a little drunk but I have been drinking for about twelve hours now. Family get together. Let me take you out tomorrow and I'll show you the real me."

Katey shook her head. "I don't think so. I'm new around here and don't know anything about you. Besides, I'm staying miles away in South Beach."

"Perhaps I think you are worth the drive," Giorgio countered.

Katey looked into his eyes again. "Gio, I am not going to sleep with you so don't think a meal out and couple of drinks will work to your advantage. Look, it's been nice meeting you but I think I'm going to leave now." She put her half-finished glass of wine down on the table she had been leaning against and turned to walk away.

"Can you at least give me your number?" Giorgio shouted after her but she ignored him and carried on walking. A group of people nearby that he didn't know snickered at his public rejection and stared at him as he staggered back into the house feeling dejected.

Not liking the rejection one little bit, he went in search of Claire. He was used to having any woman he wanted with very little effort and he needed to give himself an ego boost. He was twenty-one this month, so was he past his prime? He knew he would not need to fight for the attentions of Claire and he could always just imagine he was with the delectable, desirable and unachievable Katey. Giorgio decided that somehow, he would get Katey's phone number and convince her that she should go out with him. She would be his new challenge.

"Hey Claire!" He spotted her with a group of her friends in the hallway. "You wanna go for a walk down on the beach with me?"

Claire's face lit up. She was well aware that meant only one thing and with a ridiculous eagerness, she followed Giorgio down the path from the house that led to the dark beach, empty except for like-minded young people.

Perhaps if Giorgio hadn't been quite so drunk, he would have realised that he was being watched. Someone who had a deep-rooted and long ago started hatred for him began to follow Giorgio and Claire down the path and onto the beach. This someone had arrived at the party late but none of the party-goers would remember that, they were all having too much of a good time to know what time any one individual had arrived or indeed, left. He kept back in the shadows, trailing the drunken couple from a safe distance, not wanting to be seen at all. He shuddered as he saw Giorgio pull Claire down onto the sand, away from any light, and turned away, not wanting to witness what that animal was going to do to a perfectly nice girl like Claire. She was just being used and he walked away, out of earshot of the couple to wait for them to finish.

Sarah stirred and as she woke, she knew the bed beside her was empty. She raised her head from her pillow, opening one tired eye with effort and looked at the clock beside her bed. As the red numbers came into focus, she saw that it said it was one twenty-two. The house seemed to be silent and she only heard the crickets and other night creatures outside in the garden. This grand house that she lived in carried noise as though she lived in a cave and was rarely silent but still she heard nothing, not even the faint rumble of music from Adams room. Perhaps he had gone to join his brother at the party.

Sarah thought of calling Marco to see where he was but she knew he was out on business. He had gone cold on her earlier today when she tried to question him about his movements and he would not appreciate his wife calling to check up on him. She let the thought leave her head. She had never called to check up on him before, why should she start now?

Sarah groaned. She would struggle to get back to sleep without Marco home. She was a bit worried about him with the lateness of the hour but was aware that he had good men with him. They had probably gone for a few drinks after whatever it was they were doing and forgotten the time. She slipped out of bed and headed for the bathroom for a sip of water and a pee. She'd had too much wine earlier in the day and it was going straight through.

When she was done, Sarah went to her bedroom door and opened it a crack, listening to the night sounds. She could hear the ticking of the old grandfather clock in the downstairs hallway but no voices echoing around the house, no quiet murmur of Marco's men plotting and planning even at this time of night.

Her eyes flickered to the other side of the staircase and she saw a pale light seeping from under Adam's bedroom door. Her maternal instincts judged that, yet again, he would have fallen asleep watching T.V or reading a book. A habit of a lifetime for her youngest child.

More for something to do to keep her mind off her late returning husband, Sarah padded down the hallway to Adam's room. She knocked gently on his door but received no response and so she opened the door. True enough, Adam had been reading a book, a study book from school. It had slipped down to his lap and he was snoring. Smiling, Sarah extricated the book from his languid grip and put it on the table beside his bed. Adam didn't stir. She watched him for a moment, his face in peaceful slumber. His hair had dried naturally after his shower and had curled, so reminiscent of his father. Even though he was approaching his twentieth birthday, Adam was still her baby and she loved to watch him sleep. Her pride threatened to burst for her studious son.

After a few moments of just staring at him, Sarah switched his soft playing music off. She flicked off his lamp and crept out of the room, closing the door behind her without making a sound.

He would make an excellent doctor one day, of that, she was sure.

Sarah roused with an almost dead slowness as her subconscious heard something in the room with her. It seemed like just minutes since she had fallen back asleep although in reality, she had been in a deep sleep and now felt drugged. She became aware of a being in the room and looked again at the clock through half opened eyes. The time was now three-twelve. The bedroom door was slightly open and in the soft light, she could make out a dark shape move towards the bed.

"It's okay. I'm awake," she muttered to let Marco know he didn't have to try to be quiet as he often failed anyway. She sat up feeling groggy and switched her bedside light on.

She received the shock of her life when, instead of her husband, she saw his close friend and business associate, Gabe standing over her. He looked pale and drawn.

"Gabe? What is it? Why are you here? Where is Marco?" she threw questions at him and instinctively, she drew the cover up to her neck. Her sleepy state had left her in a state of disorientation.

Gabe said nothing but looked at Sarah, his lips were pursed so tight they were losing colour, making them pale and matching his face.

"What is it? You are scaring me!" she tried to keep the rising panic out of her voice. She threw the covers off and stood up in front of him, wondering why he was in her bedroom at this time of night. Marco would kill him if he caught him here.

"It's Marco," Gabe said after what seemed like minutes but was just seconds. His voice was too quiet, barely above a whisper.

Sarah waited, saying nothing but the blood in her veins had already turned to ice, starting to numb her. She knew that something was very wrong. She could feel that her world was about to shift on its axis.

Gabe reached out for her hand but he could not look her in the eye. He took a deep breath. "Marco was killed tonight." He said nothing more.

Sarah broke free of his grip and ran into the bathroom.

Gabe waited by her bed, feeling useless and not knowing what to do. He just listened as Sarah threw up in the bathroom, gut wrenching noises more sinister than wailing or screaming. He stood there while the wife, now widow of his dead friend and boss manifested her grief by vomiting. Gabe choked back a sob feeling desolate and heartbroken himself and for all that Marco had done for him over the years, he did not know how to help his wife now when she needed him the most.

After a while, ten minutes or so, Sarah came out of the bathroom, wiping her mouth with a cloth. She had tied her hair back into a ponytail and was looking faint and bedraggled. She looked at Gabe sitting on the edge of her bed where just a few hours previous, she had made love with her husband for the last time. A cry of anguish threatened to escape but she held it back and took a deep breath as she composed herself.

"What happened?" she asked, a quiet and eerie calm had descended on the room.

Gabe shook his head and sighed deeply. "We don't know everything. Marco was meeting someone tonight and wanted to go it alone… "

"And since when have you let him do that?" she accused Gabe, anger rising in her voice.

"Sarah, you know how he can be. I asked him, tried to insist that he take Scotty or someone with him and we fought about it but you of all people know how he can be! In the end, his word is the one that counts."

"And you have no idea who he was meeting?"

Gabe shook his head. "All he told me was that tonight he was to finish something off," he shrugged, regretful that he didn't yet know more.

"Then we need to know what. Are the police investigating?"

"Of course. But we will make our own investigation."

"Who else knows?" Sarah's voice had returned to a calmer and steadier tone.

Gabe shrugged. The news would travel fast but he didn't know how fast. Every camp had their spies in the Police Department. "It won't be long before it's common knowledge, we won't be able to keep it quiet, it's too big. I would expect the local papers to run a late edition tomorrow." The local press loved to write about the Delvecchios and this would give them a story for weeks.

"We need to get a plan in motion. Until we know who is responsible, we don't know who else they may be targeting," She looked thoughtful.

Gabe was watching Sarah and becoming increasingly concerned by her state of mind. "Sarah, do you want me to call anyone?"

She nodded. "We'd better call our allies in San Francisco."

Gabe sighed. "I meant, do you want me to call Andrea or Grace?" he tried to keep the frustration out of his voice.

Sarah looked up, taking a sharp intake of breath. "Oh my god! The kids! They can't find out about this from anyone but me." She grabbed her dressing gown and in a flurry of blue silk and satin she left the bedroom.

Gabe followed her downstairs and found her in the kitchen. She was clattering around making tea and strong coffee for anyone that needed it. She asked Gabe after Marco.

"Where is he now?" her voice had a shake to it.

"At the morgue. They will need to do a post-mortem and it may be a while before they can release him for burial. "

Sarah nodded, not wanting to talk too much about the details. She didn't trust herself not to break down and that couldn't happen yet. She needed to remain business-like despite her inner turmoil.

"You'll be able to see him from 6 a.m. He will need to be formally identified, if you are up to it," Gabe continued.

"Of course." She handed Gabe some coffee and, with gratitude, he took it and gulped back the strong black liquid. He reached for Sarah's hand across the breakfast bar, not knowing what to say or do. He had never been one for platitudes and gentle words.

The front door opened and then banged shut and Sarah knew her eldest son was home and in all likelihood, drunker than he had been when he'd left for the party just a few hours earlier. She debated with herself for a moment whether to let Giorgio sleep it off before she told him the news. She wanted to protect all three of her children from the heartbreak they were about to endure for as long as possible.

However, the decision was made for her when Giorgio came into the kitchen for a glass of water and saw Gabe and his mother holding hands.

Giorgio snickered. "Don't let my dad catch you fondling his wife, Gabe!" he was unable to resist the glib comment.

"Gio, are you alone?" Sarah asked trying to keep the hysteria from entering her voice, while subtly taking her hands from Gabe's grasp.

He nodded. "Of course. Ever the dutiful son. Dad asked me not to bring anyone home so I did what needed to be done at the party. Well, on the beach but you get my drift!" He stretched, feeling very pleased with himself. He poured some water into a glass from the bottle in the fridge and gulped it down.

"Gio, can you sit down please?" Sarah pulled out a kitchen stool and gestured for him to sit.

Giorgio frowned. He was ready for his bed, not a lecture about his lifestyle from his mother. He did as he was told though, he knew it would be easier on him if Sarah said what she had to and then, he could get to bed.

Giorgio began to get concerned when Sarah took his hand in hers. She hadn't done that in years.

"Sweetheart, I'm afraid I have some very bad news." She faltered, not really knowing the right words to choose. Trying not to choke, Sarah just said it straight. "Dad was killed tonight."

Giorgio's tears were instant. " *What?* " He choked back a sob as he tried to understand what Sarah was telling him. "Killed? How?"

Sarah shook her head. When she spoke her voice was cracking with emotion. "We don't know any details yet, my darling. A friend at Miami-Dade P.D called Gabe earlier tonight."

Giorgio looked to Gabe. "So it could be wrong? It might not be Dad?"

Sarah looked Gabe, a sudden sense of hope filling her.

"Gio, I'm sorry but I have seen him. He will need to be formally identified but we know it was your dad."

"You're *wrong!*" Giorgio shouted at him through his tears. He stood up abruptly, knocking over his stool. He threw a hate filled stare at Gabe as though it was all his fault, wanting to shoot the messenger, needing an outlet for his anger and his grief.

"Gio… " Sarah tried to find some words to comfort her son but was in such a state of agony herself that she could find no words to help start the healing.

Giorgio had fled the kitchen and Sarah heard his thunderous footsteps crashing up the stairs and to his room. She jumped as he slammed the bedroom door, the bang echoing around the house and then an eerie silence enveloped them all once more.

Sarah looked at the kitchen clock ticking slow and ponderous. It was just after 4 a.m. "When can I go to the morgue?" Sarah asked Gabe. She knew he had already

told her but her brain was incapable of taking very much in.

Gabe repeated the time with the patience of a saint.

After a few more minutes of silence, Sarah stood up. "I'd better go and tell Grace and Adam." She stood up and walked out of the kitchen, weariness filling her from her toes up. As she got to the bottom of the stairs, she became aware of loud banging and crashing noise coming from Giorgio's room. She ran up the stairs, two at a time and stopped when she reached his door. It sounded like he was trashing his room.

Sarah threw the door open and gasped in horror at the devastation inside. Giorgio's wall-mounted plasma television was still on the wall but without a screen. It had been caved in, probably with a baseball bat that had been flung through the closed window and was now resting in the flower bed below. Shards of glass from the shattered window were on the carpet below the frame. All of Giorgio's books, C.D's and DVD's were scattered across the room, cleared off the shelves in a rage.

Sarah looked at her son, sitting on his bed sobbing his heart out, with his right hand bleeding. She rushed to him and held him close.

"My darling boy! What have you done?"

Giorgio said nothing but allowed himself to be rocked like a small child in the comforting arms of his mother. He cried freely, his tears soaking through her silk pyjamas and the blood transferring from his hand to her skin as he held on to her like his own life depended on it.

Giorgio's grief was almost too overwhelming as Sarah sat with him on his bed. She could find no words to say that would take the pain away, nothing to assuage his or even her own grief so she just sat in silence, cradling her grown son in her arms. She wondered then, as she looked down on his tear stained face, if he would ever recover from this, if he would ever go back to being the carefree, loving boy that she and Marco had raised. Giorgio always had a smile on his face and a ready compliment for anyone he came across. Life was good for Giorgio Delvecchio. Or at least it had been. Marco's death was going to change life big time for everyone connected to him but Sarah feared most for Giorgio. Of her three children, Giorgio had been closest to their father and she knew, despite her protestations and Marco's denials that Giorgio was being educated and trained in his father's business. Perhaps now, she realised, it was a good thing but she also wondered if Giorgio was ready. Marco had taken over from his father at twenty five and by his own admission he had been nowhere near ready. Giorgio was a few years younger than even that.

Ten minutes had passed and Giorgio's hysterical initial grief began to subside. He choked back more tears and saying nothing, he turned away from Sarah. He curled up foetal-like and stared at the wall, saying nothing, seeing nothing but desperate for the pain in his chest to stop. He felt sick with misery and could not stop his eyes from closing. He felt his mother's hand on his shoulder but it bought him no comfort. The blackness of denied sleep welcomed him and with a big sigh, he allowed it to take him.

Sarah stayed for a while longer to make sure he was asleep. She didn't want to leave Giorgio but was painfully aware that she had to go through this same scenario twice more. She wasn't sure if she had the strength to go through it with each of her other children but she had no-one else to do it for her. Her rock had been taken from her and he would not be returning.

The front door slammed again, louder this time, causing Sarah to jump. She looked at her sleeping son but he did not stir. Grief, exhaustion and alcohol would claim him for a few hours more yet. Sarah heard Grace calling for her and she sighed. She was not ready for more grief just yet; she couldn't even handle her own. She went to Giorgio's door and called out in a soft tone.

"I'm with Gio, Grace."

Grace charged up the stairs and stopped short on seeing her mother. "Is it true?" Her face was streaked with tears and her eyes were red. Sarah hoped, with a certain degree of selfishness that she had expended her initial grief.

Sarah nodded.

Grace audibly caught her breath and her face screwed up in misery as a fresh flood of tears streamed down her face. She rushed to her mother and threw her arms around her, crying on her shoulder.

Between sobs, Grace asked what had happened.

Sarah shook her head. "No-one knows very much at the moment, we are already trying to establish what happened. All we do know is that Dad was out alone... "

"Alone? He couldn't be! He never went anywhere alone. He was too clever for that!" Grace insisted.

"Evidently not. We will find out what happened and we will find out who did this."

A door to their left creaked open and Adam poked his sleepy head out, his hair ruffled by sleep. "What's the commotion?" he asked.

Sarah left Grace and walked over to where Adam stood. He took a step away from his mother, as though denying his gut feeling of bad news.

"Darling, it's not good news. Dad was hurt tonight," she paused to gather herself. "Somebody killed him earlier this evening."

Adam half smiled. "You're kidding, right?"

Sarah shook her head. "Darling... "

"No! You *have* to be kidding. Why would you say that?" he backed further away from his mother and sister.

"Adam... " Grace tried to reach her youngest brother.

He shook his head, not wanting to believe their words and ran back into the security of his bedroom, slamming the door and causing both women to jump. They both heard him screaming obscenities behind the closed door.

"I'll go to him." Grace offered.

Sarah put her hand on her daughters arm to stop her. "Leave him be. Adam will come to us when he is ready."

"And Gio?"

"He is sleeping. He isn't in a good way so is better off as he is. Come on, let's go downstairs." She held Grace's hand and they walked side by side downstairs to the lounge where Scott waited with a sleeping Connor on the sofa.

"Gabe called me," Scott explained. "Does anyone know what happened?"

Sarah was getting sick of being asked the same old questions that she didn't have the answers to so she ignored her son-in-law. "Will you stay here with the boys? I have to go to the morgue."

"Let me come with you," Grace pleaded.

Sarah shook her head. She wanted Grace to remember her father how he had been that afternoon, full of vitality and humour, a little tipsy and soft around the edges. Warm and alive. "I need you to stay here Grace. The house will be very busy today. We will no doubt have a lot of visitors and besides, Gabe can drive me."

Grace was aware of the same sense of dread that Gabe had earlier felt. "Are you okay, mum? I mean, you seem so distant, as though this isn't Dad that we are talking about."

"Grace, I am far from okay, believe me. I am on auto-pilot right now and that is all that is getting me through at the moment. I will have my time when we have caught the bastards that have done this but until then I have to deal with it any way I can. Scott, I know you are not my personal assistant but can you call Chicago and San Francisco? Now, please excuse me as I need to go and identify my husband."

Dawn was breaking in the east as Gabe drove Sarah down the drive towards the gatehouse that guarded the Delvecchio house. Gabe still did not know what to say to Sarah and he was still struggling to understand why and how this had happened and, more to the point, why Marco had been so remiss in his own security. In all the many years Gabe had known and worked for Marco, he had never attended any meeting alone, someone had always accompanied him or was at least nearby so why had he insisted on going solo last night? Furthermore, why had Gabe let him? He would carry that guilt around with him for as long as he lived. None of it made any sense and Gabe was desolate. He stole a quick look across the car at Sarah who was staring out of the window at the sun rising over the sea, casting a golden hue on everything it touched. She had said so little to him since he had delivered the news to her. She was so calm and composed.

Accepting.

But Sarah had lived with this possibility for all of her married life. The company that Marco kept and the line of business he was in made it a high probability that one day he would not come home. It was possibly a subconscious decision she had made on returning to Marco from San Francisco all of those years ago. Gabe knew that Sarah would not trade the time she and Marco had had together to avoid this moment but she was not behaving how a newly widowed woman should. She had not cried, she had not screamed. She had just accepted her husband's death and was dealing with the situation and the problems following as a result. At least, that was how it seemed to Gabe.

Gabe made a mental note to call Cliff and Andrea as soon as he was able – Sarah would appreciate a friend around her right now. He checked the clock on the dash again and saw it was just after 6 a.m. He'd let the Bremanns sleep a while longer before he allowed the world to implode on them.

The streets were quite quiet for a Monday morning. The sun rose glorious and bright and promised another hot and balmy day in Palm Beach County although Gabe was sure the beaches wouldn't be too busy today as people made ready for Labor Day next weekend. He knew Sarah had a big party planned for all of Marco's employees and their families, that was what yesterdays barbecue was in practice for. It was heart-breaking to think that the party would be cancelled and all celebrations for some time to come.

Gabe sighed in sadness and put his foot down on the gas. He wanted to get this over and done with and was sure Sarah felt the same. He needed answers to his many questions and he wanted someone to blame and for someone to vent his physical anger on. He still had not told Sarah how her husband had died and was not sure how to. If the question remained unspoken for long enough, the police would tell her and Gabe prayed for that, coward that he suddenly was.

They pulled up outside the hospital morgue. This area of the building was still quiet and Gabe managed to find a spot right outside the door. Without speaking, they got out of the car and went through the door, searching for someone to point them in the right direction.

"Mrs Delvecchio?" A firm but kind voice called from down the darkened corridor. Sarah could not make out the person who had called out to her so she refrained from replying.

"Yes. " Gabe answered for Sarah.

"I'm Lieutenant Gray," the feminine voice spoke again and the owner came out of the darkness and stood in view of Sarah. Rosie Gray was in her early forties, jet black hair and kind dark eyes. She had on a navy blue trouser suit and her hair fell down her back. "We've been expecting you. This way please," she led them both down the corridor and after a short way, stopped by a set of double doors.

"Mrs Delvecchio, how much do you know?" Lieutenant Gray turned to face Sarah.

"About what?" Sarah was suspicious in an instant. Twenty-five years as Marco's wife had left her with an inherent distrust of the law and she wasn't going to give anything away to this woman that she didn't have to.

"About the cause of death," she glanced at Gabe but Sarah missed the look between them.

Sarah went blank. It was then she realised that she did not know how Marco had died. She had not asked and Gabe had not volunteered the information. She felt the air being pushed from her lungs as she shook her head. "I don't know how Marco died. I assumed he has been shot." Sarah struggled to take a breath as she looked at Gabe for confirmation but he just looked away, unable to look her in the eye.

Lieutenant Gray shifted on her feet. Many years doing the job had hardened her to death and destruction in the most horrific ways imaginable, but this was semi-personal and she did not relish having to tell the widow the news. "Well, let me ask you this. Did your husband have any distinguishing features? Scars, birthmarks, that kind of thing?"

Sarah frowned. "Why do you ask?"

"It would save you having to do a facial recognition at this time."

"Okay but I want to see him. I have to see him because right now, this is all too surreal and I somehow can't believe it is happening."

Gray continued. "Mrs Delvecchio, I was hoping to spare you this but the man on the other side of those doors did not die a peaceful death. We believe someone took a blunt instrument to his head."

Sarah felt the world around her spinning. She put an arm out towards the wall to steady herself but Gabe reached out and caught her. She welcomed his masculine comfort and sank into his arms. Her face was buried in Gabe's chest as she tried to catch her breath, panic threatening to overwhelm and consume her. "You didn't tell me, Gabe," she said after a moment, her voice weak.

"No, I'm sorry," he said, feeling like a coward and so very useless. "Hey! Marco had some tattoos, didn't he?" His voice sounded triumphant, thinking he had saved Sarah some pain. If the police would take the tats as recognition, he felt sure Sarah would be spared having to look at Marco's face. Gabe had seen him earlier in the night so he knew it wasn't pretty and it made him feel sick at the mere thought of having to see him again right now. He felt sure that Sarah would be in pieces if she had to go through the same thing.

Sarah looked up at Gabe, grateful for his intervention. "Yes! Yes, he did have some tattoos. He had the names of our children written on his chest." She broke into a brief smile, thinking of some far off memory. "He had it done about six months after Adam was born, knowing that I hated them! He has the boys on his right side, Gio above and Adam below his nipple and Grace on the left hand side."

Gray nodded, deep in thought.

"I still need to see him, Lieutenant Gray. I have to see him for myself," Sarah pleaded.

Gray nodded in agreement. "Okay, give me a couple of minutes and I'll come back out for you. Please wait here." She turned and disappeared through the double doors.

Now Sarah turned to Gabe. "You should have told me," she admonished him. Her words were quiet although the rage was building up inside her. She should have been given time to get used to this latest setback, rather than it being forced upon her moments before seeing Marco.

Gabe nodded. He agreed with her. "I'm sorry. I didn't know how to tell you and it never just came up in conversation. After a while, it didn't seem to be important, he is still gone. I just didn't want you to know he had suffered."

"This is me, Gabe, Marco's wife! I would have found out in the end. Besides, if he suffered, he only has himself to blame. Right now, I'm so angry with him, I could kill him myself!"

"Sarah, we will find out what happened. We will find out who Marco was meeting and why he felt he had to meet them alone."

"And will you tell me why no-one followed him anyway? God knows, he often had me followed!"

"His word was law," Gabe answered her with a quiet forcefulness. "I couldn't go against him."

Just then the double doors swung open and Rosie Gray came out with a sympathetic smile on her face. She said nothing but gestured for Sarah and Gabe to go through. Sarah put her hand on Gabe's arm to stop him, saying she had to do this alone. She followed Rosie Gray down a short corridor and then into a cold, grim room.

The room was small, with grey paint on all of the walls. A peculiar smell hung in the air. The floor was tiled white with no visible dirt or marks and the room had just one thing inside. A gurney with a white sheet covering a body.

Sarah took a deep breath. She knew it was Marco lying under the sheet just from the outline. She walked up beside him and braced herself for the inevitable. Even with the late warning, she had no idea what state he was going to be in, how much blood there might be and how bruised, battered, and distorted his once handsome face might now be. She was trembling. She wanted to be sick.

Mercifully, when the morgue attendant swept back the sheet, there was another one covering Marco's face. The only part of him in view was his upper torso with 'Grace', 'Giorgio' and 'Adam' emblazoned in italics on his chest confirming to Sarah that it was her husband. His perfect toned and tanned body that she adored and had been mistress of for many years was now lifeless and already had developed a dull waxy colour to it. She reached out to touch him for the last time but felt that he was cold, not how she wanted to remember him so she pulled her hand away as though he had stung her. Sarah felt the will to live begin to drain out of her body and although she wanted to leave, she couldn't bring herself to walk away. She was never going to see him again. She was never going to touch him again. She had loved Marco with all of her heart and soul and didn't know how she was going to live without him. A tear fell down her face and landed with a splash on his chest. Seeing him like this, getting confirmation of his death had not made it easier for her as she had hoped it might.

"Mrs Delvecchio?" Rosie prompted her. "Can you confirm this is your husband?"

Sarah just nodded, unable to speak.

"Do you need a minute?"

Sarah turned and looked at Gray, her tears having dried up with a sudden resolution and a realisation of her reason for carrying on, at least for the time being. "No, thank you. I have seen enough. This is Marco Delvecchio. I need to know what you know about how he died."

The two women walked with a steeled determination out of the room and back to where Gabe was waiting. Rosie continued walking towards what look like a cloak room and Sarah followed.

"Sarah… may I call you that?" Rosie asked.

Sarah nodded her consent.

"Sarah, I have been working for Marco for about five years now." Her voice was low and she leaned into Sarah as they walked. "This has hit us hard and we *will* find out who did this and why. All we know at the moment is that Marco was meeting with an unknown person or persons that may or may not have killed him."

"So, you don't know much then?" Sarah's sarcasm was evident.

Gray stopped and turned to Sarah and Gabe. "He was found in his car which is in the process of being impounded for investigation. There is bound to be DNA evidence in the vehicle. We believe he may have been attacked outside the car and left for dead but that Marco managed to crawl back inside. We think he was calling for help and that he was trying to make a phone call as we found his unlocked cell-phone in his hand. He died before he could connect the call."

"So he would have suffered then? He would have been in a lot of pain?" Sarah felt almost numb as she tried to get a grip on her husband's last minutes.

Her question remained unanswered. Neither Gray nor Gabe felt it required an answer.

"We can now begin the autopsy on Marco to try and find out more. We can find out what killed him and how long it was from when he was killed to when he was found. He may have more DNA evidence on him that we can use. We have police combing the area he was found in for the weapon, which may also have evidence on it. Sarah, we will find them," she assured Sarah. She reached for a plastic bag that a lady behind the desk held out for her and Rosie handed this to Sarah. "These are Marco's personal things that we have already processed and have finished with. We have kept some items for now, like his cell phone but will hand these over as soon as we can."

Sarah looked unthinking at the bag in her hand and turned away. She walked out of the building towards her car. The sun was now warm and shining. As they got to the car, Gabe took her keys to drive.

"Do you know where they found him, Gabe?" she asked.

"Sure, but you won't be able to go there though. The police will be all over it," he pre-empted her thoughts.

"Take me there anyway."

"Sarah…"

"Don't argue with me Gabe, you know you never win."

He sighed and wanted to smile at her remark but he was too heartsick. Instead, her started up Sarah's car and drove Sarah to where her husband had been killed.

They drove in silence for the journey to where Marco had met his death, each lost in their own thoughts. Sarah was now all too aware of how Marco had met his horrific and gruesome end and she fought back the nausea that once again threatened. Flashes of unwanted imagination that her mind seemed intent on showing over and over again, like an old movie stuck on its reels raced through her mind; she knew now that he would have suffered greatly, feeling every shattering blow to his skull and as she thought about it, she almost flinched as her mind replayed the events she imagined. She still hoped Marco would have lost consciousness at the first blow and not felt a further thing as he died. Sarah had hoped her husband would not have been aware that he was dying. But she also now knew that he had crawled back into his car and died; that meant he would at least have been conscious of what was happening. He would have felt the pain.

She sighed in anguish, the gentle moan of agony escaping her lips and she squeezed her eyes shut, forcing back the tears that threatened to overwhelm her. Gabe looked over at her, taking his eyes off the road for just a second.

"Sarah? Are you okay?" He knew the answer to that and he admonished himself for the idiotic question.

She shook her head but didn't say anything. She could not speak, for opening her mouth would allow the vomit at the back of her throat to escape. At the very least, she would erupt in a torrent of grief if the force of it found an exit point. Neither was acceptable. Her grief must wait until this was avenged. It would keep her sharp.

Bringing the momentary lapse under control, Sarah took a deep breath. "Just keep driving," she commanded.

Gabriel paused in thought but carried on driving. "I'm not sure this is a good idea," he ventured. "What will it prove?"

"Absolutely nothing. I just need to see the place where..." she faltered, unable to finish.

Shaking his head, Gabe nonetheless drove and headed for the location. It didn't take long, traffic was still light and doubtless they'd hit the rush hour traffic on the drive home. It was obvious when they'd hit the street off North River Drive. The area was run down and desolate; there were just a few single storey homes in a state of bad repair on this particular street, chain link fences were all that enclosed the properties encased with yellowing grass. Young women, mainly black and Hispanic lounged around on their dilapidated porches, yelling at their kids and smoking god only knew what. They seemed oblivious to the police cars and emergency vehicles parked up their street. Sarah assumed that perhaps it was such a common placed event in this area of North Miami that no-one cared anymore.

Gabe pulled over and parked the car just a short walk from the cordoned off area. After he and Sarah got out of the car, he made double sure that the expensive car was locked behind them. He didn't relish the idea of someone taking a fancy to the little red sports car and them being stranded here. Police presence was still high and several news stations were still setting up their outside broadcast units, while others were recording the news reels with the tragic scene in the background. Marco's death was big news and the news wires had been buzzing. With some hesitation, Sarah and Gabe walked towards the cordoned off area. It was beneath a busy overpass, heavy traffic above them going about their business unaware of the carnage and personal tragedy in the street below.

This end of the street was crammed with run-down buildings, long-abandoned warehouses and closed-down shops; a typical place for gangs, drugs and murder. It was the seedy side of Miami and a world away from South Beach and its tourist traps although they were just a few miles away.

As Sarah faltered, Gabe took the lead and looked around for a familiar face in uniform; he'd have one in there somewhere. He was unsure why Sarah wanted to be here and what she hoped to achieve and he for one, didn't want to be here where Marco had been murdered. He wanted to be away from here as quick as possible.

"Hey ma'am! You cannot cross that line!" a firm and almost agitated voice called out and Gabe looked for Sarah. She had pulled the yellow tape high and was attempting to walk underneath it, heading for her husband's car.

"It was my husband that died here," she told the owner of the voice, a young policemen that Gabe didn't know.

Gabe watched as the young officer's face hardened. It was evident that he knew who the victim was and was just glad that another so-called criminal was off the streets of Miami-Dade. He spoke with force and without a trace of sympathy.

"Well, I'm sorry ma'am but you still cannot cross this line. Do you have a liaison officer to help you?"

Sarah's patience was at an end and she exploded. "No, I don't! Do you know who I am? Do you have any idea who your victim is?" Her face had turned puce and she balled her fists up at her side.

Gabe hurried to her side and pulled her away from the confrontation. "Don't start with the crap, Sarah. It's not going to help. Marco never pulled the 'you should know who I am' shit, and I don't think he'd appreciate you doing it. I'm taking you home now, come on!" He tried to edge her back towards her car.

She shook him off. She would not 'come on'. She hadn't done what she had come here for. Her tormented face surveyed the scene.

Marco's black Lexus was still parked up to the curb. The driver's door was open as was the trunk. A young detective was peering in the trunk and poking around into the corners with a flashlight and it resembled a scene from a movie. A pick-up truck had arrived and was manoeuvring into position so the Lexus could be loaded on to the back and be towed away. Sarah could see no blood on the windscreen or the front seats which confirmed the belief that Marco had not been hit in his car. Marco had been found in the car so he would have had to have been very cognisant to get himself back inside after the attack. This was what Rosie Gray had told her and it looked to Sarah to be the truth. Sarah did not want to be spared the truth; she needed it, however hard it would be.

The area was crawling with uniformed police and suited detectives, buzzing around the car looking for evidence as to who had committed this crime. Sarah wondered how many of them cared about finding the perpetrator and which of them had the same attitude of the young officer, who she noticed, was still glaring at her and Gabe from the other side of the tape.

"Mrs Delvecchio?" A new, kinder voice called out from the blind side of the officer. She looked as he came into view and recognised him but couldn't name him. He smiled at her, his face full of compassion. "I'm Detective Manolo. I work with Lieutenant Gray."

"Oh yes. Do you…" Sarah cleared her throat and corrected herself. "Did you know my husband?"

He nodded. "I'm sorry for your loss," he seemed genuine. The unfriendly officer had drifted away.

Sarah had heard the platitudes of others far too many times already today and glossed over it. "Are you on this case then?"

Manolo nodded. "Lieutenant Gray is the officer in charge and I'm working closely with her. We are about to take the vehicle away." He looked to Gabe. "Maybe you shouldn't be here. Perhaps you should be with your family?"

"They're fine." Sarah replied absent of emotion, her eyes on the car behind Manolo. The pick-up was winching the Lexus onto the bed of the trailer and a police escort was ready to leave with it. Sarah turned her attention back to Manolo after a minute or so. "So, what do you know?"

He shook his head. "Nothing yet, it's too early to tell. We will keep you informed of every step and every finding. I promise you that we will find out who did this."

"Of course. But not if we find them first," her meaning was unmistakable.

Manolo paused. "You know, Mrs Delvecchio, if I find that threat to be realised, I will have to arrest you and I really don't want to do that."

Sarah looked away. "Do what you have to do, Detective, much as I will," she said and turned to walk back to her car with Gabe.

The Lexus left with the police escort and the crowd began to drift away. There was nothing else to see. The excitement was over for now.

Arriving home about an hour later, Sarah saw that Grace was still sitting in the kitchen getting another fix of caffeine. She was pale and utterly grief-stricken. She turned as she heard her mother come into the room and one look at Sarah's face confirmed the worst. Grace burst into a fresh flood of tears and wailing, headed for the comforting arms of her husband. Scott held her close, wishing he could do something to help her.

He was worried. As he held the shaking, sobbing body of his wife, he wondered what would happen to the Family now and who was going to take charge. He had called San Francisco as Sarah had asked and Frankie Miotto had said he would send people to Florida if it was required. The two families were close and they only had to ask. Scott had then called Chicago. He knew there was some sort of history with Vinnie Bonnetti and the Delvecchios but he wasn't sure what and it wasn't his business anyway. Vinnie had gone very quiet on the phone and after a minute, had said he'd be on the next flight to Miami with his son to lend any help that was needed.

The army was gathering but Scott wondered who wanted to be the general.

Sarah and Grace were drinking coffee in the kitchen when Cliff and Andrea Bremann arrived. Cliff was the family 'accountant'. He had gone to school with Marco and had been taken in from an early age with the way of life that the Delvecchios lived. Not for him the worry of morals and illegal goings-on; he was sucked in with the power and wealth. He spent a lot of time as a kid with Marco and his family and after college, came back to Palm Beach with his young wife to set up his accountants practice to deal with anything that the Delvecchios needed help with. He was expert at moving money around the world, or making investments look more legal than they might otherwise be. He had proven himself invaluable to Marco over the years.

Andrea had been pushed towards Sarah when she first came to live in Palm Beach after her marriage to Marco. The friendship had started off as forced but they soon became fast friends and Andrea was the only woman outside of the family that Sarah trusted. It was to Andrea that Sarah went when she had learned of Marco's affair with an ex-girlfriend in the early years and the one she went to when she didn't think she could live with Marco and his temper when he wanted every man that she spoke to beaten up.

Andrea was the friend Sarah missed during the 'San Francisco' years, as she called it, after she had left Marco and was living in hiding in California.

Sarah was glad of her friend now. Andrea tried to comfort Sarah but as they hugged, Sarah saw over her friend's shoulder Cliff and Gabe go into Marco's office. She pulled away from the embrace and stormed out of the kitchen and down the hallway to where the door was just closing. She pushed it open.

She looked at the assembled men in her husband's inner sanctum, her anger evident for all to see. "Don't shut me out of this!" Her voice was raised, a common temperament of hers of late. She glared at Gabe, Scott and Cliff and walked around the desk to the empty leather chair and sat down. She looked at Gabe. "What do you know?"

Gabe took a breath as if trying to gather his patience. He was used to Sarah's shows of defiance, he had seen her defy Marco for years but he had never been on the receiving end of it. He didn't like it. "We are expecting a phone call from Rosie Gray soon. She will give us the preliminary findings. We hope that this will give us something to start with," Gabe informed her.

"Someone must have known what Marco was up to."

They all stayed silent and she mistook their silence for knowledge. A light came on in her head, slowly sparking.

"Did he have another woman?" The words almost choked her as bile rose in the throat at the mere thought he'd had someone else.

All three men denied it in a rush. Too quickly Sarah thought. They all said how much he'd loved her right to the end, bowling her over with their words and strong denials.

She put up her hand to silence them. "Then what? One of you knows something."

Gabe cleared his throat. "I think, but I am not one hundred per cent sure, but I think that he had a meeting with Jimmy Caruso within the last week. It was the only thing I knew about that Marco refused to discuss much. He made some cagey phone calls to Caruso and clammed up when I asked him about it."

"Caruso? Well, that's a start. Has anyone talked to him?"

Cliff came closer to Sarah and put his arm around her shoulders. "Things take time. Why don't we wait until Vinnie and Jamie get here, then we'll have more resources."

"Of course and my husband's killer gets further away from us. I don't want the police to get whoever did this, it has to be us! Do you all understand?"

They all agreed. It was the only way.

"It's what we all want, Sarah." Gabe assured her. "When things like this happen, people will come to us. It may take a day or so for information to leak but it will happen. We have people leaning on people already so it's just a matter of time. That's all."

Sarah was not convinced. What they had no real idea on was how much Marco had confided in her over the years and that she probably knew more about his business than they realised. Marco had trusted her with some things he wouldn't trust any of them with. She knew he had looked at her with different eyes after she had tried to kill Joe twenty years ago. This now threw all of that into doubt. Why hadn't Marco told her about this, whatever *this* was?

Sarah grabbed the phone next to her on the first ring. It was only the gate house announcing the arrival of Rosa, Sal, Adina and Joe. Like Adam, Joe was home from school in California and Sarah was very grateful for having so much family around her in her hour of need. She was struggling to deal with the grief of her children as she fought to contain her own. She hoped that her niece and nephew would be of a comfort to Grace, Giorgio and Adam.

Sarah met her sister-in-law in the hallway and hugged her. The two women had always been close and Rosa was also struggling to hold back tears for her brother for Sarah's sake. Adina and Joe just hovered in the background both looking shocked and almost afraid. They were old enough to understand what might be happening and young enough to be afraid by it. They hugged their aunt in turn and offered condolences, neither knowing what to do or how to act. This was the first loss they had endured and were unprepared for grief on such a grand scale. Adina, beautiful Adina, so much like her mother stayed in the embrace of her beloved aunt for a moment longer than necessary while her brother just drifted off upstairs in search of Adam, the cousin he was closest to. Sarah prayed that Joe would be of comfort to her youngest son.

Sal kissed Sarah and disappeared into the office with the other men. Sarah and Rosa drifted back into the kitchen to where Andrea still waited with Grace. Fresh tea and coffee were needed. Rosa helped Sarah to put fresh on to keep busy while Grace sat with Andrea.

"Sal didn't tell me what happened." Rosa began, her hesitant words were barely above a whisper.

Sarah sighed. "We don't know. Marco was out alone. He got his head caved in," she replied succinctly. And without thinking about the feelings of the other women in the room.

"*What?*" Rosa's face crumpled.

"Sarah… "Andrea's voice carried a hint of a scolding.

Sarah stopped what she was doing and looked at the women in her midst. "Sorry, Ro. That was heartless. I'm just so cross with your brother right now," her voice cracked a little. "This never needed to have happened. In all the years I have known him, he never went anywhere on his own, he always went with Gabe, or Scott or Enzo. I just don't get it. I'm starting to wonder if maybe he had another woman and her husband got to him. Maybe he deserved it. I just don't know what to think or who to blame and I need some answers."

"We all need answers, Sarah. Blaming Marco might get you through the worst of this, but I don't think you are right to do it. I don't think for one minute that he had another woman. He knew how good with a gun you are!" Andrea told her.

Sarah softened a little and even managed a small but sad smile. She knew deep down that Andrea was right, that Marco had loved her and only her for over twenty years. She was glad for the time they'd had, even though it made the parting all the more difficult.

"Well what happens now?" Rosa wanted to know.

Sarah shrugged. "We find out who killed your brother and… " She didn't need to finish.

Rosa turned away and shuddered. She knew the exact meaning of her sister-in-law's unfinished sentence. Rosa despised the way her family meted out their own form of punishment, however well-deserving it was deigned to be. Her husband had been one of the men that Marco always called upon when such measures needed to be made. Rosa could always tell when Sal had been out on a job, as he put it, by the way he behaved afterwards, always on a high, almost excitable. Every time, Rosa would push it to the back of her mind and ignore it, pretend it wasn't happening. She wanted to believe in the legal system of her country and hoped that her brother's killer was tracked down by the police and dealt with in the official and proper way. She hoped so for the killer's sake as, after killing Marco Delvecchio, it would not be easy on them.

A sudden commotion in the hallway of doors slamming and raised voices turned everyone's attention from Rosa's disapproving scowl to the other side of the kitchen door. Sarah hurried over to the door and peered around. The men looked as though they were leaving.

Sarah felt her anger rise again and was determined that she was not going to be left out of whatever was occurring. "What's going on?" her voice was loud enough to make the five men stop and turn around to look at her. Cliff came over.

"We have a tip off. You need to stay here," he told her in what he hoped was a gentle but not patronising way.

Sarah took a deep breath. Why were none of these men taking her seriously? She was not the little woman to be left at home while the big, brave men went out and took care of her! She had not taken that kind of behaviour from Marco, he had learnt the long and hard way but it had got through in the end. She was damned if she was going to go through all of that again with these men.

"I don't give a crap about what you think I should be doing! If there is something to be dealt with, you can bet your life that I am going to know about it. Now, I will ask you again. What is going on?"

Despite the situation, or maybe because of it, Cliff was impressed with her attitude. He knew that neither Marco nor Gabe had ever under estimated Sarah over the years and were concessionary towards her. He himself had believed her to be a trophy wife, much like his own who just shopped and looked good. Sarah even looked good today in spite of her grief and lack of restful sleep. Maybe he shouldn't have under estimated her either. Maybe this individualism was what had stood her out from the rest of the women that tried to catch Marco's attention. Tried and failed.

Cliff looked to Gabe who nodded his assent. "We have information that confirms that Marco was meeting Jimmy Caruso on the quiet for a few weeks. We are heading over to his bar now," he told her.

Sarah nodded her thanks at this news and looked around at the men who were almost waiting for her to speak. "Gabe and I will go. The rest of you stay here and wait. Rosie Gray is meant to call soon and I'm sure there are still people you can lean on from here." She looked at her watch. It was now twelve thirty. "I also need someone to go to West Palm Beach airport. Vinnie and Jamie will be arriving within the hour." Her house-keeper came out of the dining room and Sarah grabbed her arm. "Clarice, I need you to make up the guest suite over the pool-house for Mr Bonnetti and his son and make extra for dinner tonight." Clarice nodded her acknowledgement and walked out of the French doors towards the pool and pool-house. Sarah looked at the five men around her and they looked bewildered and to be fair, pissed off. They weren't used to taking orders from a woman but in the absence of a male heir, they did as they were told, glad of some direction for the time being.

Sarah and Gabe took off again and left the house behind them. Sarah was glad to be from out of her four walls. She felt as though they were closing in on her and she was suffocating. She had to keep reminding herself to breathe, something she seemed almost eager to cease and give in to the despair that threatened to overwhelm her. The house grew smaller in the side mirror and she felt freer with every yard they travelled as if putting distance between her and the house made her forget the misery she was feeling; out of sight, out of mind.

Gabe drove again as Sarah also felt exhaustion in equal measure hit her and as the electric gate drew back to let them pass, flashes of light hit the car and temporarily blinded both driver and passenger. The road was inundated with Florida media and as the journalists and photographers realised who was in the car, they began to call her name, each trying to get the best photo of the pale woman and her companion in the vehicle. They chased down the road after the speeding vehicle, a hurricane of noise and action, but gave up and went back to settle outside the gates to wait. Someone else was bound to leave or return at some point.

"Jesus!" Sarah muttered under her breath. Of course, she had seen it all before when Marco had been shot through their bedroom window from a sniper's bullet, the culprit of which had never been caught. Again, it had happened after Joe Senior had been killed in Jupiter Beach – she had been responsible in part for that although it had not been her gun that had killed Joe. Now it seemed that the first Delvecchio to have been killed in violent circumstances in many years was again resulting in an almost permanent media campsite outside her home and the events were yet again making the news. No doubt tomorrow's local front pages would have her husband's face all over it and Sarah dared not even turn on the TV. She wondered if she would ever have time to grieve properly and in private.

As the press disappeared into the distance, taking only pictures of the back of her car, Gabe and Sarah both relaxed a little and Sarah remembered all of the times that she and Marco had evaded the press in the past. They were always very eager to get a picture of Marco, smiling at some charity bash or leaving a restaurant, he was a local celebrity in their eyes. Marco had always tried to stay elusive and private but sometimes it was hard to avoid. It was inevitable that he would always be blamed for any major crime in the county despite any apparent lack of evidence. Perhaps Marco's ultimate fate had been Kharma.

Sarah sighed. Now was not the time for reminiscing. Now was the time for action. "So what do we know about Caruso?" she asked Gabe.

Gabe shrugged. "Not much about what he and Marco were into, that's for sure. They met up last week in the bar we are going to, but he made me stay in the car. Enzo went inside with him, but was told to stay out of ear-shot. Enzo said it looked friendly enough, there were no raised voices or intimidating actions. The meeting lasted about an hour but that's it. I just want to talk to Jimmy and find out more. It may lead us somewhere assuming Caruso will talk."

"So you don't think Jimmy Caruso killed Marco?"

"Unlikely."

Sarah didn't know what to say and so said nothing. They drove in silence for a while, with Sarah just staring out of the window but seeing nothing as the sun blazed over their heads. Outside of the car and the air-conditioning, it was going to be another hot and humid day.

The bar that Jimmy Caruso owned was on the South side of Miami in a quiet area, once prosperous but now not quite so. Jimmy had claimed ownership of the bar after the previous owner, a Dutchman, had fallen foul of Jimmy in a rather expensive game of cards. Jimmy was usually at Bar Vondel from lunchtime until around early evening. After that, he could be found at his more salubrious establishments where his real profits were to be made. Bar Vondel did not attract much attention which was the main reason that Jimmy kept hold of it.

Gabe was resolute that Sarah should stay in the car while he went inside. It was not the kind of establishment that a respectable female should frequent. The area had a high crime rate, drug induced muggings and killings, some street gang related, others an unfortunate accident. Just last week, a couple from San Diego had strayed off the main drag looking for a slice of real Miami life and had been held up at gun point after flashing wads of cash and designer gear in the streets. The husband was dead after trying to play the hero and fought back leaving his wife a thirty-two year old widow.

As much as Sarah wanted to go inside with all guns blazing, she relented to Gabe's authority. He knew his business and Sarah would let him make his initial enquiries. He left her locked inside the car with her 9mm. Sarah checked her phone for messages and waited, pleased to have a few minutes alone.

Gabe pushed the red door to the bar open and the smell of stale smoke hit him at the same time as the chronically bad music. It was a dive at best and not one of Caruso's best joints. Gabe himself preferred the one in South Beach, lots of young slim women to eye up when he wasn't with one of his usual girlfriends.

Inside Bar Vondel was a lone barman. He had long hair tied back in a ponytail and a crooked nose. There were just two customers propping up the bar at the far end, each drinking beer from a large tankard. One had on a cheap looking cowboy hat and the other a cream jacket, a la Miami Vice. Neither looked up at the well-dressed gentleman who had just entered. Gabe let the door shut behind him.

The middle aged barman put down his cleaning cloth that he had been wiping his bar down with and walked to where Gabe was leaning against the bar.

"What can I get you, Sir?" he asked. His face had a look of confusion. He was puzzled as to why a man with a very expensive suit was here in his bar. This place was a hang-out for drop outs and dead beats. His question was answered with question from Gabe.

"Is Jimmy Caruso here?"

That question got the sudden attention of the two drunkards at the bar. They both looked up at the same moment and fixed their attention on Gabe.

"The Boss ain't around just now," the barman answered but Gabe didn't miss the quick flick of his gaze towards a door at the back of the long bar.

"Really. Do you know when he might be around?" Gabe pushed.

The barman shrugged. "Can't say for sure."

"Well, do you know where I might find him?"

Another shrug for an answer.

Gabe knew he would get nothing from this man and as much as he wanted to make him talk, to take his gun out and shove it in the barman's face, the odds were stacked against him with the two side-kicks at the bar. Gabe knew when to pick his battles and now was not a good time to start a fight he wouldn't win and with Sarah waiting outside for him. He would find another time.

"Okay." He pulled a Mont Blanc pen from his inside jacket pocket and, grabbing a serviette from a pile on the bar, scribbled down his name and number and pushed it towards the barman. "Have Jimmy call me as soon as. It's very important." He flashed a polite smile at him and turned away. He gave the two drunks an icy stare that made them look away as he did so.

"Right," the barman said flatly, intimating that he would not pass any message along.

Gabe walked back out of the bar and into the bright light thinking about where else he might find Jimmy at this time of the day. He slammed the door behind him and walked back to the car to where Sarah sat waiting. He got in the car without a word and fired up the engine.

"That was quick," Sarah sounded surprised.

Gabe nodded. "Jimmy's not around. So the barman said at least, although I get the distinct impression that's not the case, but... " he didn't get to finish.

Sarah was out of the car and striding across the path towards the bar. Gabe called out after her but she was gone, leaving the red door closing in her wake.

Sarah heard the door slam shut behind her and she took in the interior of the bar. The very same three men all looked up at her and Cowboy Hat wolf whistled as he appraised the rich looking well-dressed woman. Her dark hair was held back in a gold-coloured clip with not a hint of grey showing. Sarah's slender calves were encased in dark green Capri pants that gave way to a white DKNY top and she had no make-up on. Still, she gave off an air of sophistication and natural beauty. She was not the usual kind of woman who would frequent Bar Vondel.

"Where is Jimmy Caruso?" she demanded of the barman.

"That's the second time in just a few minutes someone has asked for him," the barman responded smartly.

"Unlike the previous questioner, I won't take your lies. So I ask again. Where is he?" Her hazel eyes blazed dark with anger and frustration. She was used to getting her own way. Most of the time.

Sarah became aware that Gabe had entered the bar and was standing behind her. "Sarah… " he called out as soft as he could, wanting her away from this potential explosive situation.

She ignored him and repeated her question of the barman. Sarah saw that one of the two customers had pushed back his bar stool and was ambling towards her. "I just need to know where Jimmy Caruso is. I want to talk to him about the death of my husband," her voice was beginning to break up with both emotion and anger. Why would no-one talk to them about Marco's killer? Somebody somewhere must know something!

Gabe put his hand on Sarah's elbow and tried to pull her away. She shook him off and there was a real danger that her anger would be re-directed at him.

The barman began to soften a little after witnessing Sarah's distress. He poured her a shot of a thick brown liquid, a cheap brand of brandy and pushed the glass towards her. "I wish I could help you lady, I really do, but the truth is, I don't know where he is. Jimmy usually comes in around this time but I haven't seen him since yesterday. Your man there, he gave me his number. I will ask Jimmy to call you as soon as I see him."

Sarah took the glass in her hand and knocked back the strong spirit. It burned her throat as she swallowed it and it settled in her stomach, churning a little. It made her want to drink more and get obscenely drunk and obliterate her memories of the last few hours, and drown her sorrows. Instead, she just pulled out a ten dollar bill from her purse and passed it across the bar, saying nothing.

"On the house," the barman told her with his voice full of sympathy. He didn't know this woman but he'd seen the mid-morning news and pieced it together. He knew the circles his boss moved in and knew why they were searching for Jimmy. But it wasn't his business and he didn't want to get into it with these people.

Sarah thanked the barman with just a nod and left with Gabe. Back in the car, she asked Gabe what their next move was.

"We go home and you rest. You are exhausted Sarah, and are barely functioning. You get some sleep and we can decide what the best course of action will be. I promise," he pre-empted her next words, "we won't make any plans without you."

Rest? Sarah would not be able to rest until she knew what had happened to Marco and his killers were brought to Delvecchio justice. She wanted to know why he had gone out alone. She wanted to know why Gabe allowed it – it wasn't the norm. Despite all the assurances from the men around her who knew Marco best, she had the sickening feeling in the pit of her stomach that would not go away. Perhaps he had been keeping a mistress. Perhaps he had a whole other life that she knew nothing about with another woman and God! maybe even children. He was away from home a lot, it would have been easy to have fooled her. What if Sarah had been lavishing Marco with love and attention and he had been betraying her for all of these years? Sarah had to find out if Marco had been more like his father than she had given him credit for with a love child or two kicking about somewhere. She had to find out if she had been enough for him even though it would kill her if there had been someone else.

Clarice had made a chilli for everyone even though no-one felt much like eating. It was being pushed around plates rather than down throats although this was no reflection on the housekeeper's cooking. Giorgio had woken up an hour previous and was just staring but not seeing his plate. Adam was looking sullen, staring at his mother like she was to blame for all of this. Grace was trying to keep busy with Connor and was ignoring her dinner, despite constant nagging from her husband to eat. Sarah just sat in her usual place hugging a mug of hot sweet tea.

"I'm going out again soon," she told no-one in particular. She hadn't said anything to Gabe and didn't want him to know what her plans were. He would only try to stop her. She wanted to leave and go to where she was going without any fuss. She was not hopeful that this would be achieved but she was going to at least try.

No-one had said anything about her leaving, so she stood and left the dining room. She grabbed her keys as she passed through the hallway, hearing quiet voices in Marco's office and walked out into the balmy evening air. The rain they'd had earlier had not cooled the day any and it was still hot and humid. Sarah's car was in the driveway and she unlocked it and started the engine up. As she drove down the gravel drive, she checked her mirrors but didn't see anyone coming out from the house after her. She was challenged at the gate-house but in her irritation, told them that she was going to see Andrea – her irritability whether real or fake got her through the gates. As the gates peeled back, the encamped press jumped to attention as they realised who was leaving the house. Flashes went off in Sarah's face, but she looked straight ahead and drove without concession until they moved out of her way. It was then easy to lose them in her flashy red sports car, the last gift she had received from Marco and was grateful once again for his benevolence.

Sarah's nerves began to calm once she was away from the house and all of its troubles and traumas. She turned the radio on low for background distraction and got on the I-95 south to Coral Gables. She raced passed Boca, Pompano and Fort Lauderdale, their beaches just starting to empty out after a doubtless busy day in the sun. Once through Miami she drove closer to her destination and had to rely on the SatNav to take her the last few miles. She had never been to Jimmy's house before and had no idea where it was. She had been lucky to find his address. The tinny female voice instructed Sarah to make a left turn onto Jimmy's road and Sarah was impressed with the opulence of the street. This was one of the country's richest neighbourhoods and vast, sumptuous houses lined the winding roads, hidden behind secure fences and ancient trees. The sea and its tributary canals backed onto the mansions and Sarah was impressed. Whilst it was evident that Jimmy Caruso was rich, he was not as prosperous as Marco had been. The Delvecchios still owned this part of Florida and Sarah was determined to keep it that way for her sons. Whatever the cost.

She found the house she was looking for and it was only then that Sarah began to wonder how she was going to get inside.

Remarkably, just saying her name through the intercom gave her access to the ante-bellum style house she sought. As the black gates swung open to reveal a minor national park within, she drove through and sped up the drive. There seemed to be no-one around to challenge her and she was somewhat perplexed by this. There was no way it should have been this easy and she thought that at any minute, someone would stop her car.

However, she made it all the way up the drive and to the six columned portico at the front of the house with not a soul in sight. Sarah got out of the car, thinking that maybe, she should have informed someone of her whereabouts but pushing thoughts of kidnap and murder out of her mind, she walked up to the big wooden door. She rang the bell and waited, hearing the chimes resound around the house within.

Her patience was thin on the ground and after about thirty seconds with no-one answering, she rang the bell again. Without waiting for an answer – time was short, she was tired and grouchy and still had a long drive home – she tried to push the door open, not expecting it to be unlocked. She allowed herself a small smile of victory when the door gave.

With a great deal of trepidation, she peered around the door. This was a house where people would shoot first and ask questions later, especially of an intruder. Hesitating for just a few moments and hearing and seeing nothing, she took a deep breath and pushed the door open a bit further, taking a small step inside. Her footsteps echoed around the hallway. She took a few steps further in and then closed the door behind her. Her heart was thumping fast and she felt sure she could hear it also echoing around the marble floor. Marble steps spiralled up to the first floor from the right of the hall and a darkened corridor led off from the left. Sarah dismissed both as an option and looked towards the three doors in turn opposite her. She had no idea of the layout or which way she should go.

"Can I help you?"

There it was – the challenge. At last. The gruff voice belonged to a middle-aged man, staring at her with a bemused expression on his handsome face.

She nodded. "I'm here to see Jimmy Caruso?" she made her voice as bold as she could. "I'm... "

"Yeah, we know who you are," he didn't let her finish. "Kinda been expecting you. Jimmy's through there - " he gesticulated with his chin towards the middle door and then disappeared.

Sarah turned towards the door and she relaxed a little. It was obvious that they would have been expecting her. With all that was going on, security would be tight and she wouldn't be allowed in this house unannounced any more than they would get into her house.

She opened the door and followed the corridor, her heels clicking on the marble floor as she walked. Her heart was still racing a little, exhaustion and apprehension unsettling her. A tinkle of high pitched laughter on the opposite side of another set of doors broke the eerie silence enveloping the house.

With dramatic flourish, she opened the doors and looked around her. Sarah was in a large conservatory with the Miami evening sun beating through the glass onto an array of tropical flowers and small palm trees. Another set of double doors led out onto the pool deck but that was empty.

But the eight-seater Jacuzzi in the conservatory was not. Sarah looked over to see Jimmy Caruso sat in the steaming, bubbling water accompanied by two Latino belles, both clad in bright coloured scant two-pieces.

Sarah laughed. "Is Daisy away at her mother's or something, Jimmy?"

Jimmy said nothing for a moment and then dismissed his small entourage. They walked with a surprising elegance out to the pool area, closing the doors behind them and jumped into the pool, laughing and squealing in a pathetic bimbo way that made Sarah's skin crawl. She'd never had time for such hangers-on.

Jimmy smiled and lit up a cigarette. He took a long drag, not taking his eyes off of Sarah and exhaled in her general direction. "There is much about my life that the good Mrs Caruso does not know about. I expect Marco kept similar secrets from you."

Sarah felt her heart crack a little bit more but she steeled herself from it. "If he'd carried on like you, Jimmy, I would have killed him myself. So, tell me. What do you know about my husband's murder?"

Jimmy took another long drag of his fast disappearing cigarette and regarded her with interest. He'd heard about Sarah Delvecchio and how Marco had allowed her to be privy to certain things, things that most men would not want their wives to know about. That she was in his house, alone, demanding things of him proved that the rumours seemed to be correct. He smiled at her. "Everyone knows that me and Delvecchio did not see eye to eye on a lot of things but I had nothing to do with this. What would be my motive?"

"Greed? Wanting what belongs to my sons?"

"I would never take on the Delvecchios, I have enough aggravation already and Marco left me alone to do my thing. He didn't interfere with any Caruso interests so why would I want him dead? Besides, I heard it was a plain old-fashioned mugging."

Sarah shook her head. "He was too clever for that. This was a well-planned hit and I intend to find out who ordered it. God help them when I do."

Jimmy shrugged. He was impressed with her determination and had no doubt that with her tenacity and the might of the Delvecchio family, the killer would be found and wouldn't stand a chance. It was how it should be. Still, he had to ask the question. "Are the police investigating?"

Sarah laughed. "Of course! But you know how it is. They make all the right noises but deep down, they see it as just another mobster biting the dust. A bit less work for them and a lot less crime on the streets. Why should they care?"

Jimmy knew exactly how it was. He'd been around for long enough to know that the cops didn't waste too much time on these crimes. He also knew that there would be a very high price on the head of whoever had killed Marco Delvecchio and that they would be long gone by now. At least, they should be gone if they had any sense.

Jimmy heaved his considerable bulk out of his Jacuzzi and grabbed a towel to dry himself off with. Sarah stood and waited, hoping for more from him, something she might be able to use. Jimmy wrapped the towel around his middle and walked over to the corner of the room to a table where fresh coffee and orange juice had been placed surreptitiously while they had been talking. He sat on one of the chairs and motioned for Sarah to join him. He poured two cups of coffee and passed one to his guest. While she added cream and sugar to the cup, Jimmy continued.

"I admire you Sarah and I will help in any way I can. If I hear anything at all, I will let you all know. Maybe though, you should look across towards Fort Myers, see what the Mexicans might know," he said, rather cryptically.

"Mexicans? But... that would mean narcotics and Marco would never have been involved in that!"

"Perhaps you didn't know your husband quite as well as you thought you did. I know for sure that he was working on something with Carlos Santa Cruz. Perhaps he reneged on a deal and it didn't go down too well with the crew in Fort Myers."

Sarah shook her head. "Santa Cruz?" She didn't believe it. "He is the biggest importer in Florida. Cocaine, methamphetamine, marijuana, the lot. You know that Marco took his own brother out for the damage he was causing with drugs. Joe wouldn't walk away from it. Marco would rather die than associate with such a man."

Jimmy was impressed with her knowledge but still felt that perhaps she held her husband up on too high a pedestal. Marco hadn't been as squeaky clean as he had led her to believe. It was time to put her right on a few things. He took a deep gulp of the cooling coffee before he started. "Marco came to me about six months ago. He was in deep with Santa Cruz and figured it was going to get nasty and wanted to be sure he could rely on me for help, if it came to it, which of course, he could. God knows I had no idea it would end up this way or I would have told him to get out sooner. He never said he needed help to sort it; I would have given it to him for free. Like I say, I don't know what issues he had with Santa Cruz, but there was something."

"In deep, how? You must have some idea!"

"Sarah, in all honesty, he didn't elaborate. The less people knew, the better. That was his ideology."

Sarah had to agree with Jimmy on that at least. Marco had been bleating that out for all of their married life. She'd had no idea that Marco was mixed up with the Mexicans and Sarah needed to know what he was into and why. It was becoming more and more evident that her husband had not confided very much in her at all.

"Where is he? I have to go and see him," Sarah said suddenly, having made her mind up. She stood up to leave as soon as Jimmy gave her an address.

"Who?" Caruso was confused.

"Carlos Santa Cruz."

Jimmy stood and took a firm hold on her arm. "That is something I can't allow. Not on your own," his eyes had gone black with anger. Like Marco's used to do when she defied him.

"You think he would harm me? A woman?"

"He won't care about your gender or your circumstances if you cross him. Santa Cruz has no scruples and no rules and if he did have a hand in killing Marco, he won't care a fuck about killing you, excuse my language. Everyone knows how he operates and he would enjoy taking you out, concerned as he must be about our form of revenge. He may even take your boys out next, not wanting to take a chance on Gio or Adam coming after him."

"Are you saying you think that he had Marco killed?" Sarah spoke, her voice just above a whisper.

He shook his head. "Not for sure. Let's face it; Marco pissed a lot of people off in his time and it could be any one of a number of people. I'm just saying that my money is on Santa Cruz."

"Then this cannot go unpunished. To hell with the law, they would just deport him to carry on with his murderous crimes back in Mexico City or whatever God-forsaken hellhole he comes from!"

"I need to call Gabe. I have to tell him what you are going to do! Have you gone completely mad, woman?"

"I won't go alone Jimmy, of course not," Sarah spoke calmly to placate him. "I have my husband's army to call on plus the combined forces of Chicago and San Francisco. But I have to go. I have lost my husband. My children have lost their father. If Santa Cruz has nothing to do with this, he has nothing to fear and I will drop it. But at the very least, I want to know what possible business he had with Marco."

Jimmy was resigned to the fact that Sarah was going to do whatever she wanted to do and whatever she felt was necessary. Marco had never been able to control her, what possible hope did he have? Besides, it was not his place or his business to try to do so. "Fine. Call me if you need help, I can always send more bodies if you need them."

Sarah felt comforted by his words. She knew that Marco and Jimmy had a colourful history and for Jimmy to offer her, Marco's widow any assistance at all was a bridge half rebuilt. She was grateful to Jimmy for his help and she would make sure he was paid back when this was all settled. She shook his hand and left without saying another word.

It was late when Sarah arrived home. Downstairs was in darkness apart from Marco's office which Sarah crept past, not wanting to draw attention to herself and have to answer any awkward questions. She felt like an errant teenager once again. She could see the lights from under the boys' doors upstairs but she ignored that too. As much as she wanted to be a mother to them and bring them the comfort that they needed, she felt like she didn't have it in her anymore. She assumed Grace had gone home and Andrea too and didn't know where Rosa might be. Sarah headed for the dining room, she knew there was a bottle of brandy there and she needed a drink, just to help her sleep. She headed to the drinks cabinet and poured herself a large one. She stood in the dark and gulped the drink back and as it hit her stomach and burned through her body, she swayed on her feet. Exhaustion was getting the better of her and she yearned for sleep. The door opened quietly and a long familiar face peered around the gap, backlit by the light from the hallway.

"Hey. Gabe said you'd snuck out. I guess some things never change. How are you doing?" Vinnie switched the light on as he walked into the room and over to where Sarah stood.

Sarah was so pleased to see her brother-in-law that tears of relief threatened to fall. She choked back the tears and smiled up at him. "Do you really want an answer to that?" She looked up into his green eyes and felt more comforted than she had at any time in the last twenty-four hours. Sarah was so glad that Vinnie was here that she was unable to express it. She wanted to fall into his arms and feel his strength flow into her. She was also afraid of how she might react if there was any physical contact.

Vinnie shook his head. "Purely rhetorical. Do you mind if I...?" He left the question unfinished as Sarah was already pouring him a drink. They walked over to the large dining table and sat on opposite sides cradling their drinks in their hands.

"Where have you been all evening?" Vinnie asked.

"Just out. Trying to make sense of everything. One thing I have figured is that there is no sense in any of this. Every time something gets uncovered, it leads to more questions. The police don't care, they see it as 'in-house tidying'. No-one appears to know anything so my mind keeps circling back to the same thing. Marco had another woman."

"That's absurd and irrational."

Sarah shrugged. "Perhaps but what else can I think?"

"Think the best of my brother, at least until we know the truth. I don't believe for one minute that he was involved with another woman, he loved you too much. This is not the work of a jealous husband."

They sat in silence for a moment while Sarah thought about that. "So do you believe this is a professional hit then? There are no hallmarks or calling cards, none at least that we have been made aware of. It wasn't a regulated hit, it was too messy."

"True. Not every faction leaves clues or any obvious signs behind. That's why I believe it to be the work of someone else who is outside our... way of doing things," Vinnie finished a little awkwardly.

Sarah nodded. She understood what Vinnie meant despite his clumsy words. It was not the work of an Italian Family or local gang, not a professional one at least and her mind came back around to Carlos Santa Cruz.

"Have you heard of Carlos Santa Cruz?" Sarah asked a little tentative.

Vinnie looked hard at her. "The name has been brought to my attention, yes," he sounded cautious and that intrigued Sarah further.

"In what capacity?"

He shuffled on his chair, buying a few precious seconds to find a non-committal answer, not wanting to fire up Sarah's imagination and give her more fanciful ideas. "We get newspapers in Chicago too, you know," was what he came up with. Pathetic even to his own ears.

Of course! The idea hit her and a light in her brain went on. What a wonderful invention the internet was. She could do her own research and investigation in the privacy of her bedroom and no-one needed to know what she was doing or why.

"Vinnie, I'm so very tired so I think I'll go to bed now. Do you have everything you need?"

He nodded. "Clarice has fixed up the pool room for me and Jamie. I gather you have a full house tonight."

"I think so. I don't know if Grace and Rosa have gone home or are staying but I'm sorry we can't get you in the main house. I hope you'll be okay there tonight."

He assured her that they would be fine and saying goodnight, they went in opposite directions – Vinnie out through the kitchen and out to the pool house and Sarah up the stairs to the empty master bedroom.

Marco had kept a laptop in his closet with some personal documentation on it and she hoped that as computing wasn't his strong point, that it would be easy enough to guess the password so she made a bee-line for that. She was unprepared for the stab to the heart that she felt as she walked into his closet and was surrounded by his clothes, all hanging lifeless around her. His cologne was still attached to them and Sarah physically ached for Marco. She breathed in his lingering scent. Waving off the despair that loomed and resisting the urge to hold his clothes against her, she grabbed the laptop, closed the door behind her and set the machine up on the bed.

As it was firing up, Sarah put on her comfy pyjamas and settled in for a long internet session. The first thing she did was put the name Carlos Santa Cruz into the search engine and was not at all surprised by the many hits it returned. Sarah searched for a newspaper entry and clicked on the first one she found. It didn't tell her anything much. It was about some charity event the Mexican had hosted to raise funds for the African needy. She glanced down at the computerised columns with a lack of interest and began to think that she was wasting her time.

Then she saw Marco's name in the last paragraph of the article.

The journalist had finished the piece by mentioning other persons of note at the function and Marco Delvecchio was a rich benefactor to the charity that Santa Cruz was assisting. He had donated fifty thousand dollars to this particular charity and while Sarah knew Marco had donated a lot of money to various charities and helped wherever he could, she wondered why the two were involved in this. The newspaper was dated over a year ago. She wanted to know why Marco had donated such a large amount to an organisation that built hospitals for AIDS patients in Johannesburg – he was always proud to showing off which charity he donated to, why not this one?

Sarah clicked back to the main list on the search engine to try and find out more from the other entries. There was a small piece about Carlos being arrested around ten months ago for some immigration infraction but that had all been efficiently cleared up by his lawyers. She discovered that Carlos had a wife and two daughters and on delving a bit further into his family life, learned that his son had died at the age of eleven from a drive-by shooting near the family home in Mexico. This was what had necessitated the move to the US ten years ago and Florida in particular.

Other than that, there was nothing newsworthy, nothing to give Sarah any ideas about the man she was convinced had had a hand in her husband's ordered murder.

Releasing a heavy sigh and no longer able to keep her eyes open, she shut the laptop down. Exhaustion had overtaken her need to delve into Santa Cruz' private life and she knew the only way she was going to know what had happened was to see Santa Cruz face to face. Tomorrow she was going to do just that.

Tuesday

The light crept around the edges of the heavy curtains, so bright on the outside but very dark in the middle, almost pitch black. The blinding light in the corners made it extremely hard for Sarah to open her eyes any more than just a crack. She tried but it hurt her head too much as though someone was stabbing her through the eyes. Then she became aware of the pain in her chest.

Someone was kicking her. Hard. Dead centre of her chest. Right on the breastbone. Every time her heart pumped, the boot drove in, slamming hard in time with the beat and with a force she had never known, never experienced before. Her arms flayed, trying to stop the beating but the pain just kept coming, ramming downwards, towards her abdomen making her want to throw up again, something she had been doing on a regular basis since Marco had been killed. It felt like her sternum was going to shatter into a thousand pieces and Sarah knew it would kill her if she received one more blow. Who were they and why were they kicking her so hard? Who hated her this much that they wanted her to suffer such extreme pain and maybe death? She was unable to open her eyes to see who was inflicting the blows on her, so she clung on to the image of her three beautiful children and grandson and of her husband. But, on thinking of Marco, the kicks got harder, the boot drove deeper into her soul, slamming into her core.

With a gasp, Sarah opened her eyes. Bewildered, she looked around and found that she was in her own bed, alone in the semi-darkness. There was no-one beating her or kicking her. She moaned aloud as she realised the physical pain in her chest was her grief exposing itself. She once again realised that her beautiful beloved husband was gone from her life forever and she fought to stop the tears escaping from her. She allowed one to go but knew that anymore and she would never be able to stop. Her pain was too deep. But she would not seek solace in her tears until Marco's killers and the people responsible for all of this heartache were dealt with, in the old-fashioned way. It was a way that she abhorred and had fought against for many years now but she knew it was the only way. It was what Marco would have wanted. She was loathed to admit it, but it was what she also wanted.

Sarah sat up and reached across to the bedside cabinet. Her hand found the plastic yellow bag she had placed there yesterday, unmolested since she had taken possession of it. She tipped it up and emptied the contents onto the bed in front of her and looked at her husband's belongings; a black and gold watch, not over expensive and one that Marco had used for every day. Sarah opened up his wallet and was struck by the photograph inside. She saw the smiling faces of their three children, taken around Easter time this year when they had last been altogether as a family. Hidden behind this was another photo and Sarah smiled. It was of her, a little worse the wear for drink and wearing very little! No small wonder that Marco kept it hidden for personal viewing only. There was also around five hundred dollars in bills and a few loose quarters, his driving licence was hidden away in another pocket.

Then Sarah saw his wedding ring on the bed. Smiling through the pain, she picked it up and put it on her finger but it was much too large even for her biggest finger. She didn't want to lose it or hide it away so she would put it on a chain around her neck. She had worn hers that way through several years of separation.

Taking a deep breath, she pulled herself out of bed and headed downstairs to face another day. It was still very early, just before 5a.m. and far too soon for anyone else to be up and around. She welcomed the peace despite the fact she'd had just about six hours of deeply troubled sleep.

Sarah sat in the kitchen and stirred her cup of hot steaming sweet tea. Bloody hell! She missed him. It had been just over twenty four hours since she'd last seen him and it was already killing her. The empty void in her chest, the forever overwhelming anguish that was threatening to annihilate her. And part of her wished it would.

"Sarah?"

She spun around to face the voice and for a split second, she thought it was Marco. Her smile faded before it had settled and she slapped herself mentally as her eyes came to rest instead on the handsome face of his brother.

"Vinnie. You're up early," her tone was flat to hide her disappointment.

He just nodded. "You sleep okay?"

Sarah looked up at him at the dazzlingly dumb question and decided it didn't warrant an answer. She was too weary. Vinnie realised what a stupid question he'd asked almost straight away.

"You know, I thought you were him. Just then. Daft, isn't it?" she muttered.

"Of course not!" he rushed to reassure her. "There is no right or wrong way of dealing with grief and you have to do whatever you feel is necessary to get through this. It will take a long time, maybe forever. Gradually the pain will ease but it may never leave you," he set about making some coffee, needing to put a bit of distance between them.

"I've lost a lot of friends over the years, Vinnie, but nothing prepares you for this. Mind you, I don't know why I should be surprised, with the company we keep. I suppose it's a miracle Marco lived for as long as he did. The amount of times he's been shot at, I should be grateful that he lived to fifty-seven."

"Maybe, but it doesn't make it hurt any less."

Sarah nodded in agreement and looked into her brother-in-law's dulled eyes. They too were full of grief at losing his brother. The two had been very close despite living in different states. They had spoken often on the phone and Vinnie and Jamie had visited every six to eight weeks, although it was rare that Marco would go to Chicago, citing the cold as an excuse. He had loved the Florida heat.

"Is the pool house comfortable enough for you?" she asked.

"Yeah, good thanks. I left Jamie still sparked out – he was up late with Gio. Jamie says he is a mess."

"I don't know how to help him, Vinnie, or any of them. Grace at least has Scott but I'm so worried about all three of them."

"They'll get through it. I'm not going anywhere for a while and if there is something I can do to help, I will do it. For any of you," his meaning was unmistakable.

Sarah wanted to take him up on his offer but just didn't know how to ask him. Vinnie picked up on her hesitancy.

"What is it?"

Sarah smiled in spite of herself. "How do you do that? Just the way… " her weak smile vanished.

Vinnie knew what her unfinished sentence would have been. "We had the same father, the same intuition. Besides, I've known you for a lot of years so I know when something is on your mind. Tell me."

Still, she hesitated.

"Do you think I would ever deny you anything? Especially now?"

Sarah wrung her hands together. "I can't ask Gabe, he would just lock me in the cellar. He's always been tolerant of me, but this? I know I can't ask him."

"So then ask me."

"Santa Cruz." She couldn't look Vinnie in the eye.

Vinnie narrowed his eyes in suspicion. "Again with this?"

Sarah nodded. "Do you know how I can get to him?"

"Why?" Vinnie could not keep the irritation out of his voice.

"Marco has been meeting with him for the past few months and I want to know what those meetings were about. I want to know if Santa Cruz killed my husband."

Vinnie might have laughed if he hadn't known that Sarah was deadly serious – he had known her for many years and knew that when she had an idea she was like a terrier with a rabbit – she wouldn't let it go. He looked at her for a moment, pondering his next move, his next words and stalled for time. He wanted her to give this up, to grieve for Marco like any wife would but he knew she would not give up until it was over. Sarah was too stubborn and too determined and if someone told her no, she would be even more tenacious.

And he could no more say no to her than Marco had been able to. Besides, if he tried or worse, suggest she leave it to the boys, she would have his testicles on a plate. The best he could come up with was that he would see what he could do but he knew it was only going buy him enough time to take a shower and make a call and he wasn't going to kid himself otherwise.

True to form and less than two hours later, Sarah was hunting Vinnie down. She walked up to the pool house doors and knocked quietly, hoping he was inside and not wanting to awaken her nephew. She opened the doors without waiting for an answer. Vinnie was inside, pacing up and down the far end with his phone stuck to his ear. His face suggested that his call wasn't going well. He saw Sarah and beckoned her in.

"Okay. Yes, I got it. Eleven today. Okay," was all of the one-sided conversation that she got but she realised that it was not meant for her to understand. Vinnie disconnected his call and smiled at her. He motioned for her to go outside and followed her, shutting the door behind him so as not to wake Jamie up and permit him to overhear their conversation.

"Against my better judgement, I have a meeting with the Santa Cruz number two today."

Sarah shook her head. "Not good enough. I need to see HIM. No-one else is acceptable, I thought you understood that."

"It's the best we're gonna get," Vinnie shrugged.

Muttering under her breath about the ineffectiveness of men, Sarah walked away and back to the main house.

'What do I have to do to get this meeting arranged?' she thought to herself. She was determined that somehow she would get to see Santa Cruz. She was convinced that he had something to do with this mess.

Slamming the kitchen door behind her, she went straight to Marco's unoccupied office. It was empty for the first time since yesterday afternoon and she relished the peace. She sat in Marco's soft leather chair and set about searching through his desk drawers. There had to be something to find, something he had hidden away. She knew where he kept the keys to his locked bottom drawer but maybe he had a secret compartment somewhere in the desk? She started with the locked drawers first, the larger ones at the bottom. Sarah pulled out a pile of papers and flicked through sheaf after sheaf but nothing seemed relevant. She found no mention of the name of Santa Cruz in anything although she knew Marco would have known better than to write anything down. Or would he? His last movements had been against everything he had been schooled in, he was too important a commodity to take a meeting on his own and yet he had gone ahead and done just that. Perhaps writing something incriminating down was not outside the realms of possibility.

The door squeaked opened and Vinnie poked his head around. "I can't get any closer to Santa Cruz at the moment. We need to take baby steps but I will get to him. Give me some time," Vinnie was almost apologetic.

"Hmmm. In the meantime, perhaps you could help me."

Vinnie stepped into the room and closed the door behind him. He perched on the edge of the desk next to Sarah and looked down at the reams of paper at her feet. "What are we looking for?"

"I don't know."

Vinnie looked at her and wondered for her sanity. He was also struck by how beautiful she still was even now and the years and good living had been extremely good to her. Her dark hair was pulled back into a loose ponytail, showing off her slim neck. The lines on her face were natural and elegant and usually covered with a small amount of make-up but he had never known Sarah to cake it on, she had never needed it. Even in her grief and with very little sleep, Sarah was stunning. Vinnie checked himself. They hadn't even buried her husband, his brother yet. Nevertheless, he realised that long hidden feelings were re-emerging that should never be allowed to surface. Twenty year old, one-sided emotions were seeping back that he had tried to suppress with a loveless marriage to someone else and a move away from Florida, back to Chicago. He tore his gaze away from her.

Vinnie knelt down beside her and began to sift through the piles. After almost an hour, Sarah threw several sheets of paper in anger. Their search had revealed nothing and the feeling of helplessness was returning once again. No-one seemed to know anything. No-one seemed to care. She didn't know where to turn to next.

"Let's go and get some breakfast." Vinnie said as he sensed her hope fading with his own. He helped her up off the floor and they walked into the kitchen where they found Gabe putting on some fresh coffee. Sarah glanced at Vinnie with a silent plea. She did not want Gabe to know about the meeting with Santa Cruz's associate later that morning and Sarah was thankful as Vinnie nodded almost imperceptibly in acknowledgement, catching on to Sarah's wishes.

"Morning Gabe. Is there any fresh news?" Vinnie asked.

Sarah turned back around and left the room. She was sick of rehashing the same old conversation around with different people when no-one had the first clue. Even she was clutching at straws with this Carlos thing, but until she met with him, it was all she had to believe in. She looked at her watch; it was just after nine. They would be leaving for the Gulf Coast soon. She needed some peace so went outside with the intention of deciding what she was going to say to Santa Cruz's man. She had no idea and thought perhaps she should leave it to Vinnie to talk to him.

Within minutes and before Sarah had had any time to think about it at all, Vinnie came looking for her. He just gestured with his head that they were leaving and without saying another word, headed for Sarah's car. The drive would take a couple of hours and for the first few miles, neither spoke. Sarah eventually broke the silence when she asked Vinnie what he was going to say.

"I need to see how the land lies. We can't go in with all guns blazing accusing him of killing Marco or you and I will both end up dead. I need you to say nothing. I know there is no point in me asking you to stay in the car, I spoke to Gabe yesterday and he told me what happened in Jimmy's bar."

"Did he also tell you that it was my persistence that got us here today?"

"No, because he doesn't know where 'here' is. He is not aware that you went to Jimmy's house last night and threatened to tell his wife about his companions in the Jacuzzi... "

"Then how do you know?" Sarah frowned.

"Lucky for you, I took the call from an irate and concerned Jimmy Caruso while you were on your way back last night."

"It's nice that he is concerned for my well-bring."

Vinnie laughed. "He was only concerned that you would tell Daisy!"

Sarah was a little indignant. "Does he not think that I have enough to worry about? I don't give a fig about what Jimmy Caruso does or with whom or where, and I don't owe his wife anything. Did he think that I might side with his wife? As far as I'm concerned, those two deserve each other."

"Jimmy's not that bad!" Vinnie protested in good nature. He paused and looked across at Sarah for a brief moment. He knew what was going through her mind. "You do know that Marco wasn't like that, don't you?"

"I guess so," Sarah replied quietly. Her rational mind was far away but she admitted that she would be wrong to accuse Marco of having an affair. He had too much to lose and she knew that he had loved her.

Sarah must have drifted off into a sleep for the next thing she was aware of was a change in engine noise as Vinnie pulled off the main road. They were in a car park.

"Where are we?" she asked, her voice drugged with sleep while trying to stretch in the car.

"At a manatee nature reserve. It's public and Enrique Guzman asked us to meet him here. Remember, it's in our best interests for you to stay quiet and let me do the talking. Please," he was almost pleading with her.

Sarah made no promises but just nodded with a huge amount of reluctance and they got out of the car. Sarah stretched her arms above her head and yawned, feeling a little more refreshed and eager for this meeting. She followed Vinnie as they took a gravel path which was sign-posted for the boardwalk nature trail and wondered why these people could never meet in a bar or a library or somewhere normal! She knew that Marco had been forever going off to some random place, a supermarket, a tourist ferry, even, when the kids had been little and at school, he had been known to meet people in the playground at home time, all to fit in and not look too out of place. Regardless, Sarah was just two steps behind her brother in law.

She knew when they were approaching Enrique Guzman. He was a short, fat little man with an outmoded clump of hair that seemed as though it had been just stuck on the top of his head. He nodded in acknowledgment at Vinnie, having a sixth sense as to who he was and scowled at his female companion. Guzman fell into step beside Vinnie and the three continued walking along the boardwalk with the swamp below them and mangrove trees to their side. Insects bit at their faces and all three were continuously swatting them away.

"Does she have to stay?" Guzman stopped and asked Vinnie in a thick Spanish accent.

"Yes. This is Sarah Delvecchio and she is personally involved in this. Marco was her husband."

"I don't like to do business with women. They should not be involved with a man's business."

Sarah began to spout feminist invective at him, but Vinnie stopped her with what he hoped was a calming hand on her arm. They continued walking.

"Sarah is not involved in this meeting, she is just going to listen to what you have to say. We know Marco was somehow involved with Carlos and we know that they had been meeting over the past few months. We just need to know if it had anything to do with the events of Sunday night."

Guzman scowled at Vinnie. "You have some front, my friend. You come to us and ask outright if we had anything to do with the murder of a man? I should be insulted; I know my boss will be."

Vinnie did not want to fire shots across the bow and he had hoped his words would not be construed as an act of war. Not without the Delvecchio Family blessing. He did not have any authority in Florida and he needed to placate Enrique. "No insult was meant, Enrique. A great damage had been done to the Delvecchio Family and we need to know what happened and who is responsible. We are not suggesting that Mr Santa Cruz is responsible, just that he may know who is and might help us out a little. It has been implied that Marco met with Carlos – can you tell me what these meetings were about?"

Sarah couldn't keep quiet any longer and couldn't help but to add her thoughts to the conversation. "If not, I want to speak to your boss. I'm sure he will be more forthcoming."

Vinnie was fuming but did not reprimand Sarah. Not here in front of Guzman, it would show a divided front and that was not the image he wished to portray. He glared at Sarah while they waited for a response.

Guzman turned to leave the way they had just walked down. "My boss won't deal with a woman either," he spoke to Vinnie. "I'm afraid you have had a wasted journey." He smiled as though he was enjoying himself at Sarah's and Vinnie's expense.

"Mr Guzman. We know that Carlos was meeting with Marco. We also know of Mr Santa Cruz' recent issues with the INS, issues that we can make re-appear if necessary. I understand that his family, his wife and his two daughters have had death threats issued against them in Mexico and that it would be far safer for them to remain in the US. It would be a terrible shame, a tragedy even, if they had a deportation order issued against them... " Vinnie issued his thinly veiled threat.

This stopped Guzman in his retreating tracks. He spun around and had a look of vile hatred on his face, glaring at both Sarah and Vinnie in turn. "I heard you Italians were unscrupulous bastards. You would condone the murder of three innocent women just to get what you want?"

Vinnie shook his head. "No, I wouldn't. We don't, as a rule, go after family members, just perpetrators but we need information and I will make this happen if you don't co-operate with us. We will get this information in any way we can."

"What are you hiding from us? Did you kill my husband?" Sarah asked.

Guzman laughed. "Why would we do that? Why would we want to kill the head of the Delvecchio Family, the man in charge of South Florida?" He sneered. "Marco made us a huge fortune, an unlimited mountain of American Dollars. He was our cash cow."

"What do you mean by that?" Vinnie urged him to explain.

"He refused to have anything to do with the narco business, has done for years, which left us free to run it as we saw fit. He didn't even want a percentage, just turned his head to the whole thing. He did not allow any of his people to get involved which kept the streets clean for us to do with as we pleased. That was one of the reasons Carlos moved here; he would have no competition and no interference from anybody else, no-one that we fear or can't eliminate. Marco Delvecchio made that all possible."

"So he didn't even take a cut?" Sarah asked.

Guzman laughed again, finding the revelations hilarious. "No way! He was far too pious for that! Just his refusal to let his people get involved is enough to keep our pockets lined. I hope that will continue with... who *is* taking over from him, by the way?" His contempt was obvious.

"I am," Sarah told him. "And you still haven't told me what the meetings were about."

Guzman looked at Sarah and walked over to her, finally acknowledging her presence. "I don't know and that's the truth. It was a personal matter between Carlos and Marco, no-one else was ever involved. Ever."

"Then it is obvious that I need to speak to your boss. I can see that you have no authority here so I will speak to the man at the top. So go back to him today and tell him to call me."

Guzman laughed and began to walk away. "That's never going to happen, lady!" he called out over his shoulder.

"Then the INS *will* be calling," she called after him.

Guzman hesitated just for a second, just long enough for him to miss a step and then he was gone around the corner, swallowed up by the mangrove trees and swamp. Vinnie grabbed Sarah's arm and began to frogmarch her back towards the car, ignoring the strange looks from other nature lovers on the walk.

"What part of 'say nothing' did you not understand?" He seethed as they hurried along.

Sarah shook his hand off of her arm. "How dare you speak to me like that? You are not Marco and nor will you ever replace him!!" Tears sprang to her eyes and she wrapped her arms around herself in a protective manner as if to try another way to shut out the pain.

Vinnie backed down and took a step away, shocked by his own behaviour. He looked at his feet as he apologised. "You're right, I'm sorry. That's just about the way he would have behaved, isn't it?" he smiled at her. "He would often call me to say that he had pissed you off again. My brother could be a brute at times, sometimes necessary at work but never at home. I should never have said what I did and I am sorry," he waited for Sarah's forgiveness but it did not come.

"No, you shouldn't," she turned away from him and walked back to the car. Once Vinnie had caught her up, she asked, "Do you think it will have worked? Will Santa Cruz talk to us?"

"I hope so. If you are still convinced that Santa Cruz had something to do with it, we have no place else to go. We can get the INS to visit and lay a few threats down but I don't know if it will get them to talk. If they get deported, we'll lose them for sure. We just have to hope that they get scared enough to talk to us without us having to carry out the threat. Let's go home."

They headed back towards the East Coast.

Sarah and Vinnie arrived back in Palm Beach just after three, after a leisurely drive and a pit stop for food. Sarah had wolfed down a chicken burger, feeling hungry for the first time in days but they had to stop after half an hour for her to bring it back up. Evidently, her grief was still playing havoc with her digestive system.

Outside the house, an unfamiliar car was parked and Sarah hurried inside to see who was visiting. She had hoped Santa Cruz had beaten them back home and was ready to impart some vital information but was surprised when she found Rosie Gray in the lounge talking to Rosa.

"Sarah, I've been trying to call you," Rosa stood up as Sarah entered the room and tried to subtly extract Sarah's movements from her.

Sarah gave nothing away. "It's okay Ro. Hi Lieutenant Gray. How is the investigation going?" She sat on the sofa opposite the police detective and looked eagerly at her.

"Well, we have given the Lexus a good going over. As you know, we believe your husband was attacked outside the vehicle and have not found any evidence to suggest otherwise. We have not traced the murder weapon but we are still searching the area around where Marco was found but it could be anywhere by now. We think it was blunt metal object, like a baseball bat, so we are looking for something like that. We also found chips of blue paint in Marco's hair; do you know what that might be from? Had he been decorating?"

Sarah would have laughed at the notion of Marco painting anything had the situation not be so serious. Instead she looked at Rosie Gray and shrugged.

The detective ploughed on. "We did find something strange in a black plastic wallet in the trunk of his car, in the well, instead of a spare tyre. Can you shed any light on this?" She passed over the wallet.

Sarah examined it and straight away recognised Marco's handwriting, a series of numbers written in his scrawl. She thought it might be bank account numbers but the sets were too long for anything she was familiar with and she was only privy to a handful of account details that Marco had. She wracked her brain, desperate to think of something useful that might bring an end to this nightmare but her head hurt too much. She handed it back to Rosie with a shake of her head.

"I'm sorry. I didn't have a great deal to do with Marco's businesses," she told a half-truth. "Are they overseas bank account numbers?"

"Quite possibly. We have someone looking into that area." She hesitated a moment before continuing. "Sarah, you know you can trust me, right? Whatever you tell me will be dealt with sensitively," she implored Sarah to come clean with her.

Rosie had been a willing and devoted employee, working for the Delvecchios for a great many years now although she had never met Sarah or been in her close circle. Rosie was a close acquaintance of Gabe's after the two had met around fifteen years ago when she had pulled him over for a minor driving infraction and a broken break light. As Gabe had wound the window down, Rosie had straight away realised who the man in the car had been and what this might mean for her. She had felt stymied in the police force, convinced she had been passed over for promotion because of her sex and couldn't get past being a beat cop even though she was damn good at what she did. She had let Gabe off in the vague hope that he would remember her and help out in any way he could. Rosie knew that Gabe had some control in the police department and this was her subtle way of letting him know he could rely on her.

Later that same evening, Gabe had met her off her shift and they had gone out for dinner, during which, they had had a full and frank discussion about where her career was headed and whether they could be of mutual benefit to each other. A few months later, she had been promoted to sergeant and the Delvecchios's minor issues were disappearing from the police files. Rosie Gray worked her way up to lieutenant in homicide but she let her presence be felt in any investigation that the Delvecchios were mentioned in and she squashed most of them.

The love affair she'd had with Gabe came to a mutual ending soon after although they remained friends and in regular contact. Marco had felt that they were both too high profile by now and it would not be in either persons best interests to be known to have a formal association with the other; it would raise too many questions. Marco had felt that Rosie was too much of an asset to them.

So Rosie stayed single, worked too many hours, got Giorgio out of lots of trouble and cared for her elderly aunt. It was her life and how she liked it. She was paid a small fortune by her standards by the Delvecchio Family and saw no reason to jeopardise that. She met with Gabe on a regular basis and updated him with anything that pertained to the Delvecchios and if they were being targeted by any law enforcement agency. Gabe would give her names of any one that was giving him trouble and often fitted them up for crimes they had not committed, just to get them out of his way or to take the heat away from himself or his men. Rosie had no guilt about this – her main concerns were survival of the Delvecchios, her pay-day and if truth be known, her own life.

But Sarah did not know any of this and she wanted to do things her way. She was not aware of just how much she could trust the cop standing in front of her.

"I know that," she snapped. "But I don't know what those numbers relate to and that's the truth. If I find out, I will be sure to call you. I want to know who killed Marco and if I knew anything that would help you to catch them, I would tell you."

Rosie sighed. She was not so sure that was the truth. Detective Manolo had informed her of Sarah's threat against Marco's killers and knew the police had just a short time to catch them before the Delvecchios did. "Okay. Just one more thing. We found some prints in the Lexus, several sets which indicate that the owner of them was in the car for a while. They don't belong to anyone we have on file so we are unable to match them at the moment. Whoever they belong to has a clean history."

Sarah nodded, understanding what this meant. Marco had always kept people on his books, usually fresh immigrants, illegal and not so, that had not had any contact with the police. This meant there would be nothing traceable to the Delvecchios. That way, if Marco needed something a little risky doing, he had people he could ask and know they would not be traced by the police. The moment the police had them on record rendered them expendable. They were very well paid and also aware of the risks. Sarah had no doubt that Santa Cruz had such people on his books which meant that if Santa Cruz had used such a man to carry out the hit on Marco, they may never be tracked down.

Rosie was disappointed to realise that she was hitting a brick wall here. She had expected it of the family, but not of Marco's widow. She had hoped that her long association with the Delvecchios would have built some trust of her in them, but it seemed it was not to be the case. "Well, I'll be going then if there is nothing else you need to tell me?" she left the invitation open.

Sarah shook her head. "Let me show you out." She needed some time to herself to digest the events of today.

Giorgio's phone was ringing again, the tinny sound of a My Chemical Romance song filling his head with noise. He checked the caller display – it was Claire. Again. He hit the voice mail button, knowing she would leave another too perky message for him to call back, hoping he was coping and she was there if he needed someone to talk to. It would be another message that he would not respond to.

Giorgio got up from his messy bed, checking his watch as he did so. Time seemed to have slowed down since Sunday and he was in no real hurry to be anywhere. Usually at this time on a Tuesday, he'd be getting ready to go the Riverside Club with Jesse. The club was nowhere near a river and he had no idea why it was so named, but he always had a good time there. He and Jesse would spend the late afternoon there, shooting some pool, maybe have a light bite to eat and start drinking early on so he'd be ready for the club's Ladies Night. There was nowhere else he would rather be on a Tuesday night even though he never had any problem attracting girls due in part to his natural charm, good looks and the Delvecchio confidence assisting him. On a Tuesday night there could be vacationers and out of towners, girls, women who didn't know who he was and this gave him a fresh challenge. Sometimes, he enjoyed being turned down and having to use his talents, rather than his name to attract the women. If all else failed, he could flash the cash. But he would never let on that he was Marco Delvecchio's son. First born son and heir. The Prince of Palm Beach.

He was beginning to feel the weight of responsibility that the unofficial title now carried. He knew that his playboy days were most likely behind him and it was possible that he was going to be thrust into the role of King of Palm Beach. And he was scared.

Not scared of dying, like Marco had but of failing. Death came to everyone in the end, it cannot be cheated and Giorgio knew he had a lot of living to do yet. Failing was not an option for him if he was to take over from Marco. He knew he had a lot to live up to and he still had plenty to learn. He didn't want to let anyone down, especially his father and especially now. The thing was, he didn't know what to do next. He had not been groomed for the sudden and violent death of his father; they hadn't got around to covering that topic. Marco had not told his son what to do in the event that he died unexpectedly and in the brutal way that he had and left him as head of the family and grief-stricken. Marco was supposed to be around for a good few years yet and Giorgio's position in the family had not been set in concrete. He wasn't yet twenty-one and still a kid in his eyes and in the eyes of others. Giorgio had been asking himself if he had it in him to be the man he was supposed to be and much sooner than was planned. He still had not come up with a satisfactory answer. He felt sure his father's men did not have enough respect for him to take over just yet, he could see it in their eyes. They – Gabe, Cliff, Sal even Scott – just saw him as a bit of a joke, out to have the time of his life and do as little as possible in return, to do just enough to get by. If they weren't ridding him of nuisance females he'd grown tired of, they were being sent to the Police Department to bail him out for yet another misdemeanour. Even when he'd been drunk enough to punch out at a cop, he'd been okay and he'd known all along that he would be. His family knew enough people in enough places that that incident had just meant a night in lock up while he sobered up and got taught a lesson. He was home having a hot shower and a lecture from his parents by mid-morning the next day. He'd even had his allowance stopped for a week after he and some friends had trashed an empty house down by the beach. His mother had wanted him taught the value of things but Giorgio, at seventeen, had just found the whole thing hilarious. He'd bummed some money off of his sister who, like most people, found it hard to say no to her brother.

Giorgio smiled now as he recalled that that was about the time that Marco had decided his son needed a living. He knew Giorgio was not academic and Marco would be able to find something within his own organisation that he'd be good at. The pay was lousy to start with, he had to prove himself like all newbies but Giorgio was pulled through the ranks and he excelled at every task he was given. Sarah had protested but she was no match for her son and her husband combined, so with Marco promising – with crossed fingers behind his back – that he would never let their son do anything immoral or illegal, she relented and had to give in to them. Giorgio gained more experience than Sarah realised, even to this day, under the guidance of his father, uncle, and brother-in-law and cut his teeth in all parts of Marco's business and he enjoyed it. The money, the power and the notoriety. All of it.

Given a few more years, Giorgio would have been accomplished enough to have taken over from Marco when he decided to retire. But now? It was just too soon.

Giorgio wandered over to the window and peered out. He frowned. His mother was talking to that police detective, Rosie Gray. The lieutenant nodded at whatever it was that Sarah was telling her and speaking back. The conversation didn't look heated or anything other than business-like. But Giorgio began to get the distinct feeling that he was being excluded from everything, although he was in part to blame for that. And it angered him. True, when he had been told of Marco's death, he had literally fallen apart. He knew his behaviour would be forgiven but now was the time to behave with dignity, just as his mother was trying to. He had to get himself into the centre of things, find out what was happening and take charge. It was what Marco would want, Giorgio was sure of that.

He headed into the bathroom. First, he had to get himself cleaned up and make himself respectable before he went downstairs and stepped into his father shoes.

Wednesday

"Wherever it is you are going, I am going with you!" Giorgio's face was glowering in an image of his father that made Sarah's heart ache. His eyes were turning darker and his face was crimson with anger while Sarah was trying but failing to placate her son.

"I said no, Gio," she tried to put authority in her voice but it was having no effect on her changed son. Last night, he had come downstairs clean-shaven and fresh from his shower and he had been a different person since. He seemed now to be taking the lead and Sarah knew that no amount of opposition from her was going to alter whatever path he had placed himself on.

Giorgio knew he was winning. He shook his head, denying her any influence in this conversation, not letting her for a minute win back the upper hand. "It's not about what you say anymore. All bets are off. Dad wanted me to learn his business and take over after… " his voice faltered for just a second. "Well, here we are. He would want me to find out who did this, not you. He did a good job of teaching me." He put a comforting hand on her lower arm, as if to tell her that she did not have to worry about him anymore, he knew what he was doing and could handle this.

Deep down, Sarah knew her son was right. She had no real clue as to how much Marco had been teaching him, but she thought, despite all of her nay-saying, Giorgio would know much more than she had hoped for. She had known her husband too well to think anything else. Giorgio was almost a grown man, almost twenty-one and she knew that he would be making his own decisions from now on. Plus she no longer had the strength to oppose him. She thought she had known about Marco's business – she certainly knew a lot more than most wives in her position did –

but it now seemed that Marco had kept many things from her including how much Giorgio handled for his father.

In addition, Sarah did not want a scene in the hallway where mother and son stood. It was too close to the office where Gabe was sequestered with the other men and she did not want them to know of her's and Vinnie's plan. They would insist that she change her mind and this was something she would not agree on. Sarah's single option was to keep Giorgio sweet and take him along.

Giorgio looked towards the office door. He knew that whatever his mother had planned, she did not want anyone to know about it for whatever reason. "I suggest you let me go with you," he said with a vague hint of malice in his voice that made Sarah want to slap her eldest son. He was sometimes too much like his father.

Sarah acceded to his demands. "Okay," she held her hands up in defeat, knowing she had lost this battle. She had not wanted Giorgio to know about the plan she had hatched that even Vinnie had tried to talk her out of. But nothing was going to stop her from having this meeting, not even her angry, grieving son tagging along. Looking again towards the office, she wondered if any of the men within its walls wanted to find who killed Marco or if they were all just looking for a seat at the head of the table. It appeared to her that it was just Vinnie on her side, his allegiance blind and he stood by the front door watching the standoff between mother and son. He smiled as Giorgio won. The boy had had a lifetime of watching his father contest with Sarah and knew which buttons to press. "You don't say a word to anyone, Gio. Do you understand?"

Giorgio shrugged as he walked out of the door, the closest thing to any sort of commitment that Sarah was going to get.

Sarah drove this time with Giorgio in the passenger seat and Vinnie in the back.

"So where are we going?" Giorgio asked to no-one in particular as they left Palm Beach behind.

"Fort Myers," Sarah responded succinctly.

"Any reason?"

"To talk to the man I believe killed your father."

"Sarah… " Vinnie warned from the back. He wasn't convinced of Santa Cruz's guilt and knew this would be an act of war if Sarah got it wrong.

"Who is it?" Giorgio's voice was pinched.

"Carlos Santa Cruz."

Vinnie sighed in agitation but the conversation went on without him.

"The Mexican drug dealer?" Giorgio was well informed. "Why would you think it was him? Dad never had anything to do with drugs."

"No, he didn't," Sarah agreed. "But he had been meeting with Santa Cruz and if it wasn't to do with drugs, what was it about? We met with one of his honchos yesterday and I got the feeling that he was hiding something. He was cagey, defensive."

"And you think that means he killed Dad," Giorgio stated, his voice full of scorn. The evidence put to him was not convincing and he had the same feeling of reasonable doubt as Vinnie.

"Maybe, maybe not but I think that he knows something though," Sarah continued, ignoring her son's tone. "I want to talk to Santa Cruz and find out what he does know and why he was meeting with Marco."

"And you think you'll get close enough to ask him?" Again, sarcasm.

"Clearly, your father did not teach you everything, kid!" Sarah smiled to herself.

Giorgio faced the road ahead, scowling and trying to sit on a retort that wanted to escape. He hated it when Sarah called him that, as she so often did. He was going to have to do something that would make everyone take him more seriously. He needed to make people aware that he wasn't a kid anymore and he was ready to step up. No-one had called his father a kid, or done anything other than do as he told them (with the possible exception of Sarah) and Giorgio knew he had to get to the same place as his father had been otherwise this was never going to work.

Sarah swung her Jeep into the already busy parking lot and searched for a spot to park. After a short drive around, she found one and fronted into it. Everyone gathered themselves together and got out into the hot sun, Sarah stretching as she did so and waited for her son and brother-in-law to catch up. Two long drives on consecutive days were not doing her exhausted body any favours and she knew she needed to rest. Perhaps tomorrow.

Confidently, she strode into the single-storey police building, a large white block surrounded by the parking area and lush green grass, which was being watered by the sprinklers. An elderly gentleman was tending to a flower bed in the far corner. Sarah announced who she was and who she was meeting to the friendly smiley cop on the front desk, who asked her to wait in the plastic chairs.

She didn't have long to wait. Within a few moments, a stocky man with short black cropped hair and a big grin came out through the doors to greet her. His blue eyes sparkled as he walked over to Sarah, Giorgio, and Vinnie. His waist band was a little too tight and his ample middle was bulging below his blue checked shirt. Still, Sarah had to admit he was good looking. She knew that he went back a long way with Marco, that he had been on the Delvecchios's books for a good number of years, ten at least, and he could be relied on. Marco had approached him before Adam had even started school for a returned favour that the detective was glad to oblige. Marco had brought a debt of Foley's from a tough but small Irish contingent on the Gulf Coast and Marco had wanted to call Foley's favour in. The Irishman was glad to help out as he knew that Marco may well reciprocate and help him out with some other financial matters he needed some assistance with, regardless of how much deeper he would get himself into. Foley had been passed over for promotion on a number of occasions for reasons that he would never care to admit and he had many bills to pay. He had an ex-wife and a son in Louisiana, neither of which ever spoke to him, but he was duty-bound to support them both financially until the son finished school. Foley now found himself in a position of power and was helping the Delvecchios out more than he had anticipated but the financial rewards were worth the potential risk. His ex-wife now never called him to scream at him for money and he had managed to procure a condo on the Gulf Coast that he would be able to retire to. He even managed to sleep most nights.

"Hey, Mrs Delvecchio? I'm Detective Foley. Please come through this way." His voice had a very slight Irish accent to it. He gestured towards another doorway and Sarah rose to follow him. Giorgio was just a step behind her and she turned to warn him with her eyes. She was reluctant to allow her son to come with her but she knew he would just insist and make another scene which she wanted to avoid at all costs.

"You don't say a word!" she warned him again, knowing she had little choice but to let him be a part of this. Giorgio just shrugged and followed her while Vinnie waited in the reception area for her to be finished. He knew between the three of them, they could handle this.

Foley showed them into a small square, grey painted room with no windows and just the standard table inside with a chair either side. On one of the chairs sat a Mexican man.

Carlos Santa Cruz.

He looked up and dared a half smile as Sarah, Giorgio, and Foley entered the room. "Mrs Delvecchio." he knew who Sarah was although the two had never met.

"Mr Santa Cruz. We meet at last," Sarah acknowledged him and sat in the chair opposite. Foley closed the door behind them and he and Giorgio leant against the back wall, just watching the drama unfold and ready to leap in and offer assistance if necessary.

Santa Cruz leaned back in his chair and visibly relaxed, obviously now feeling safe and untouchable. This woman had no authority here and he knew it. "So, am I to understand that you have taken up with the Fort Myers Police Department?" he asked Sarah with obvious derision.

"Not at all. Neither am I here to act as your lawyer." She replied.

"Then... ?"

"You are here because I need to talk to you."

"I have spoken to my lawyer on the phone. He has told me not to talk to the police until he gets here."

"As I said, Mr Santa Cruz, I am not with the police. Besides, your lawyer is going to be somewhat delayed. Your man yesterday made it very clear that we would not be able to meet with you so I had to find another way."

He smiled again. "You are a very resourceful woman, Mrs Delvecchio. Your husband was a lucky man. So tell me, why do I deserve all of this attention?"

Sarah leaned forward and laced her fingers together in front of her, resting her forearms on the table. "I want to know what the meetings you had with my husband were about. I need to know if you killed or had Marco killed or if your meetings were in any way connected to his death. His people are all for just taking you out but me, well, I may be English by birth but I am all for American justice and would rather have proof of any wrong doing before a man is executed."

That condescending smile again. Sarah wanted to slap it off his face but dug deep and found the strength to refrain. It would serve no purpose.

"No, Mrs Delvecchio, I did not kill or order for Marco to be killed. Neither did I want him dead as he inadvertently made me a lot of money, which I know my colleague informed you of yesterday."

"Yes, he did say something about that but I didn't find his words convincing enough."

"I like my people to be evasive, it helps my cause."

"Indeed. But then perhaps you should understand about my cause. The cause I am fighting for my sons and my daughter, for my own peace of mind."

He nodded in sympathy as though he understood. "I am sorry that your husband is dead, I truly am. I can assure you that neither I nor anyone connected to me had anything to do with it."

Sarah leaned back. "It's strange but everyone tells me that. Someone killed him and I am going to find out who it was. This won't sit easy but I have learned from my husband over the years not to be too squeamish about such things."

"Perhaps you should leave it to the police, with you being such a believer in American justice."

"We both know that's not going to happen," Sarah said. "So, what did you two meet about?" She changed to a different tack.

Santa Cruz sighed heavily. Sarah was good but he had no intention of telling this woman anything about his business. He was from the old school where men's business did not mix with women. He never understood Marco's rumoured enthusiasm for telling his wife about his business and it was a line he himself was never going to cross with his own wife or any other female. "I cannot tell you," he shrugged, indicating finality on the matter.

"Hmmm, I thought you might say that," she turned to Detective Foley with an air of pretend reluctance. "You can make that call to INS now, Dennis."

He nodded and left the room without saying a word. She saw Giorgio's brow was furrowed but he stayed silent, just taking it all in, wondering where his mother was going with all of this. Sarah turned back to Santa Cruz.

He was shaking his head and laughing, hamming it up for her benefit to show he was not afraid of her threats. "That doesn't scare me, Mrs Delvecchio. I know there are no grounds for deportation, my records are clear. I shouldn't even be detained here and I will sue the Police Department for this. Maybe get your friends fired!"

Now it was Sarah turn to smile as she played her trump card. "You may be safe for the moment. But what about your wife and your daughters? What if their criminal records are 'discovered'? What about their pending extradition order?"

His eyes clouded over with a modicum of fear for his family. "There are no criminal records and no extradition orders," he insisted.

"Are you sure about that? It is easy to 'add' things to police rap sheets, my youngest son is a whizz with computers. I understand that the paperwork is being signed off right now and your family will be picked up in the next hour or two. Your daughters will be dragged out of their classrooms in front of all of their friends. Your wife, I believe she goes to the gym on a Wednesday lunchtime and then meets with friends for a late lunch. She can be picked up by the police with no effort at all. I have been told that all three are on the manifest for a flight to Mexico City on Friday afternoon. It's not the safest place for the Santa Cruz family to be alone especially when the bosses of some of the cartels are tipped off about their arrival." The threat was undeniable.

She could see that Carlos was shaking with rage when he answered although he tried to keep his voice level. "I don't know what you want from me. I have already said it has nothing to do with me and these threats are below the belt. Your husband had higher standards than this and he lived by the rules. No families. Why are you threating my family?"

"As I have already said, I will do whatever I need to do to find my husband's killers. *Anything.* So are you going to tell me what I need to know? Time is ticking."

"I don't believe even you could have my family deported."

Sarah shrugged. She was enjoying herself. "Are you willing to take that chance? You know we have lots of friends in many places. Just for the want of a little information, you would risk your family? Wasn't your son killed in Buena Tiempo? Can you take a chance that your daughters will be safe when they go back on Friday? How long do you think they would survive?"

Santa Cruz thumped his clenched fist hard on the table which made Sarah jump a little. Giorgio continued to watch, almost fascinated. "You are a cruel bitch! Perhaps Marco wanted to die so he could be rid of you! I'm sure he'll be waiting in hell for you." His face was puce and he was almost foaming at the mouth.

"Yes, I'm sure he will. Until then, I will be hunting you," she stood up and pushed her chair back. "I'd like to say it has been a pleasure meeting you but clearly it has been a waste of everyone's time. Enjoy Buena Tiempo."

With Carlos Santa Cruz screaming obscenities in Spanish at her retreating back, she and Giorgio left the room. Foley was waiting for her, his face expressionless.

"Did you make the call?" She asked him.

He nodded feeling almost saddened. "Delore and the girls are being picked up as we speak. They will be on that flight on Friday unless he comes around." He hesitated for a moment. "Are you sure this is what you want?" Foley seemed reluctant at being Sarah's co-conspirator in this. He knew exactly what would happen the moment that plane landed in Mexico and while he wanted Marco's killer found and dealt with, he didn't want it to be at the expense of three innocent lives. Santa Cruz perhaps, but not his family.

"Don't question me! If you don't like my methods, perhaps you'd better get in there and try and talk him around. That's the only way to stop this now." She snapped at the detective and stormed down the corridor and out to where Vinnie stood waiting for her and Giorgio. She was furious. Sarah's patience was at an all-time low and she did not want people second guessing her, especially when those same people had been paid in excess for their loyalty. It was now time for them to step up and pay back some of Marco's previous generosity.

Thursday

Breakfast had been a sombre affair, much like it had been every day since Marco had died. Sarah's family ate a quiet breakfast with just a small amount of muted conversation to punctuate the silence. Nobody wanted anything cooked just cereal and toast and juice plus gallons of coffee. It seemed no-one was sleeping particularly well. Grace had mumbled that she wanted to go back to her own home, she felt useless and restless just hanging around waiting for nothing and her infant son's routine had been disrupted. He was in a constant state of fractiousness. Sarah understood – if she could have gone somewhere else she would have jumped at the chance. Grace promised she would stay in touch and would be there for when the time came to start arranging the funeral. They were still waiting for Marco's body to be released.

After the atmospheric meal, Sarah took her newspaper outside to the pool. She didn't want to be in the morgue-like house. It had become very empty. Grace, Scott and Connor had gone home straight after breakfast; Adam had skulked off to his room closely followed by his cousin Joe who was keeping close to Adam on instruction from his mother. Adina had gone back to her apartment in the city and Rosa had gone with her to settle her back in although in reality, Sarah sensed that Rosa was struggling to be around her sister-in-law. She knew Rosa couldn't understand why she was being so calm, so distant and not ranting or raving. Rosa had told Sarah that she was afraid she would say something she might regret if she stayed around her for too long.

Sarah flicked through and glanced at the paper but didn't take any of the words in. She was in that horrible state of limbo following a death and preceding a funeral, where nothing could be done except to sit around and wait. The police were no further forward in their investigation but Sarah half hoped they never would be. She was getting the feeling that this was personal and it had to be dealt with in that way. However, after the meeting with Santa Cruz yesterday, she felt stymied and unsure how to proceed or which way to turn. She had all but excluded Marco's former clique from the events of the past twenty-four hours but was thinking of bringing them back in. They might have some fresh ideas. However, she was also concerned that they had their own agenda and making their own plans and that scared her a little. No, she decided, she would wait for Vinnie to rise from his slumber and they would discuss their next move.

Giorgio ambled down the path to sit with his mother. Neither said a word, just smiled at each other and enjoyed the conversation-free company. Giorgio was also waiting for Vinnie to wake up as he had his own ideas of where to turn to next but also didn't want to include Gabe in his conversation.

"Sarah?" Gabe's loud voice broke through the quiet of the morning as he shouted down from the house. "You have a visitor!"

Judging from Gabe's uncouth introduction, Sarah guessed it to be Andrea perhaps or at least someone that she knew well, so she was astonished when she saw who it was coming down the path towards her and Giorgio.

Striding along was a bemused looking Carlos Santa Cruz. He was alone and looked somewhat bedraggled and unkempt, probably as a result of his night in lock-up. It was evident that he had come straight from jail to Palm Beach rather than go home to freshen up first and Sarah surmised that he didn't think this impromptu visit was worthy of the additional time and effort it would take to shower and shave. Perhaps he now understood the urgency and was racing against time to save his family.

Giorgio stood in respect to the older man as Santa Cruz approached.Sarah remained seated and defiant. She squinted up through the sun's glare as he stood in front of her. He appeared to be ringed by a halo of sun although he would never pass as an angel.

"Hello," he said and he nodded curtly to Sarah and Giorgio in turn. She gestured for him to sit and glanced up at the house where Gabe, Scott, and Enzo all stood on alert but distant at this unexpected visitor. She said nothing and just waited while he sat. Giorgio also waited in silence.

Carlos cleared his throat. "While I do not like your ethics, I appreciate your fervour," he began. "A night in a Florida jail evidently run by the Delvecchio Family is not my idea of a good night out. My innocent wife and daughters are also in jail awaiting deportation due to some imaginary charges!"

"It is regrettable but as I told you yesterday, I must do whatever it takes," Sarah told him without a trace of remorse as she stared at him, her face cold and free of emotion.

"Despite my giving you assurances that we had nothing to do with any of this? Despite all of that, you somehow conspire to have me and my innocent girls thrown in jail?" His eyes blazed.

Sarah said nothing but kept eye contact with her visitor.

"Lady, you have some power behind you," he marvelled with something close to admiration.

"My husband was a very powerful man and we all owe it to him to find out what happened and bring some justice to the situation."

Giorgio shifted in his chair. He was desperate to get in on the conversation but had to admit to himself that his mother was doing okay without him. It was obvious that she didn't need his input just yet.

"I came to give you this," Santa Cruz handed Sarah a brown file.

Sarah hadn't noticed him clutching this before. It was about half an inch thick and she could make out Marco's scribble on the front cover. Sarah took it hesitantly. She was nervous as to what the file might contain.

"What's in it?" her voice remained strong belying her true feelings.

"It should prove to be an interesting read for you. It is what Marco and I have been working on and meeting over for the past few months and the results of much hard work and worry. You will make of it what you will. I have not been able to come to any conclusions with it and I think Marco was also struggling. You are very resourceful, perhaps you will have better luck."

Sarah opened up the brown leaf file and made her initial thumb through rapidly. Inside there were many loose sheets of paper, some bound together with a staple, others had luminous post-it notes attached with scrawled notes in Marco's messy handwriting. Looking through the reams of paper, some original, some copied, Sarah knew that amongst them were bank statements but they looked as though they were English banks. London Shires. She'd never heard of it and although it had been quite a while since she had seen anything like that, she was sure that's what they were. Most of them listed just two transactions a month; one for five thousand and one dollars going in and then two days later, an outgoing transaction for exactly five thousand dollars. Both were from and to an unknown source with just a line of numbers as a clue. Sarah continued to flick through and saw photographs of an unknown woman and a younger man that looked as though taken under surveillance; scraps of paper with what appeared to be coded information; others with what seemed to be an address in Dallas; dates, all sorts of useless information that Sarah did not begin to understand.

She looked up at Santa Cruz. "This is all very well, Mr Santa Cruz, but none of it makes any sense. What makes you think this is enough to cancel your family's travel plans?"

He shrugged as though in agreement with Sarah. He did not understand the contents of the file either despite having compiled it with Marco. "What is not listed in that file is the fact that two months ago, Marco received a death threat. He received a letter to his business address in Palm Beach which said that he was being watched and someday soon, he would meet a fitting end to his murderous life – the letter's words, not mine," he almost apologised.

Stunned, Sarah looked away. She couldn't bear to look at the face of the man who knew months ago about the fate of her husband but had still been unable to put a stop to the tragedy.

"So why would he tell you and not anyone in the Family?" Giorgio took over while Sarah was unable to find any words.

"Marco told me because we think the same foreteller of death also threatened my sister. The letter said that Calliope would be killed as soon as he had dealt with Marco. Calliope lives in Mexico under an assumed name with her family. As you rightly said yesterday, the name of Santa Cruz is not revered by all in my home country."

"But how does your sister know my dad?"

Carlos shrugged. "As far as I and my sister are aware, they do not. Marco had told me that they had never met; he didn't even know I had a sister. I do not shout about it for her safety."

"I still don't know how relevant any of this is to whatever is in this file," Sarah spoke up after recovering her composure a little. She looked at the now closed file on the table in front of her and did not want to re-open it. It seemed to hold too many secrets that her fragile heart could not cope with exposing.

"I don't know if it has any relevance," Carlos confessed. "I believe that after the mystery person threatened Marco and Calliope, Marco started delving into the past to see if there was any connection. Perhaps my father knew his father. Marco had no clues and was looking for absolutely anything that might shed some light, however irrelevant it may appear. He found the bank transactions about six weeks ago as a result."

"And when did you last see him?" Sarah asked.

He thought about it for a few seconds. "Maybe three or four weeks ago. He came to my house to talk to me and said he was making progress. He thought he knew who was making the threats to both him and my sister and why but wouldn't tell me. He wanted to be sure first. I'm sure you understand the reasons for his secrecy."

Sarah narrowed her eyes in suspicion and tried to work out what was going on in Santa Cruz' head. She didn't trust the Mexican in front of her – he was too important a man to have come to Palm Beach with this vague information and deliver it in person and she wondered why he was really here. Had he made this all up just to rescue his family? Should she make the call to Dennis Foley and get him to stop the extradition to Mexico City tomorrow? Perhaps Santa Cruz had an ulterior motive that he didn't want the Delvecchios to find out about because he was right about one thing; they were a very powerful force and Sarah was straining to hold back its fury for the damage it had suffered.

But on the other hand, it was undeniable that there were documents in the file that Marco had been working on; his handwriting was all over it. Maybe it might help. Perhaps he should be given the benefit of the doubt, at least for the time being.

Giorgio cleared his throat and looked at his mother. It was obvious to him that she was done talking. "We appreciate you coming all this way to see us, Mr Santa Cruz," he said, the epitome of politeness and respect, while standing up ready to show their visitor out.

Santa Cruz said goodbye to Sarah but she did not acknowledge him, her mind was already elsewhere, staring across the pool as the September breeze rippled across the blue water. She had no idea if what she had just heard was the truth but she had to find out whether there was any relevance to it, how it all fitted in. She knew she would have to pick up the investigation from where Marco had left off but first she would have to sift through everything and try and piece it together to work out her next step. She had no idea where it would lead to but it was at least something to occupy her mind. Standing suddenly, she hurried up the stone path towards the house, calling for Giorgio, Vinnie, and Gabe as she did so.

"Why was Santa Cruz just here?" Gabe asked Sarah as he followed her into Marco's office. There was just a hint of agitation in his voice that he had been excluded from something.

"To give me this," Sarah handed him the file without taking her eyes off the computer screen that Giorgio was working on. She was leaning over his shoulder watching intently although he was only just firing up the system.

"What is it?"

"We're not sure. Two months ago someone threatened to kill Marco and Santa Cruz' sister, Calliope. Marco was trying to find a connection between the Delvecchios and the Santa Cruz'. What's in that file is everything Marco had been able to find out and what Gio is going to try to do is find out the relevance of the contents."

"A death threat? Marco would have told me," Gabe scoffed at the suggestion that something so vital would have escaped his attention.

"Yeah, you'd think." Gio muttered.

His mutterings were not quite low enough to evade his mother's radar ears and he received a gentle clout around the head for his show of disrespect. "Whatever Marco's reasons for not telling anyone but Santa Cruz, we will find it. Recriminations will not help us right now."

"Does anyone know if Santa Cruz actually has asked his sister if she knows any reason why she and Marco would receive similar death threats and if she knows Marco?" Vinnie asked.

Giorgio answered. "He hasn't asked her because he can't have any direct contact with her. He is afraid that if people back in Mexico know who she is related to, there will be recriminations and reprisals. I've heard the drug lords down there don't have any scruples and don't give a shit about who they take it out on, just anyone they can get their hands on. They don't care."

There was silence for a while and then Vinnie hit on an idea. "So why can't one of us call her?"

"Sure, if you can track her down and find a number."

Vinnie picked up the now famous brown file and began to leaf through it. He looked at all of the various series of numbers he came across, searching for something that might be a Mexican telephone number. "What's the DDI for Mexico?" He looked up and saw everyone looking blank and Vinnie sighed in frustration. "Useless," he muttered and continued searching. "Hey, wait a minute – what's this? I've found a number here with a '214' pre-fix. Anyone know where that is?"

"Dallas," Giorgio spoke up without looking away from the screen. "I have a long-distance girlfriend from there. It's going nowhere," he shrugged but smiled as he thought of a naked Sally. Great girl and great in bed. Big distance between them geographically so she couldn't pester him too much although she did like her daily phone calls. Maybe he should put her out of her misery and end the so-called relationship. It wasn't worth the aggravation and he didn't get enough out of it.

Vinnie shook his head at his nephew although it was very hard to disapprove and he suppressed a smile. Giorgio was no different to his father, his uncle or his grandfather. He put it down to Delvecchio genes. "Dallas. Why Dallas? Who is there?" he asked more to himself than he expected an answer and continued looking through the file. "Maybe it's a go-between for Carlos and his sister."

Giorgio sighed. "I think we should call Adam, he's way better on a computer than I am and I don't know what else to try." He sat back in Marco's chair as frustration got the better of him. He knew should have paid more attention in tech class.

"No! I don't want Adam involved in this," Sarah was adamant on this point. She had better plans for Adam that would not involve a life of corruption and immoral behaviour. She realised know that she was too late to save Giorgio but she'd be damned if she would allow Adam to fall by the wayside and waste his good and expensive education.

Vinnie looked up. "Jamie is pretty good on a computer and can hack into most systems that just have basic security. He has spent a lot of time sitting in front of a screen doing god knows what. Let me go and drag his ass out of bed - he needs to start to earn his keep." With that, he left the office and headed to the pool house to wake his lazy son up.

"Gabe, do we know anyone that would be able to trace where the money in the London Shires bank account goes to and from?" Sarah too, was beginning to get frustrated.

Gabe nodded as he thought. "Yeah, I think so. Let me make a call and I'll let you know in ten minutes," he said. He also left the room, taking his mobile phone out of his pocket and dialling a number as he went.

Sarah took the opportunity of Gabe out of the room to call Detective Foley as she felt Santa Cruz deserved a stay of execution at least. He had co-operated as much as he was able, she was sure of that. As Sarah spoke to Foley, she could hear the relief in his voice that he was not sending three women to a certain death and promised Sarah he would see to it.

Friday

"Yes, ma'am. We have two king rooms booked for tonight for one night. We have both of you on our fourth floor, which is the executive floor and you can take a complimentary continental breakfast in the executive lounge between 6 and 10 a.m." The perky receptionist at the airport hotel at Dallas Fort Worth trilled in her Texan accent.

Sarah smiled and handed over her credit card for the pre-approval for both rooms. She couldn't expect Vinnie to pay for this trip out of his own money, it had been her crazy idea and she had had to work hard to talk him around. She knew that he thought it was a complete waste of time but she had told him she would go either with him or without him.

After the formalities, Sarah and Vinnie took themselves to the fourth floor. They declined assistance with their baggage as they were both travelling light. She had a small overnight bag with her and Vinnie carried even less – just a suit carrier which contained the bare essentials for the night.

They rode the elevator in silence and stepped out when the mechanical male voice announce the executive floor. Following the signage down the hall, they soon found their respective rooms, 426 and 434, the safety of a few rooms apart. Sarah had wanted it that way.

Sarah turned to face Vinnie after she had swiped her card through the reader to gain entry to her room. "So, do you want to meet me back here in half an hour?"

"Sure." He smiled at his sister-in-law and then made his way a few doors further down the corridor to his own room.

Sarah stepped into her room for the night and took in the spacious, neutral coloured room. It was the type of room that could put you anywhere in the world, all very generic. There was no indication in the furnishings or décor in the room to suggest that you were in Texas.

She put her bag down on the bed and checked out the bathroom. Again, it was spacious, functional, clean and sterile. It would serve its purpose. Sarah sat down on the bed and pulled out her mobile phone to call Giorgio.

"Hey, we're here. Any developments?" she asked her son when he picked up the call.

"Nothing new. Jamie has been working on it since early this morning but he's just an amateur hacker. We need a professional, which Gabe is working on. Jamie was lucky to find a name in Dallas, he is struggling to discover anything else. The address matches the one Dad had written down so maybe we are on the right track."

"Maybe."

"So what time are you meeting with this woman?"

"In about an hour. We are going to head over there soon."

"Do you think she might talk to you now that you have made the journey to Dallas?"

"She intimated that she might if we met up with her. I think she just didn't want to talk over the phone, she is nervous about something. It seems to me that she has something big to divulge and I just hope that it gives us some answers."

Giorgio stayed silent. He was unconvinced.

"I'll call you once we come away from there. Remember, if the police call, I have just gone away for tonight for some time alone."

"For breathing space, yeah, yeah, I know the drill." But Giorgio was not impressed. He did not see why Vinnie had to go along with his mother. And overnight. He did not want to think about it. "I'll speak to you later then," he said and disconnected the call.

Sarah sighed. She knew Giorgio was unhappy about her and Vinnie being here together, they had had a big and somewhat heated discussion about it earlier that day. She couldn't convince Giorgio that there was nothing going on, that Sarah just wanted to talk to this mystery woman face to face and that Vinnie had volunteered to come along. She was bothered by Giorgio's sudden attitude towards her. Since Wednesday, he had become more authoritative and she was aware that she was no longer able to control him, that it was becoming more the other way around. He was taking up the mantle of being the top man and it appeared to Sarah that he was becoming more disapproving of her actions than his father had been on occasion. Sarah had always been able to talk Marco around but she doubted she would be able to do so with her son for much longer. He was not a child any longer. Marco's death had elevated him almost overnight to a grown man and he was now stepping up and leaving her behind. He would not need her for much longer.

There was a loud knock on her door, startling her and Sarah realised with surprise that the half an hour had flown by. She picked up her bag and opened the door to Vinnie.

"Ready to go?" he asked.

Sarah just nodded and stepped into the corridor, closing the door behind her. She followed Vinnie down the hallway towards the elevators. Neither spoke.

The doorman found them a cab within moments and Vinnie gave the driver their destination address. As they drove away from the airport towards the city centre, Sarah just looked at the Texan countryside flying passed her. The silence was helping them both to plan what they wanted to say to Melanie Boulter.

Late last night, Gabe had called upon an unnamed contact within the FBI, a low grade paper pusher at the Miami Field Office and pretty much off the radar from her superiors. She was a technical analyst in the financial crimes department and Gabe used her only when necessary. He had given her the London Shires bank account number as that was all the information that they had so far. Gabe wanted to know where the money was coming from, if it came from a Delvecchio, when it had been set up and also, perhaps more importantly, where the money went to. The contact had come back to Gabe soon after with the information required and had advised Gabe the account had been set up in the Mayfair,

London branch of the bank by a John Harris. The initial transaction appeared to have all been above board, the correct paperwork and financial checks had been made and all of the I.D's had checked out. She had so far been unable to trace where the deposits came from but had confirmed with accuracy that the outgoing transaction went to a bank account in the name of Melanie Boulter of 2568 South Avenue, Irving, Texas and even supplied her telephone number.

Melanie Boulter had not been forthcoming over the telephone and had come across as frosty. She had said it was difficult to explain over the phone. Sarah had told her she would come to Dallas if that was the case but Melanie was even more hesitant by that suggestion. She confided to Sarah that she knew who she was and was terrified of being caught up in the wrong thing but that she wanted to explain the entire situation. Rather reluctantly, she had agreed for Sarah to come and visit and promised that she would try and resolve her questions. Vinnie would deliver all kinds of pain to Melanie if she did not.

So, here they both were, in Dallas, speeding towards who knew what possible fairy-tale and most likely a waste of time but until Sarah could bury her husband she had nothing better to do.

Melanie's house was a small one in the middle of suburbia, in an older neighbourhood. The houses on South Avenue were mostly single-storey dwellings surrounded on all sides with grass, some green and lush, other gardens were browning and withering in the heat. Melanie did the best she could and her house had a wraparound porch and was enclosed with a picket fence in need of a repaint. Her grass was green and vibrant, sprinklers were watering the garden when Sarah and Vinnie's cab drew up outside. A tyre swing hung from a large tree at the side of the house, unused for many years judging from the ample growth of grass beneath it. A new silver Ford sat in the driveway to the left and Sarah surmised that five grand a month extra income would enable you to buy a new car every once in a while.

The front door was open and Sarah looked up to see a woman a little younger than herself leant against the frame. She waited while Vinnie paid for the cab and told the driver to come back in an hour for them before they walked up the driveway together. Clearly Melanie had been looking out for her visitors and she stood unsmiling, waiting for them to arrive and get inside the house. They were ushered inside unceremoniously and Sarah hesitated as she looked at Melanie, unsure of the secrets she held. She looked a little familiar but Sarah could not think where she might know her from. She was pretty sure the two had never met but something was niggling at her. Was this Marco's lover? Did he have another family with this woman? The possibilities were both endless and frightening.

"Please, won't you come in?" Melanie asked, almost in desperation as she looked up and down her street to see if any of her neighbours were watching. Sarah wondered what or who she was afraid of and why.

Sarah took a deep breath and stepped into the hallway as Vinnie followed just behind her. Melanie closed the front door quickly almost catching Vinnie's jacket tails in the door. He scowled at her but she paid him no mind and showed them both into a chintzy room with oversized and overstuffed sofas. The dark wooden floors were strewn with patterned rugs that clashed with the flowered sofas and overall, it looked very old-fashioned.

Melanie on the other hand, was the complete opposite. She had very short cropped red hair and a butterfly tattoo on her neck. She wore black leather trousers that clung to her skinny hips and legs and a black cropped tee-shirt completed her ensemble and showed off more tattoos on her toned arms. Her nose was pierced and there were several ear-rings in each of her lobes and a ring through her eyebrow. She was just a few years younger than Sarah but they could not have been more different – surely Marco would not have had an affair with this aging punk?

Then it hit Sarah why Melanie looked familiar to her. She was the woman in some of the photos in Marco's file. Sarah kept this nugget to herself for the time being. She wanted to see what Melanie was going to say first. Sarah stole a surreptitious glance at Vinnie on the opposite chair and she could tell that he was now aware this was the woman in the photos in their file but he just sat quiet, waiting for Melanie to speak.

When Melanie did finally speak, her voice was so soft that she sounded like a little old lady and not the aging punk trying desperately to cling to her disappearing youth. She looked so out of place in this chintzy house in the suburbs of Dallas. Marco had always scoffed at women who tried to hide their real age, saying he felt the natural look was so much sexier. He couldn't stand women who had surgery which discounted most of the women he rubbed shoulders with in Palm Beach. For that reason, Sarah felt sure Marco and Melanie had not had an affair but she had to be sure.

"Can I ask you one thing first?" Sarah ventured. "Did you have an affair with my husband?" She tried to keep her voice level but it threatened to crack with every word.

Melanie laughed with a high pitched tinkling tone. "Lord no, honey! Men have never been my thing, if you get my drift."

Sarah smiled with relief and she felt a weight lift from her shoulders that had been sitting there since the Dallas trip had been arranged. She felt she could deal with almost anything Melanie threw at her now.

"So what then?"

"Well, it's such a long story that I hardly know where to begin."

"Why not start with who John Harris is?" Vinnie prompted. His voice was gruff and unfriendly.

"John Harris?" she looked confused.

"Yeah, the guy who has been paying you five grand a month for the last twenty-seven years."

"Oh. John Harris doesn't exist. It was kind of a – what do you call it? – a kinda made up name."

"It sounds exactly like that. So, who has been paying you and why?"

"You're not giving me time to tell my story." Melanie complained in her southern accent. Sarah doubted it was Texan. Southern – definitely. Texan – not a chance.

"We don't have time for stories, just cold, hard facts." Vinnie's eyes bored into Melanie's like daggers.

Melanie flinched as she realised that this was not a man to be messed with. She took a deep breath. "Okay, well, John Harris was a cover for Joe Delvecchio. The money has been coming from him."

Sarah froze at the mention of the name. Joe was dead. She knew he was dead because she had seen Vinnie pull the trigger and watch as the bullet tore into his head and kill him in an instant. She had seen his lifeless body on the slab in the morgue when she had accompanied Marco to identify his brother. She had been to his funeral for Christ's sake and cried crocodile tears for anyone watching to think it had been a terrible and upsetting murder and that she was shocked and horrified by the events. Marco had hoped that those events were enough to make her put her gun away and not want to take the law into her own hands again and for a while, it had worked. Now, she was itching to dust off her gun again and shoot someone. Justifiably so.

Vinnie stood up. "Sarah, we are leaving. This woman is a fucking crackpot and we have heard enough!" He was furious although trying but failing to control his temper.

"No. Please wait!" Melanie pleaded. "I know it sounds strange, I know Joe died many years ago but he had the payment set up two years before he died and notarized by a lawyer friend of his – Nico or Rico or something like that. The arrangement was to continue indefinitely and be paid out of his estate until the beneficiary died."

"Joe's estate was willed to Marco. It never got changed even after the two fell out, I don't know why. Marco was the sole beneficiary." Sarah remembered quietly, almost to herself. She recalled the time just after Joe's funeral when Marco had found out that he now owned all that his brother had. Marco had never approved of how Joe accumulated his wealth, most of it through drugs and cat houses and he swore that he would never touch the money. He told Sarah he would one day bequeath it to a charity but over time it had been forgotten about and had just sat there, amassing interest and growing ever bigger for all of these years.

"I don't get why Joe or Marco would be paying you anything. Just who the hell are you? And who is Joe's beneficiary?" Vinnie was even more confused and began to think that his father, Marco and Joe's father had been hiding another secret illegitimate child for all of these years. He himself was living proof of Giorgio Delvecchio Senior's inability to keep it in his trousers. Just how many indiscretions had he committed?

"I'm just an old friend of Joe's. I did some work for him way back when."

"What sort of work?"

Melanie then became reluctant to say anything further. She stood up and walked over to a cheap looking cabinet by the wall. There were tasteless looking wine and champagne glasses on display through the etched glass at the top and two drawers at the bottom. Melanie opened one of the drawers and rifled around inside for a moment. She soon found what she was searching for, for she closed the drawer and walked back to Sarah and Vinnie. She handed over the photograph.

"That was Raymond when he was four months old," she said with pride in her voice.

Sarah stared at the picture of the baby and her heart leaped. The child looked just like Adam had at four months old. Beautiful dark brown eyes, and dark wavy hair and a stunning Delvecchio smile on his chubby face. It was evident to see and Sarah struggled for words. The room began to swim before her eyes.

"Who is Raymond?" Vinnie asked, taking the picture from his sister-in-law's shaking hands. He looked in concern at her; she had gone very pale.

Sarah stuttered. "Is he Marco's child?"

Melanie smiled patiently. "No, he isn't Marco's child. He is Marco's nephew, Joe's son."

Sarah and Vinnie just sat motionless in their chairs, floored by this latest piece of news. None of it made any sense to either of them but it also seemed irrelevant to how and why Marco had died.

Nevertheless, Sarah felt some compassion rising in her knowing that there was an orphaned Delvecchio child out there somewhere. She felt the need to comfort this child – man that he now would be – and wanted to know where he might be.

"Joe came to me with the baby when Raymond was just three months old. He said the mother wouldn't or couldn't look after him, I don't remember which he said. Joe asked if I could look after him, to adopt him and raise him as my own. Well, of course, with me having an aversion to men, this would probably be my only shot at motherhood so I jumped at the chance. I didn't want or need to know anything about Ray's birth mother or the baby's background. I knew Joe well enough, or so I thought, so I agreed. He would support us both financially until Ray was of age."

Sarah shifted in her seat. "And you have no idea who Raymond's real mother is?"

Melanie shrugged. "I never wanted to know. As far as I am concerned, Raymond is my chid."

"And where is the prodigal nephew now?" Vinnie asked.

Melanie shook her head. "I have no idea. I haven't seen him for about two years now. I tried to tell him, maybe a little too late, that I was his adopted mother and it got ugly. I should have told him sooner, when he was little maybe so he had time to get used to the idea. Ray can have moments of... well, he can be unhinged, if you get my drift."

Vinnie passed the photograph back to her. "The apple doesn't fall far from the tree. Does he know who his father was?"

Melanie took a deep breath. "Yeah, I told him. It was kind of hard to keep quiet when he was holding a knife to my throat. It was like all the years of nurturing and all the love I had given him had just been swept away. The look in his eyes – it was like he hated me." She looked at her feet as though she was ashamed, as though it might be her fault that her adoptive son was a psycho.

Vinnie muttered something almost incoherent, something more about like father like son. Sarah caught his drift and shot him a warning look; this was not the time or the place for recriminations. Ray had not grown up around his father so why should he have turned out as bad as him? Surely such things were not in the genes so why would Raymond have the violent traits? Her own children had the genes of Marco and Sarah knew all too well what he had been capable of but Grace, Giorgio and Adam were not like their father in that respect. Well, she conceded, she wasn't so sure about Giorgio but the other two were well rounded human beings.

"Do you think Raymond could have found out who his birth mother is and that maybe he went after her?" Sarah asked.

"Perhaps. I don't know how he would ever track her down. Joe's arrangement with me was always informal, the adoption was never legalised so there was no paperwork other than the monthly stipend. When I heard Joe had been killed, I assumed the secret would have died with him."

"So what did you say to Ray? I mean, he must have asked you how you knew his father."

"I told him I worked for him, that's all."

"Worked for him – how?"

Melanie stood up somewhat agitated and began to pace the room. "Look, I'm not proud of what I did, okay? But I was young and I had a habit. One that indebted me to Joe."

Sarah nodded in understanding. Drugs. Again.

Melanie continued. "I would fly into Mexico and back to various places in the U.S. Dallas, Atlanta, Miami. I would carry… things, stuff for him."

"You were a drugs mule?" Vinnie was astonished.

Melanie nodded. "I guess that is the word for it. For me."

Sarah didn't hear Melanie's last words. Her mind was racing. Mexico. Santa Cruz. Was there a connection there somewhere? She knew there must be, it was just a question of finding it. "Where in Mexico did you meet with Joe?"

"Oh, just various hotels near the airport. Nothing glamorous and always under the radar. I would fly in and almost straight out again. In with one airline and back with another."

"Was Joe ever with anyone?"

"Nope, I always met with him alone."

Sarah sighed in frustration. She knew the connection was there but she couldn't piece it together yet although she knew she was close. Just a few more pieces to find.

"Melanie, why were you so hesitant to talk to Sarah on the phone? You could have saved us a trip out here?" Vinnie asked.

She shrugged. "I guess I was scared. I knew what Joe was, who his family are and it scares me. I had hoped it was all in my past, in Ray's past and then all of a sudden here it is, right in front of my face again. Maybe by seeing you, I hoped that it wouldn't bite me on the ass but I reckon it still will somehow."

The three of them sat in silence for a while. Sarah got the feeling that they had got all of the information they were going to from Melanie and then a thought hit her.

"Do you have a recent picture of Raymond?"

Melanie nodded and disappeared down the hallway. Sarah just looked at Vinnie, both floored by what they had learnt in the past hour. They could both hear Melanie opening and closing drawers in the bedroom and after a few minutes, she came back with an eight by six and she handed it to Sarah.

"This was taken on the last Christmas we had together, which I think was two Christmases ago."

Sarah gasped. She had seen this guy before. He was the mystery man in the photos with Melanie that she had at home in Marco's file. Only in this photo, he was smiling and happy with a shiny red paper Christmas hat on and covered in paper streamers. He looked like Adam.

He looked like his father.

Vinnie stood to leave and placed a hand on Sarah's shoulder while still staring at Melanie. "If you think of anything else, be sure to call." It was more of a barked order than a request and Melanie had a 'fuck you' look on her face and Vinnie doubted that they would ever hear from her voluntarily again. Melanie knew her monthly payment was about to end and she owed neither Sarah nor Vinnie anything more.

As they left the house, their cab pulled up with perfect timing. Sarah was astounded that an hour had passed; it seemed like no time at all since they had entered the house and been spun a tale of who knew what. Truth or fiction, Sarah couldn't tell yet. But she would find out.

Once inside the taxi, Sarah called her son.

"How are you getting on?" she asked Giorgio.

"Good, I think. We have found out that the money went into the London Shires account from an unused account of Dad's. It was originally Uncle Joe's estate although Dad never changed the details over." he enthused, pleased to have a discovery to impart to his mother unaware she was now in receipt of these facts.

"No. Your father never approved of how Joe made the majority of his money and wanted nothing to do with it."

"So the payment continued to be paid into the L.S bank. It's where it went that you might be interested in," he enthused.

"Let me guess, Melanie Boulter?" This was not news to any of them.

"Uh-huh, but once there, half of it had being going into an account in the name of Raymond Boulter for the last eighteen months."

Okay. That makes sense, Sarah thought. That was about the time Raymond found out the truth about his parentage so perhaps he blackmailed Melanie into giving him half the money. She was certainly scared enough of him to jump to his demands. To Giorgio, she asked, "Has there been any activity on Raymond's account recently?"

Giorgio couldn't contain his excitement. "Yes! There have been regular withdrawals in the last six months from various ATM's around South Beach."

"Now *that* is interesting. Who found this out?"

"Someone Gabe knows."

"So Adam is not involved?"

"No, but he is asking questions."

"I'll be home early tomorrow. We've missed the last flight home now."

"You should have taken the plane, as Gabe insisted. You could have come home tonight." Giorgio was peeved about his mother staying away the night. With Vinnie. Especially when it was not necessary.

Sarah picked up on the gentle chastisement in her elder son's voice but chose to ignore it again. She would talk to Giorgio when she arrived home and let him know that everything was above board.

"I'll be home in the morning," she said again with more strength in her voice. They said their goodbyes and hung up. The cab was just pulling up outside the hotel.

They walked back to their respective rooms each lost in their own thoughts. Vinnie was still of the impression that this whole trip had been a right royal waste of time. It was interesting to learn that he had another nephew but didn't feel the need to get to know him and also couldn't see how this might be related to Marco's murder. He wanted to get back to Palm Beach and he would just have to humour Sarah in her quest as he couldn't leave her to run off on fool's errands alone.

Sarah fumbled around in her bag looking for her key card. Vinnie hesitated outside her door.

"What is it?" She asked him. Sarah could be more astute than he sometimes gave her credit for.

Vinnie twisted his hands together in apparent anguish. "I was just wondering whether it would be appropriate for me to take you out to dinner tonight."

Sarah blinked twice, shock overcoming her and then she relaxed and smiled. "Well, I suppose we do have to eat so we may as well keep each other company. It's fine, Vinnie. Your brother wouldn't mind."

Vinnie let out a huge breath as though he had been holding it in while they spoke. "Okay. About eight then?" It gave them two hours.

Two hours with which Sarah didn't know what she was going to do with. Since Marco had been killed, she had not had any time to herself, no time to think or dwell on the events. She wasn't sure she wanted to be on her own right now, filling in time, watching endless mindless programmes on T.V and forcing herself to think about her husband. Think about never again seeing his sexy smile; the naughty twinkle in his dark eyes when he was lustful or the curly edge to his graying hair when it was wet and clung to the nape of his neck. He would never amuse her again with his temper; never bring her a cup of tea in bed or dance around their bedroom naked after his morning shower. He was forever gone from her life and she couldn't bear time alone to think about that or the implications.

"No Vinnie. Please come in with me just for a little while. I can't bear to be alone right now." Sarah swiped her key card and entered the room, switching the lights on as she did so.

Vinnie followed her inside and locked the door behind them both. He was aware of a sudden and drastic change in Sarah and he hoped that she wasn't about to shed her first tears for her husband. He wasn't sure what he was going to do if she did.

"Are you okay?" he asked as she sat down on the end of the bed.

She shook her head slowly. "No, Vinnie. I don't want you to be shocked by what I am going to ask of you now and feel free to say no but will you make love to me?" she looked up into his green eyes that were frozen in surprise.

Despite Sarah's request not to be shocked, Vinnie could not help but to be so. He looked at his sister-in-law sitting on the edge of her king-sized hotel bed looking up earnestly at him. She had a pleading almost desperate look on her face and he wondered what her agenda was. But he also felt something stirring deep inside him and he couldn't say no. Like he knew he should do for both of their sakes.

Instead, his mind drifted back to over twenty-five years ago to an afternoon in a London hotel when they had made love before. It had taken him some time to get over her then when she had gone back to Marco and for a good few years, it had rightly so, cost him his relationship with his brother. Vinnie wasn't sure what hold this woman had over him then or now other than perhaps the wanting of something or someone that you cannot have. But his feelings then and his hesitancy now made him think that perhaps the heat of love or lust had just cooled to a glowing ember rather than being extinguished altogether. In any other circumstances he would have thrown her back on the bed and taken her with the rapacity that he was fighting with then.

"And you think my brother wouldn't mind that either?" his voice was husky when he asked the question.

Sarah shrugged. "I daresay that he will kill you all over again when you meet him in the fires of hell but he is not here now. He has gone. He has left me. You are here and so I am. Two consenting adults."

"And what happens when we leave Dallas?"

Sarah shook her head. "I don't know. That's too far in the future for me to think about. All I can think about is the next few hours, just you and me. I need to feel you inside me. I need to feel something other than numbness and a great gaping hole in my chest. I can't promise you anything and I don't want you to expect anything of me other than what I can give you right now." She stood up and took a tentative step towards Vinnie.

He offered no resistance, no step back away from her so she took his inaction as consent and reached behind his neck. She pulled him towards her and kissed him almost shyly, testing the water. Suddenly Vinnie came alive under Sarah's lips and responded with absolute passion, his tongue probing and finding hers. He pulled her body to his, crushing her to his own desperate body. Sarah reached around and pulled his shirt over his head, springing free a button as she did so. She kissed his smooth chest, so different to his brother's hair covered one and began to feel breathless and giddy. Her hands moved down to his belt and she stifled a girlish giggle as she struggled to undo the clasp on his belt for a moment before freeing the buckle and moving onto his zip. Before she was able to push his trousers down, he had unbuttoned her blouse and his fevered tongue found her hard nipples. The two fell back on the bed breathing heavily, Sarah kicking off her shoes at the same time as her skirt was peeled away.

Vinnie lay on top of her, looking into her eyes, trying to read her before they reached the point of no return. "You're not going to pretend that I am him, are you?" Doubt clouded his eyes as he saw himself falling into the abyss again.

Sarah didn't respond with words, just wrapped her legs around his hips and forced him into her before he might change his mind. "It's just you and me, Vinnie." She whispered into his ear, pulling him down to her and began to kiss him. Vinnie began to move with her, ecstasy evident on his face.

Sarah's mind was not on other people's opinion of her, or her dead husband as his blond brother thrust into her again and again with increased force. She felt safe and wanted once more and knew she would not give Vinnie up a second time. She didn't know how things were going to work out or be explained once they returned to Florida but they were going to find a way. Right now though, it was just the two of them and she needed this.

With a start, she realised Vinnie had come to a grinding and breathless finish. He buried his face in her neck and offered his apologies for not being able to wait for her. However, Sarah realised that it would give them a good excuse for another round later, after dinner.

"You owe me, Bonetti! And after dinner, I will collect," she teased him as she headed for the bathroom.

She looked back and saw his satisfied face and boyish grin.

He had realised the implications of her words, that there would be another time for them to be together. Despite the circumstances, Vinnie didn't want to be dropped by Sarah again and was hoping for something more permanent. He was more than aware that Marco had not even been buried yet and so they would have to either cool it or keep it clandestine until a suitable period had elapsed but Vinnie was prepared to wait. He was going to need Giorgio on his side at least and he couldn't risk upsetting him.

He knew he would also do anything for Sarah.

Saturday

On their flight home, the two illicit lovers tried to plan how they were going to continue to spend time together. It was not going to be easy and they both realised that there was nobody who would be happy about Sarah and Vinnie taking up together. Sarah wanted to spend time with Grace, Giorgio and Adam and this was paramount above all else. They were not under any illusion that her children would understand how Sarah had gone from their father's bed to their uncle's bed in such a short time span and she wouldn't be able to explain it to them. She barely understood it herself. If she were to take a step back and think about it, Sarah would be shocked by her own behaviour – Marco hadn't even been buried yet – because she had loved her husband with all of her heart. She had excused her actions by telling herself that this was just a way of coping with the extreme grief although others might just call that denial. So, just ten minutes from landing in West Palm Beach Airport Sarah and Vinnie had come to the decision of cooling their fledgling relationship until such a time that Grace, Giorgio and Adam might begin to understand, even if that was a year down the line.

Arriving back at the house, it was back down to the business of finding out who killed Marco. Gabe was sequestered in the office again, taking charge of a meeting which put Sarah's back up slightly. Vinnie wanted to bring them all up to date with the events and discoveries of the trip to Dallas although he was still of a mind that it was a waste of time as far as finding his brother's killer, at least. Sarah didn't want to be in on it, rehashing the same old stuff and getting disapproving glances from her son and all the others. Vinnie promised her that he would update her on anything relevant as she headed outside to find Rosa.

Rosa was sitting on the patio with Grace. The two women had not long arrived with their husbands and were quietly talking. They fell silent as they saw Sarah walking down the path towards them.

"Where have you been?" Grace asked her mother, her voice accusatory.

Sarah answered with a stern stare — she did not want to be spoken to by her daughter in that way. "You know full well where I have been, Grace. Looking for your father's murderer." She sat down on an empty chair and watched Connor play in the grass with some bright coloured plastic toy bricks. He was at the stage where he enjoyed throwing toys but grizzled when he could not retrieve them. His grizzling irked Sarah today.

After a suitable and dramatic pause, Sarah continued. "I have been to Dallas."

Neither Rosa nor Grace said anything but waited for Sarah to continue. It was not lost on either of them that Vinnie had accompanied Sarah to Dallas and both couldn't help but wonder in what capacity.

Sarah continued, "It's quite difficult to explain and we are not yet sure of the connection but we have found out that there is an undiscovered member of the Delvecchio family," she made the revelation in a whisper as though it were a great piece of gossip that only select ears should hear.

Rosa frowned.

"Dad had an affair?" Grace's voice was full of hurt as though it was she that had been wronged.

Sarah smiled. "No, darling. You have another cousin. Your Uncle Joe had a child before he... he died. A boy. He's about twenty-six now."

"Joe had a son? Why did he never mention it? Who is the boy's mother?" Rosa threw questions at Sarah without giving her the opportunity to answer any of them.

"Now, *that* is the million dollar question. We don't yet know but we are trying to establish that. Joe gave the child to a female friend of his to raise, money every month to support him, although

Marco had been paying the stipend after Joe died, and again, we don't know if he was even aware that he had been paying it. It was all a no questions asked scenario until now, anyway. We've been to Dallas and spoken to Ray's adoptive mother but she doesn't know very much. Joe just turned up one day with a baby and asked her to keep him."

"So is Ray coming to meet us all?" Grace was excited at the thought of having a mystery cousin and her face lit up in a happiness that had been missing for a few days now.

Sarah shrugged. "No idea. He hasn't been heard from for about two years now. He and his mother had a falling out and he now he has just vanished." She decided to keep quiet about the part where he might be in South Beach.

"So how has this story suddenly come to light after all of these years?" Rosa was intrigued. She was the only family member who had any guilt or remorse about Joe's demise and now here was a chance of redemption.

Sarah signed. "It's a long story and I am still trying to piece it all together. It all started with Carlos Santa Cruz and sometimes I think it is just a wild goose chase as we just keep going round in circles. Now, I'm starting to wonder if Joe worked for Santa Cruz in any capacity but he has denied having any relationship with any Delvecchio and I am inclined to believe him." Again, she missed out vital facts, such as her appalling deal she made with Santa Cruz.

"Joe used to spend a lot of time in Mexico, long before he became involved in the personal use of narcotics." Rosa mused, her eyes taking on a long ago remembered look.

"Really?"

"Yes, he'd fly down every three months or so for a vacation, so he said. You and Grace were in California at the time but Marco used to wonder if he had met a senorita down there and we had hoped he was getting over Lydia and Sam. Then it became apparent about his side-line and Marco dismissed the idea of vacations. Joe was just building up his new business."

"Well that's what Santa Cruz' business is so I guess it is quite possible that the two of them were working together on the drugs thing. Melanie told us she used to smuggle drugs into the U.S for Joe. Perhaps Joe was a Santa Cruz distributor in the beginning. Santa Cruz was and always has been a major cartel for cocaine, perhaps that's how Joe got his 'big break'."

Grace interjected. "Ah, but what if Joe had met a woman down there? All men have their needs, especially when on vacation. Add in alcohol and recreational drugs. Maybe he got said mystery woman pregnant and after the baby was born, he bought it to the US as he wanted it but she didn't and… "

"Jesus Christ!" Sarah jumped up as the realisation hit her. Of course! It was so bloody obvious! "I'll be back in a minute," she said and she ran up the path towards the house. She clattered into her husband's office oblivious of the men inside who were still involved in their meeting. She didn't care that she had interrupted them, this was a breakthrough.

Gabe stopped speaking and smiled at her, trying to show tolerance as he had learned to through years of similar interruptions. He had watched Marco try to curb his temper every time she had done it to him but it had still never deterred her.

"Did anyone find out where Calliope Santa Cruz is?" She was breathless from her charge up the path. "Or a phone number or anything at all?"

Blank stupefied faces stared back at her as though she was a mad woman.

"Oh never mind!" she muttered and turned back round, slamming the door behind her she headed to the kitchen. She found her bag on the counter where she had dumped it on her arrival home and rummaged around inside as she searched for her cell phone. Finding it and seeing the battery dead, she swore and charged into the lounge to use the land line. As she dialled Carlos Santa Cruz's house, she didn't expect to get anything other than an answer phone.

"Hello?" A female voice answered after just two rings.

"Mrs Santa Cruz? Hi! This is Sarah Delvecchio. I need to speak to your husband urgently, if he is available." Sarah was still a little breathless.

There was a sharp intake of breath down the line. "I don't know how you have the nerve to call my house after what you have done to me and my daughters! Do you have any idea how terrified my girls were?" The scathing voice was thick with its Spanish accent.

Sarah had forgotten until then that she had almost had the Santa Cruz women deported. She smiled to herself at her faux-pas. "Yes, yes, I know but I need to speak with your husband. Please put him on the line if he is there." She hoped Dolore would be too afraid of any possible consequences not to do as she was asked. Sarah laughed out loud when she realised the woman had put the phone down on her. She hung up and then walked back into the office.

"I need one of you guys to make a call for me," Sarah demanded. She ignored Gabe's scowl which was showing signs of being less tolerant each time she went into her husband's office.

Vinnie jumped to attention first and he left the room with her. Once back in the lounge, he stole a kiss from her.

Sarah smiled at his audacity. She had enjoyed the chaste kiss. "I need you to call this number back and charm, coerce and cajole Mrs Santa Cruz into getting her husband on the line or to call me back. I need his sister's phone number in Mexico and I need it today," she smiled again, and left him to it. She went to check if she would be able to get the Delvecchio jet in the air that day. She might need to go to Mexico.

Thankfully, no-one needed to fly anywhere that day. Vinnie had used all of his considerable charm offensive on Dolore Santa Cruz until she promised him that Carlos would return his call, which he did at around five later that day.

He swore blind to Sarah that he did not have a contact number for Calliope, it was just safer that way. However, he could get a message to her via several contacts in Buena Tiempo but it might take a day or two.

"My plane is on stand-by and waiting to take me to Mexico City – can I have the contacts as I absolutely have to get hold of her today." Sarah was not going to let him off the hook that easily.

"What is this about? Why the desperation?" Carlos wanted to know. He felt he had been forthcoming enough with the Delvecchios.

"I think I know who her stalker is but I need to find out more information from her. Things that only she would know, before you ask."

Carlos paused. "I should say no. My sister is a vulnerable person with a fragile state of mind. You will make things worse for her. She may not be able to cope with your style of questioning; I know first-hand how you work and what happens when you do not get your own way. However, I also know that you won't be giving this up and a phone call is less intrusive than a doorstep visit, so I will make the call for contact."

"I knew you would see it that way. When is she going to call me?"

"I will ask her to call you but I cannot make her call you." He hung up.

At eight o'clock that night, Sarah's newly charged mobile phone buzzed. She looked down at the unknown number on the display and prayed.

"Hello? Is this Sarah Delvecchio?" A faltering voice in unsure English asked.

Sarah's hoped soared. "Yes it is. Calliope? I am glad you called."

"Carlos say I call you. Muy importante."

"Yes it is important. Calliope, I need to ask you, did you know Joe Delvecchio?"

The fraction of a second of hesitation confirmed to Sarah that she had. Now she had to find out how.

"Yes, I knew him. Many years ago. Now, I am happy. I am married." Calliope sounded stressed already.

Sarah did not want to push her away too soon. This conversation could be imperative to her investigation. "I know and I am sorry to have to ask you these questions but I wouldn't trouble you if it wasn't vital. Can you please tell me how you know him, what happened?"

"Sorry but no. My husband does not know and I do not want him to find out. It was a long time ago."

Sarah felt she was losing her. "Okay," she paused. "If I ask you a question, will you just answer yes or no? Would that be okay?" Sarah assumed Calliope's hesitancy was due to her husband being in earshot of their conversation.

A moment later – "Okay."

Sarah put her cross examining lawyer hat on and thought about how to phrase the questions. "Did you have a relationship with Joe?"

"Yes."

"And this was before you were married?"

"Yes."

"And was it a serious relationship?"

"For me, yes."

"Did your family know about it or did they know who Joe was?"

"No. We met in a nightclub in town."

"And he just wanted some fun." More of a statement than a question but Sarah had known her brother-in-law well enough to already know the answer to that one. "And then you got pregnant?"

A barely audible yes came from the Mexican end of the line.

"Did Joe want the baby?"

"Yes. But not me."

"You didn't want the baby?" Sarah couldn't hide her surprise.

"I did. I mean he didn't want me."

Bastard, Sarah thought to herself but wasn't sure why she might have been surprised by this revelation. Joe had pretty much always been very self-centred. "So, he didn't want to marry you and instead took the baby away when it was born?"

"Yes."

Sarah thought about this for a moment. The Santa Cruz' were an old-fashioned practising Catholic family and this would have brought scandal on them. Their unmarried daughter with an Italian-American drug dealer. It was entirely possible that none of the family knew Calliope had been pregnant, keeping it to herself and she could have disappeared to have the baby. This would have made it easy for Joe to take the baby away undetected and it most definitely would have turned Calliope into a fragile state. Sarah knew that if she had had to give any of her babies up at birth she too would have had a breakdown. Joe had maybe returned to Mexico at just the right time and taken the baby away with him to live in the United States. Why Joe had not brought the baby up himself, she had no idea and maybe would never know. He certainly had the means to raise a baby. There were still things that didn't make sense.

"Did you ever see the baby again after Joe took it away?

"No, I didn't see either of them again. My son would be twenty-six by now." She now sounded brave and unafraid of saying anything out loud.

"Calliope, is it possible that anyone could have found out about this? Could it be that your son knows about you and is holding a grudge?"

"Well, I don't see how. Only Joe knows he is the baby's father. I had the baby in Miami so he would be born in America and no-one there knows who I am. I come home after the birth and marry my husband a year later. I try to forget all about it."

Sarah had so many more questions to ask but was aware that she had intruded enough into Calliope's past. It was evident that bringing it all back was a painful experience and she was struggling to cope with the terrible events that she had been through. Sarah wondered how terrified Calliope must have been to have given up her baby to a father as bad as Joe turned out to be. She decided to wrap up the conversation.

"Thank you, Calliope. I know how hard this must have been for you and you have no idea how much I appreciate your honesty." She told her.

"My brother – he does not know about this."

Sarah heard the unspoken plea in her voice and realised that she was the keeper of a secret so long buried that it should stay buried. If anyone found out about this, the woman on the other end of the phone could lose the life she had painstakingly built up over the last twenty five years. But Marco had taught her well enough about how to keep deep dark secrets and she would not betray this one. She promised Calliope that no-one would find out from her.

Giorgio left the office feeling very frustrated. No-one was listening to him. They were none of them getting anywhere fast and he wanted to punch something or someone, he didn't care which. He poked his head around the lounge door and saw his mother on the phone to someone, talking conspiratorially with her back to him. He didn't want to know who she was speaking to. He just wanted to get away from the house for a while. The family had a condo in the Bahamas and he was thinking that perhaps he could get away there for a few days. Just for a break. His phone rang again and he saw it was Katey. Jesse had somehow got hold of her number and passed it along to him. Giorgio had called her late last night and left a message. Now she was calling him back. He smiled.

"Hello Gio."

"Hello sexy Katey. I'm glad you called. I was just thinking about you." He lied but she would never know.

"Nice thoughts, I hope?"

"*Very* bad thoughts actually." That wasn't such a lie.

"Well, why don't you come over and visit? My house mates have gone out for the evening and the house is empty."

God! He loved her accent. No wonder his father had been so smitten with an English woman for all his life. The accent was just so sexy. He didn't think about Katey's invite for long. He was already picking his car keys up as he said goodbye.

As Giorgio drove his black Porsche south, the drive and the thought of Katey began to calm him. They had only been introduced last week and had spoken just once before, the night Marco had died. He had seen Katey around at other parties but for some reason, he did not have the courage to talk to her. He had never before been tongue tied over a girl and he wondered why this one was different. He laughed as he guessed it was because she refused to go to bed with him but she had heard about his alleged reputation and was refusing to be added to his list. That just made the challenge more interesting although he had been crushed at first. It was rare, if ever, that Giorgio got refused by a girl, particularly one he was very attracted to.

Katey was in Florida on a three month trip researching for a book she was in the process of writing. She was house sharing with two other girls to keep the costs down and it was just a few blocks from the fine sandy beaches of South Beach, party town. Giorgio loved it there. Katey was a curvy sexy girl with almost jet black hair and an easy smile and he was so eager to see her that he pushed his Porsche to the limit. He didn't care about speeding tickets. Let the cops write him a ticket; he could add it to the pile of other unpaid ones he had at home. That reminded him – he must get someone to sort them out again.

He pulled up outside Katey's house having memorised her address. He was determined to be on his best behaviour and play the long game with her. But he was resolute that he would win her around.

Katey greeted him at the door wearing a kaftan over her bikini, revealing plump breasts that made Giorgio need to push down his urges. She was a stunner! He gave her a chaste kiss on the cheek and took the beer bottle she held out for him.

"Stupid question, I know, but how are things?" She asked in her crisp accent as they sat down on the sofa.

He sighed. "You know, still difficult. We aren't any closer to finding out who did it, and the cops don't seem to care. We can't even arrange the funeral yet and I think my mother has taken up with my uncle already. Discretion is not a word they are familiar with," he said sarcastically.

"Discretion is not for everyone." Katey took a swig from the beer bottle and Giorgio eyed the bottle with envy as her lips encircled it. He looked away quickly. This was going to be less easy than he imagined. He was sat very close to her as the other chairs in the cluttered room were chock full of magazines, discarded clothing and college books. Katey was sitting with her bronzed legs curled up underneath her and was enjoying watching her guest squirm. "What makes you think they are having an affair?" she asked. "Was it happening before... Sunday?"

Giorgio shrugged. The sparkle had left his brown eyes as he remembered the reasons for him leaving Palm Beach for a few hours. "I don't know. I know there is history but it was never something that ever got discussed at home for obvious reasons. It's kind of like the taboo subject at Christmas! But they both took off to Dallas yesterday and stayed the night claiming they'd missed the last flight home even though they both took an overnight bag. Our family owns a private jet and they could have taken that. It's almost like they planned it. Why else would she want to be away at a time like this?"

"Well maybe... " Katey said slowly as she thought about it for a moment. "Maybe it's too hard for your mum to be at home at the moment. Perhaps the thought of not waking up next to your dad is too much to bear. Perhaps a sterile hotel room eases the heartbreak a little. Don't be too hard on her, Gio. It's tough on all of you, I'm sure but she was married to him for a long time and it must be awful." Her words were soft and sympathetic, non-judgemental.

"I know but I just wish she would talk to me, tell me what's going on. I know there is something that she is keeping from me." Giorgio took another swig of his beer, letting the cold fluid flow though him, calming him. "Do you want to go out and get something to eat?" He changed the subject, eager to forget about the situation at home.

Katey thought about it for a moment. She liked the idea of being seen out and about with Giorgio Delvecchio, the gorgeous, handsome blond rich play boy from Palm Beach. "So long as I don't have to sleep with you, Gio," she teased and jumped up to change into something for the evening.

Giorgio followed her into her bedroom and watched as she changed. His mouth began to water as he watched the forbidden fruit strip almost naked in front of him and put fresh clothes on. "Would that be such a bad idea?" he mused.

She looked at him and nodded. "It would be a terrible idea. I'm not going to be another one of your conquests, used, abused and forgotten about. I would rather we just stay friends."

"We could be friends and lovers… " He suggested.

Katey laughed. "No, we can't! When have you ever called a girl back after sleeping with her?" She slipped into a pair of black pumps and after grabbing a jacket, Katey pulled Giorgio into the balmy Florida night.

"Anyone would think you have known me for years instead of just a few days." Giorgio mumbled as they walked along.

"I know your sort. Rich, good-looking, thinks all women want to wrap their legs around your hips. Not this one, matey. I have too much self-respect and besides, I really enjoy your company. You are a great bloke, Gio, and perhaps you should respect yourself a little more."

He stopped walking and turned to look at Katey. "There's a royal telling off, if ever I've had one. I thought my mother had the monopoly on that." Giorgio looked hurt by Katey's words, perhaps because there was a slight needle of truth to what she had said and perhaps Giorgio didn't like it.

Katey took his arm and they began to walk again. "No it's not. It's just an observation." They had reached Ocean Drive and turned right towards a café that had wonderful views of the Atlantic and Katey had taken a liking to the establishment. She wasn't sure they would get a table at this time on a Saturday but it was worth a try.

As luck would have it, the restaurant owner knew Giorgio and found him the best table on the patio outside. As they sat, Giorgio ordered a bottle of red wine and two glasses.

"So do you think I should mend my ways?" he asked as he lost himself in her dark brown playful eyes.

Katey laughed. "You do whatever you think you need to do. I would just hate to see you hurt or worse – trapped by some silly girl who claims you have got her pregnant. You would attract that sort of person."

"I'm too clever for that," he assured her.

"Gio, have you ever been in love?" she asked him earnestly.

He thought about it for a moment. "I think so, once. I was fifteen. She was twenty-two and she stole my heart and my... "

"Enough!" Katey laughed. "I get the picture."

The waiter arrived with their wine and poured it for Giorgio to taste. He took a sip, accepted the bottle and Katey's glass was filled.

"So you'll be too drunk to drive home tonight," she stated." Do you have somewhere to sleep? I can't see you getting comfortable in that small car of yours."

Giorgio looked sheepish. "I was hoping you might have a sofa I could crash on."

Katey smiled. "I guess so. Just no funny business. I really do mean it when I say I am not going to sleep with you."

It was the worst challenge Katey could have inadvertently issued Giorgio. He decided then and there that he was going to clean up his act and win Katey over. His life was changing in many ways and this was just another change he was going to have to deal with. He was going to have to step up in the family business and make some decisions and take on the responsibilities that were undoubtedly heading his way and it was time he stopped behaving like a gigolo.

It was Katey who forgot to behave responsible that evening. She guzzled wine like it was the end of the world before she'd started on Mai-Tai's and it was the very sober Giorgio who helped her home.

"Too much sun," she slurred, her words almost incoherent as he helped her into her bedroom. The rest of the household was in silence, her flatmates having turned in hours ago. Giorgio took off

Katey's shoes and thought about undressing her but he knew he would never be able to prove his innocence if he did. Instead, he folded the blanket over her and lay down beside her. Curling up in her bed, he put a protective arm around her as she snored heavily through the wine and numerous cocktails.

Sunday

Giorgio was the first to awake and was thrilled to find he was still holding Katey in his arms. Such was the extent of her drunkenness of the night before that she had not moved all night. Giorgio smiled to himself and buried his face in her hair. Then his memory recalled that his father had now been dead for a week and his heart lurched in fresh heartbreak. The small anniversary hit him all over again and he felt sick at the thought. He breathed in the smell of Katey's hair and tried to block out the memory and concentrate instead on the present and the living. It was now mid-morning and he knew he ought to make tracks to Palm Beach as he was both needed and required there but here, he was happy to be isolated from all the issues that awaited him. Here, lying in bed with Katey it felt safe and uncomplicated and he didn't want to move and break the spell. He didn't yet want to return to his new reality.

Katey moaned as she began to come around from her near unconscious state. She became aware that someone was in bed with her and holding her tight and she twisted her head to see the smiling face of Giorgio next to her. It wasn't unpleasant but she remembered her resolve.

"What did you do?" she asked, her voice full of suspicion, her black mascara smudged around her eyes and her hair was in a tangled mess.

Giorgio laughed. "Absolutely nothing! You have my word on that, Katey." He got out of bed to show that he was still fully dressed. "I just didn't feel like sleeping on that sofa in there. It doesn't look very comfortable. Look – I didn't even undress you, just took your shoes off," he said, smiling.

Katey looked down at herself with some doubt. She could prove nothing and so mumbled that she was going into the shower.

She stumbled out of bed and headed down the hallway towards the bathroom. When she returned some twenty minutes later, she looked and felt much better. Her face was free of the claggy make-up and her hair had been washed and styled. She still had the pale pallor of someone who was hungover, complete with the black circles under her eyes as though she had not slept in weeks. Giorgio still wanted her, even then.

"You owe me breakfast," she told him.

Giorgio laughed. "How do you work that one out? I got dinner last night and I paid for the numerous cocktails you had afterwards!" His protest was good natured and he had every intention of buying her breakfast. He would buy her absolutely anything she wanted.

"I put you up for the night for free," was Katey's counter-argument. "Besides, I don't believe you didn't even cop a feel. You had motive and opportunity."

"I wish. So you get dinner, drinks, a handsome escort and breakfast. What's in it for me?"

"My gratitude," she smiled and kissed him on his stubbly cheek. "That's it. Come on, I'm starving!"

When Giorgio drove home later that day, he was still smiling to himself. He'd never been so completely refused by a woman before and she intrigued him further every time she slighted him. He adored her accent, that was a given. He found it bizarre that he loved that she wouldn't sleep with him; it made the wanting of her all the more acute and he knew it was just a matter of time. He had faith in himself enough to know that she wouldn't be able to keep saying no to him, he just had to bide his time and not push the issue. She would want him eventually if she didn't already. He was confused as to why he didn't feel it necessary to call up one of his many willing female admirers, perhaps the able Clare again and use her to relieve the tension brought on by Katey's steadfast refusal of him. He found that the hardest thing to understand and he wished his father was still around for him to talk to. Nothing made any sense now but at least he was smiling again.

When he arrived home a few hours later after a leisurely drive back, Giorgio sought out his brother-in-law. Scott was in a conference with Gabe and Vinnie but he managed to drag him to a quiet corner of the house.

"Any updates?" Giorgio asked Scott, getting the serious stuff done with first.

Scott shook his head. "Nothing yet. We are still searching."

Giorgio nodded in acknowledgement and stayed quiet, looking at a spot on the wall behind Scott. He was suddenly unsure about asking Scott about this but had no-one else to ask. Giorgio needed advice. "I need to ask you something but this cannot go any further than us two. Not even to my sister."

Scott shrugged. He was good at keeping secrets especially from his wife.

Giorgio shifted on his feet. He wasn't comfortable being in this position, like an unsure child and he tried to think about how best to say it before it came out all wrong and he looked a bigger fool than he felt. "At what point did you realise you were in love with Grace?"

Scott looked at his brother-in-law and his first reaction was to make fun at him and laugh. But as he looked hard into Giorgio's face, he realised that Giorgio was serious and this was no laughing matter. He knew what Giorgio was alluding to and Scott was quick to realise just how hard this must be for him.

"I don't know exactly but very early on. I was much like you are now Gio. I wanted to sleep my way around the county and thought numbers were the way to go. I treated many women very badly and I thought I was doing them a favour by letting them have a piece of me. I didn't consider their feelings and I'm sorry for that now. You know Grace and I got together on her eighteenth birthday and I thought I was going to lose my genitalia when your dad found out! He knew what I was like back then and was looking out for his daughter, which I get now. He shouted at me for around twenty minutes and I have to admit that I was terrified. He had a real temper on him as you know and I still can't quite believe I got away with all my body parts intact. But it made me take a long hard look at myself and I didn't want to be the person I was anymore. I wanted Grace. I really liked her - let's face it, what's not to like? But I wanted to make her my girlfriend and it didn't take me long to realise what a great decision that was. I also knew that I wanted to spend the rest of my life with her and the other women, however much they still threw themselves at me were just invisible from then on. Grace was the only one for me, although I can't tell you how many proposals of mine she refused!" He laughed, caught up in a private memory.

"So what did you do?"

"I didn't give up. I gave her plenty of time and space and carried on as normal." Scott paused, "How is this relevant to you? You can't be interested in mine and Grace's history?"

Giorgio's face crew crimson which made them both laugh. "I've met someone," he mumbled to his feet. "We are friends but that's all and she won't take it any further. She thinks I'm a tart – her words, not mine! She is just amazing and it's got to the point now where I wish I had cleaned up my act earlier so she wouldn't have heard all the rumours, true though they may be. Sad, huh?"

Scott shook his head. "You will just have to work hard at proving to her that you can be different, that it's all in the past and you want her to be your future. I'm sure she won't be able to hold out for long from what I have heard about you!" He winked and Giorgio laughed.

Grace walked into the room at that moment and stopped short as she caught her husband and her brother laughing together. She was unimpressed, thinking it showed disrespect to her father. The look she gave them silenced them both and wiped the smiles away.

"Gio, we need you in the lounge. We have some news for you now you have shown up."

Adam felt as though he was still in a daze. It had been a week and he was still unable to function like everyone else seemed to be doing. He couldn't get up from his seated position at his computer desk, his limbs felt as though they were made of lead and to move them would require all of his energy, which Adam had discovered had all been sapped from him after hearing his mother's dreadful news last Sunday morning. He knew he was behaving in an appalling way and that he should be with his family, what was left of it, as they searched for the person who had killed his father. Adam was aware he should be with them as they all worked through the grief that ensued but he couldn't bear to be around any of them. He didn't want anybody's company. He knew he had always been the weaker sibling, the one who couldn't control his emotions and he certainly couldn't deal with this situation. He hated the thought of the conflict and the coming confrontations as the family endeavoured to find the killer. This was why he was away at college, why he wanted to be a doctor so he wouldn't be called upon to 'help' his father in any way. That was Giorgio's calling. This was proof enough if it were needed that Marco had chosen the correct son and acceding to Sarah's request by allowing one of the Delvecchio boys to have a proper career. Adam would have fought his father every step of the way if he had insisted that Adam join the business and was glad that it had never come to that.

However, none of this stopped Adam from feeling excluded when Giorgio went off with their father on some jaunt loosely disguised as a business trip or venture. Whenever Giorgio had been part of a meeting and the office door was closed with Adam on the wrong side, he felt a simmering resentment towards his elder brother that he struggled to push down; he didn't want to end up hating Giorgio. That was why Adam had decided to become somebody important in his own right and someone that his parents and his father in particular, could be proud of.

There was a gentle knock at his door and his mother's tired, drawn face peered around the frame, not having waited for Adam to answer.

"Darling, could you come downstairs for a minute? There is something we need to discuss." She spoke as though worried her normal tone and volume might shatter her fragile younger son.

Adam nodded but said nothing and she withdrew, closing the door behind her. She needed to give Adam time to compose himself. It hadn't escaped her notice that he had been crying again, his eyes were red and puffy.

Taking a deep breath, Adam called on whatever energy reserves he had left and walked on unsteady legs to the bathroom to run some cold water over his face. He knew he looked a mess but he wasn't going to apologise for that. He looked and felt like what he was – a wreck. He splashed water on his face and combed his fingers through his dark wavy hair. He stared at his reflection in the mirror and wondered what life would hold for each of them now. Then he headed downstairs to be with his family.

He found each of them in the lounge and they all looked up as he walked in. He sat down in a single vacant chair as far away from everyone else as he could get and looked down at the dark brown wooden floor to focus on a speck of something on one of the rugs while waiting for someone to speak. It wasn't going to be him.

Sarah looked around at her family and began. "I have just had a call from Lieutenant Gray. They will be releasing Dad tomorrow so we can start with the funeral arrangements."

Grace looked up bewildered and started to cry again. "But they haven't caught who did it yet! How can they release him?"

"Rosie said they have all of the evidence they are going to collect from him. They have no wish to prolong our misery and are happy for the… for him to be released."

Giorgio looked up with fresh tears in his eyes. All of his earlier buoyancy and happiness had vanished. He wished Katey was here.

"I need to know what your thoughts are for the funeral," Sarah continued.

"I can't deal with this," Adam muttered and stood up and charged out of the lounge. He needed the sanctuary of his room. Sarah let him go; she would talk to him later when he was on his own.

"So are the police giving up?" Grace asked with anger in her voice.

"Of course not!" Sarah was quick to soothe her. "They have all they need right now and have assured me that the investigation is continuing. As is our own." She didn't want Grace to know any details yet but the Delvecchios had a good lead that had been established earlier that morning and it was being followed up with renewed vigour. Sarah had after a struggle been able to convince Gabe, Vinnie, and Scott that Ray Boulter had something to do with Marco's death in some way or other. He had been the one that had threatened to kill Marco and that at least, deserved to be investigated and for Ray to be found. Jimmy Caruso had been spoken to last night as Ray was last known to be in Jimmy's area so the Carusos were now looking into where he could be and had ears to the ground, so to speak. Someone matching Ray's description had been seen in one of the better bars in Miami Beach and so the watch was out although by the time Jimmy had dispatched men to the bar, Ray had disappeared again, if indeed it was him. They all hoped the disappearance was a temporary one but it was a starting point.

Grace knew she would never get the whole story from her mother. She sighed as she wished she had been more like her mother from the start of her marriage and that her own husband would be as free with his information as her father had been with Sarah. Grace was aware that there was more than met the eye with the current state of affairs but she would never be privy to it. Even Giorgio kept her out of the loop. Instead she did the dutiful daughter thing.

"I think the funeral should be as soon as possible. Dad has had enough delays and deserves some peace. I am tired of being in limbo and want to be able to get on and grieve for my father instead of just feeling this incredible anger. Just as soon as possible." She stood up and left the room having nothing more to say on the matter.

"I agree," Giorgio said and stood up to leave. He needed some alone time and headed towards the beach for a walk and some air. At the moment, he could only think about Katey and being alone with her again. He knew his father deserved for him to think about him and in his state of mind, he had thoughts of just one thing. He called her.

"Why don't you come and spend a couple of days with me?" he asked her after the usual pleasantries had been exchanged.

She laughed. "You are a trier, Gio, I'll give you that."

"Babe, we have plenty of spare rooms here, it's a big house. Besides, after your snuffling and snoring last night, I don't want to spend another night with you." He smiled as he spoke. Nothing could be further from the truth.

"Snoring? I don't snore!"

"Evidently you do when you have had a drink. Please. Come up for just a few days. I will have the guest suite made up for you and it's on the opposite side of the house to my room... "

"Is now a good time? I mean, with all that is going on?"

"Believe me Katey, now is the perfect time. I need some sanity in my life right now and I reckon you are about the only sane thing I know of."

There was silence on the other end of the line for a moment while she thought about Giorgio's words. "Okay. I'll be there tomorrow around lunch time. Spare room though, Gio." She warned him again wanting to make it perfectly clear.

Giorgio couldn't help but smile. He felt like he had won the lottery. Bit by bit, Katey was coming around to his charms.

Monday

Sarah woke up and the first thing she was aware of was the need for Vinnie. Actually, if she was honest, she wanted Marco but the realist within her knew that was never going to happen and Vinnie was as real as it was going to get. He was as close to Marco as she would ever be close to again. But Sarah also knew that she shouldn't be alone with Vinnie at the moment; it wouldn't be the right time for the family to find out about them and she couldn't trust herself to be platonic friends with him. She would have to wait until at least after the funeral.

Today was the day that she arranged her husband's funeral. Grace, Giorgio, and Adam seemed happy to leave it all up to her which meant no disagreements over the details but Sarah had still hoped that they would have wanted some input. Rosa had called last night and wanted to help out with it all so at least Sarah would not be alone and for that, she was grateful.

Sarah skipped breakfast knowing that anything she ate wouldn't have stayed down anyway and headed off to Rosa's house to collect her. The sun was shining again today and Sarah hoped to get a couple of hours chill time later by the pool. She was looking so pale and pasty at the moment. After leaving Rosa's house, they drove just outside of town to the funeral home in silence. Neither woman had much energy to talk about anything of substance and didn't want to waste what little energy they did have on small talk.

They left the funeral home two hours later and both felt drained. They had arranged the funeral for the coming Wednesday and Marco was to be buried in the family plot at the Catholic Church, along with his mother, father, and brother Joe. Sarah and Rosa had picked out a closed casket, both realising that Marco would not be in a pretty state to be viewed, given the nature of his death. They knew this would cause consternation amongst some of the mourners but that was neither of their concern. Both wanted Marco to be remembered as the handsome, laughing sometimes scowling man Sarah had been married to and Rosa had grown up with and not the beaten, broken and some might argue, neglectful man who had arrived at the funeral home while they were there, discussing the particulars.

Sarah and Rosa decided to go and grab some coffee while they recuperated from their ordeal. It was just past eleven thirty and Rosa needed to talk to her sister-in-law about something important.

As they sipped their drinks in companionable silence, Rosa leaned back in her chair and eyed Sarah up over her mug. She had to ask and now was the time.

"Sarah, what's going on with you and Vinnie?"

Sarah looked up in shock and surprise at the question. She tried to keep her face neutral and not give anything away. "Nothing. Why do you ask?"

"It's something Sal said. He was concerned that you and Vinnie went to Dallas together. The guys have been talking and, well, I'm concerned for you."

"Yes, I told you we went to Dallas. To find Marco's killer." She bristled at the implication. Or maybe she realised Rosa was too close to the truth and that scared her.

Rosa thought about Sarah's answer and conceded there might be truth in it. "Gabe said he made the jet available to you but you both decided to go commercial and therefore missed the last flight home. Gio made it clear that he wasn't happy about it either."

Sarah thought about it for a moment. "Look Ro, I know it looks bad but there really is nothing going on. Yes, we went commercial and I knew we'd miss the last flight back but I needed to get away for a night or two. I'm sure no-one would begrudge me that. I needed to wake up somewhere unfamiliar where I wouldn't expect to still see Marco lying on the pillow next to me and having my heart broken all over again when I realise that I will never see him again." She choked back a little sob and caught her breath. "It was just a little trip and we had separate rooms, he was down the hallway." She felt proud of herself for being able to tell the truth, for not lying in her statement. She also felt a little shabby that people were talking about her in such a way, gossiping and sniping.

Rosa reached across the table and held Sarah's shaking hand. "Sarah, no-one would mind if you and Vinnie got together at some point. It's just too soon right now and would look as though you never cared a hoot about my brother."

Sarah took her hand away from Rosa's. "I see. So what is the proper mourning time in the twenty-first century before I am allowed to take up with another man?" Her tone was full of anger that she was struggling to control.

"Sarah, don't get upset with me, I didn't mean to make you angry. I just thought you might want to know what people are thinking."

Sarah stood up and glared down at Rosa. "People? Or you, Rosa? I have loved your brother for more years than I can remember as you well know and I cannot believe that you of all people would think so little of me! I think it's best if I leave before one of us says something that cannot be unsaid." She threw a fifty dollar bill on the table. "That should over the drinks and a cab home for you." Sarah walked away with Rosa calling after her. She could hear Rosa telling her to come back and talk, that she didn't mean it to sound as maybe it had.

Sighing, Rosa gave up her protestations and let her go. She knew Sarah was in a bad way and the two would make up soon enough – they had been friends for too long.

Giorgio had wanted to introduce Katey to his mother but when Sarah raged into the house in such a bad mood and stormed upstairs to her bedroom, he thought it could wait a little longer. He wanted it to be right and for Katey not to be scared off.

Giorgio had shown Katey to the guest suite where she would be staying for the next few nights, or as long as she wanted to stay and he had also shown her where his room was, just in case. Once

Katey had been settled in, they both went and sat by the pool for a few hours. Giorgio was thrilled to have her all to himself.

After a swim to cool off from the intense heat, they were sitting drinking peach tea that the house keeper had brought out for them, chatting and laughing among themselves.

"Oh! I meant to tell you, I have some photographs from the party we went to the other week. Remember? The one that David and Mark had at their beach house. I printed a couple out to show you."

Giorgio smiled. "The party where you gave me a public dressing down?"

Katey blushed. "I'm sorry. I've been pretty hard on you, haven't I? I just… "

Giorgio waved her semi-apology away. "I know and it's fine." He didn't feel that she needed to say sorry, he was winning her over now and it was going to make the victory all the more sweeter. "Anyway, these photos?"

Katey was already rummaging around in her bag looking for them. "You were pretty wasted towards the end and I don't know what you remember so I thought this little trip down bad memory lane might be fun. There are some crazy pictures of you and Jesse there, a few of your butt." She giggled.

God, I am an asshole, Giorgio thought to himself as he took the pictures Katey was holding out for him. She leaned over to commentate on each of the pictures, giving Giorgio a good eyeful down her bikini top as she did so and he struggled to keep his gaze on the glossy prints and not her flesh. She started to go through who was who in the pictures, who went home with whom and so on.

Suddenly Giorgio's blood ran cold. His eyes were glued to a face in the photo, unaware of Katey's continued chattering as he stared hard at the photo. There he was with Jesse, very drunk, laughing into the camera lens but, the man behind them was just staring into the camera lens with a hard, almost vicious look set like concrete into his face.

"Who is this?" he asked so quietly and through gritted teeth that Katey stopped her chatter and looked at Giorgio, almost afraid of his tone.

"Oh, that's Steve. He is David's cousin and visiting from Ohio... "

Before Katey could finish her sentence, Giorgio was off and running up towards the house in his bare feet. Katey stood up bewildered by his behaviour and watched his retreating back, not daring to call after him.

Giorgio was in his father's office like a shot. The room was empty for the moment, for which he was pleased as he didn't want to have to explain his behaviour to anybody. He rummaged through the deep bottom drawer of the desk until he found what he was looking for –the Santa Cruz file, as it had become known.

Giorgio spilt the contents of the file across the desk and started rifling through the papers and photos until he came across the specific one he was looking for. He picked it up and analysed every detail of it, particularly the face of the grinning man with the ridiculous Christmas hat on. The one in which Melanie Boulter and her son were celebrating Christmas together, happy and smiling. He looked again at the photo that Katey had just shown him from David and Mark's party, the one of the cousin from Ohio and Giorgio was in no doubt that they were one and the same person. He was now tanned and slimmer than the pale smiling man in the first picture but Giorgio was absolutely certain he'd got this right.

He rushed back out to where Katey was reclining on a chair, lapping up the sun. She opened one eye as she heard him approach. "What's up?" She asked him.

"Where does 'Steve' live?" he asked.

She shrugged. "I don't know. I met him just the once."

"Katey!" Giorgio was more frustrated than angry but his temper was quick to flare in any case.

"I don't know, Gio. I'm sorry." She sat up in her chair and looked at him as she came to decision. She reached under the chair for her bag and pulled out her phone. "I can call David and ask him, that's the best I can do."

Giorgio fell back onto his recently vacated sunbed and put his head in his hands. He felt out of his depth in more ways than one. Katey put her arms around him.

"What's the matter?" She asked.

He answered by handing Katey the photograph of 'Ray' and his mother. She took it from him and studied it and then, frowning, she picked up the one of 'Steve' from the party. "Is this… ?"

Giorgio was nodding. "We know him as Ray Boulter and we're pretty damn sure he killed my dad. I need to talk to him."

"Well, if he killed your dad, shouldn't we call the police?"

Giorgio laughed and looked at Katey in a sympathetic way. The trouble with out of towners was that everything had to be explained to them. He wondered how his dad and explained 'things' to his mother all those years ago.

"No, Katey, we don't call the police. We will deal with this, or at least, I will. But I need to know where your friend lives."

She kissed his cheek and dialled David's number. He picked up after two rings.

"Hey David, it's Katey. Great party last week." She smiled at Giorgio in a 'trust me' way and listened to what David had to say. "Yep. Yep. Uh-huh. Listen, I was wondering, your cousin Steve. Is he single? He is? Great! I don't suppose you could give me his number?" Giorgio shook his head to tell her that he needed more than a number. Katey just smiled at him. "Okay. Is that a South Beach number? That's where I am and it would be great to meet up with him." She nodded and signalled for Giorgio to grab a pen from her bag. "Apartment five, Martindale Court, Lenox Avenue, yes, got it. Listen David, don't tell him I was asking after him. I'd like to surprise him. See you then and great to catch up." Katey disconnected the call and smiled at Giorgio. "You owe me, Delvecchio."

Giorgio smiled and leant over to kiss her. She allowed him a lingering kiss and was more than just a little disappointed when he drew away, eager not to overstep the boundary she had lain down. Besides, he had more important issues to deal with right now.

"You can collect any time," he teased.

"Okay, well I want you to tell me what you are going to do with that information."

Giorgio shrugged non-committal. "I just want to talk to the guy, that's all."

Katey stood up. "Okay, we'd better go then."

Giorgio fought the urge to laugh. "We?" Jesus! She was so naïve! "No, my English Rose, *we* will not be going anywhere. I can take you home or you can stay here and chill for a few hours but I am going to see Steve or Ray, or whatever his name is on my own."

Katey knew more about Giorgio's world than she would let on and she also knew the possible consequences of giving him that address. She had known that she would not be able to go to South Beach with him and, on reflection, wasn't sure she even wanted to go. She had seen movies and read the papers and knew the horrors of what might happen. She told herself that as long as she didn't see it, she was not a part of it and it didn't exist.

"Well, I don't want to go home and neither do I want to stay here on my own. It feels awkward. Why don't you drop me at Worth Avenue and I can maybe shop while you're gone. Then you can take me out for an expensive meal tonight to make up for your absence," she teased.

"I thought you had no money?" He asked as he picked their things up to go back inside.

"I don't but window shopping costs nothing."

Giorgio took his wallet out of his back pocket. He handed Katey his credit card and pin number, telling her to memorise it. He had a complete feeling of trust with this woman.

"You can't buy me, Gio. I don't want your money," she held out the card for him to take back.

He looked chastened. "I'm sorry, I just wanted to do the right thing. There are no strings attached and I thought it was a nice thing to do."

She kissed his lips again, their earlier encounter making her ache for more. "I am happy to window shop. Besides, you know how much I can drink so I don't think even you can afford to clothe me *and* take me out!" She teased as they headed back up the path towards the house.

Giorgio headed south. He was getting tired of driving to South Beach on what seemed to be a daily basis, but he felt he was onto something at last and the family needed a break. If nothing else, he might clear up the mystery of who Ray was and meet his cousin into the bargain.

He made it in just under an hour and followed his Satnav's instructions to Lenox Avenue. He found Martindale Court and pulled up across the road, looking at the run-down apartment building. It was plain and quite dilapidated with a poorly kept pool deck out to the front. Giorgio watched a while as people came and went and let thoughts run through his head as to what to do next. He knew he would have to play it on the fly as he had no idea what to expect, if Ray would be prepared for his arrival at some point but he knew without a doubt that if Ray had killed Marco, Giorgio would never get another crack at it. Ray would go underground and no-one would ever hear from him again and Gabe, Sal, and Scott would string him up if they lost what might be their only chance at getting to Ray. Giorgio checked under his seat but knew he hadn't come prepared.

Jimmy Caruso was on his speed dial and he called him up. No pleasantries, Giorgio told him straight what he needed and that he needed it quick. Jimmy said he'd send someone over and within ten minutes, one of Jimmy's men got into the black Porsche next to Giorgio and handed him a package.

"Jimmy says it's on the house and he doesn't want it back. It's clean," the man told Giorgio and got out of the car without saying another word.

Giorgio took a quick peek inside the plastic bag and saw the gun he had asked for and plenty of bullets to go with it. He was banking on needing just one if his suspicions were correct.

He sat in the car for a while longer as he tried to establish if the occupant of apartment five was home or not. He had not seen any movement from that particular premise and the curtains were drawn, giving an impression of emptiness. Perhaps Ray was a night owl and slept through the day; the continued financial support Ray received from the Delvecchios would help him to support such a lifestyle.

Giorgio made his mind up to go in anyway. He wanted to get this over with and get back to Katey. He got out of the car, the gun hidden in the waistband of his jeans, his white shirt overhanging and hiding it. He zapped the car door locked and activated the alarm before he walked across the street, keeping it casual as possible He did not want to draw attention to himself from the people going about their business in the street. He hoped he was hiding the inner turmoil he felt and made every effort to keep his face looking calm; Giorgio felt sure he was about to face his father's killer.

The gate to the apartment block was closed but not locked and it opened with the grind of neglected and rusting metal. Giorgio closed it behind him, looking around all the while to check if he had been spotted. The place was empty. He had thought people would be making the most of the late afternoon sun and relaxing by the pool, much like he wanted to be doing but on closer inspection, Giorgio realised why the residents perhaps favoured the beach to the pool area. It was a stagnant, murky mess covered in rotting leaves and dead insects. Giorgio thought he saw a dead bird floating on the surface and he shuddered as he moved forward, towards the steps that would take him to the upper floor of the apartment block.

As he stood outside Ray's apartment, he took another look round and was grateful to see no-one around, no-one watching him or taking any notice of him. The whole courtyard was deserted. The place was shabby in the extreme and un-cared for and Giorgio began to get the idea of the sort of low-income families that might live here. He thanked God yet again for his father and his grandfather's hard work that allowed him the privileged lifestyle that he led.

Giorgio listened intently for signs of life from within number five. He put his ear to the door and was sure he detected some TV noise so he knocked on the door.

"What?" A slow and lazy voice from inside yelled in answer.

"Hey, Steve? Open the door?" Giorgio yelled back hoping he sounded casual and friendly while trying to ignore the violent and murderous feelings he was having.

Either the occupant of the apartment didn't recognise Giorgio's voice, or he didn't perceive the danger he was in for just a few seconds later, the door was yanked open and Raymond Boulter stood there looking at Giorgio Delvecchio, a brief look of stunned surprised registered on his face.

Giorgio smiled at the reaction and pushed past his cousin, closing the door tight behind him before Ray could come to his senses. He looked around the sparse room. "I like your place, man."

"How did you find out where I live?" It was obvious that Ray knew who Giorgio was and the most likely reason he was here.

"Ways and means, my friend." Giorgio kept looking around until he was satisfied that it was just the two of them. He pulled out his gun and turned to face Ray. "So, cuz, is it true? Did you kill my father?"

Ray laughed. "Put that piece of shit away! You don't scare me."

Giorgio moved closer to Ray. "Did you kill him?" he asked again, menace in his voice. "I know who you are. I know you threatened to kill my father and now, fuck me! He's dead!"

Ray just kept smiling. "Aww, that's so sad Gio. I'm sorry daddy is dead. I can sympathise. You know that my father was also murdered when I was just three. At least you got to know your dad." His tone was anything but sympathetic and carried heavy sarcasm.

"And we all know about your so-called father. Your dad was a drug-dealer, drug addict, pimp and he liked young boys. He tried them out himself before he sold them on the street. How the fuck you were ever conceived is beyond anyone's comprehension. I just want to know why you killed my father."

"Revenge. You should know all about that, isn't that what you mob boys live for?" Ray sneered. "Your dad killed my dad. I killed him. Now we are even and that's how it goes. You Delvecchios completely fucked up my life. Joe was the only one who cared in the slightest and your dad, your precious Don Delvecchio had him killed. His own brother."

Giorgio laughed a humourless laugh. "Joe was not killed by the Family. He was murdered by some spaced out junkie who needed a fix, probably one of his own rent boys."

Ray backed slowly away from Giorgio. Giorgio still had the gun on him but he was beginning to waver. This was not going how he had hoped. And Ray was picking up on that.

"And you believe that story?" Ray asked. He was looking around the room, seeking a way out but he had to keep Giorgio talking until he found one. "I had you down as being a bit more savvy than that, Gio. That is the story everyone is led to believe, sure. I expect Gabriele Carminati made that one up and your stupid father went along with it. Gabe was always the one with the balls — he should have been the head of the Family and then, perhaps, none of us would be in this predicament. Your *father* ordered the hit on Joe and your *mother…* " at the mention of Sarah, Ray laughed, " …tried to shoot Joe but your 'uncle' — and I used the term loosely — Vinnie was the one that took the killing shot, doing away with him and his business associate." By now Ray's eyes had turned black with the passion and anger he felt as he relived the tale he had been told. He knew that he had the upper hand, that Giorgio had not been privy to this information.

Giorgio rallied. "Jesus Ray! You are more stupid than you look if you believe that! Fuck, even if it was true, Joe still abandoned you at birth. He abandoned your mother and took you away from her. That says a lot about the sort of man he was and I don't know why the hell you would show him any kind of loyalty."

Ray shook his head. "Because of your father, Joe never had the chance to make it up to me. I know that one day he would have come and taken me away from the lesbian nut-house I grew up in."

Giorgio laughed. "Your father a queer, your mother a lesbian? No wonder you are so screwed up."

"Maybe but what's your excuse? So, are you going to kill me now?"

Giorgio smiled and nodded. "I would get great satisfaction from that. But first I want to know why you didn't leave after you killed my dad. Even a dumb shit like you must have known that we would come for you? "

"I knew you'd try. But I wasn't finished. I wanted you dead next. Stupid me for not getting on with it quicker but I didn't think you'd find me so quick. I didn't have you all down as such intelligent beings."

Giorgio raised his gun again and Ray braced himself for his last breath.

But before Giorgio had the chance to shoot, there was a knock at the door. Ray smiled in triumph. "Now what?"

Giorgio shrugged. "You'd better answer it." The way he was feeling, he'd be happy to shoot whoever was the other side of the door as well. Just to keep things tidy.

Ray sauntered across the room to the front door. As soon as he had drawn the lock back, the door was charged from the other side, knocking Ray off his feet. He sat there dazed for a moment, before the powerful arms of Vinnie picked him up by his collar and threw him onto the threadbare couch. Gabe came in behind and serenely closed and locked the door behind him. Both of them looked at Giorgio that told him he would be in for trouble later.

Giorgio was unperturbed. He just smiled and raised his gun to Ray's temple. "Gentlemen, you are just in time to witness the execution of the killer of Marco Delvecchio." He said with dramatic flourish.

"Gio," Gabe's words held a warning to stop. It was enough to make Giorgio lower his weapon. "An eye for an eye."

"I know, Gabe. That's why… " He did not look away from Ray's face as he spoke.

"Your father did not die by gunshot," Gabe reminded him.

Giorgio looked up at Gabe and then to Vinnie, who was nodding in agreement. He looked back at Gabe again as realisation hit about what they were telling Giorgio to do. He smiled and looked back at Ray. "No, he did not. Tell me, Ray, how *did* my father die?" He asked the now terrified man on the couch, who had also realised that his death was going to be drawn out and painful and not the quick bullet to the head that he had gambled on. "Oh yes," Giorgio continued as if he had just remembered the terrifying way his father had died. "The Coroner's report said he had been shot in the knee before he died." Without any further warning, Giorgio pumped a bullet into the kneecap of the now cowering, pleading man. Ray screamed and swore at Giorgio as tears began to stream down his face. Giorgio became concerned about neighbours hearing. "Shut the fuck up! Did my father scream and wail like a baby?"

Snivelling, Ray shook his head. "I'm sorry," he whispered.

"Sorry ain't gonna bring my dad back, cuz. Did you show him any mercy when you beat the shit out of him?" Giorgio asked, a calm veneer settling about him. The bullet to Ray's knee had been like a shot of Valium to him.

Ray shook his head. "I won't beg for my life," he said as he looked up into Giorgio's eyes. He was determined not to give any of them the satisfaction.

"There would be no point Ray. You ain't getting out of this one and you are going to die very, very painfully."

"Stand up!" Vinnie demanded of the injured man. "It's time to go."

Without arguing, Ray stood with a great effort and he hobbled along as he followed Gabe out of the building. He looked around him, desperate to find someone in the street that might be able to help him out. But no-one was around at this time of day. He could also feel the knife pressing into his kidneys, held there by Vinnie as he walked him to the car. Regardless of who might be around to come to his rescue, Ray knew one wrong move would see the knife plunging into the depths of his body. Ray thought for a moment that this might be a quicker and less painful death than the tortuous one that was doubtless planned for him but the moment passed before he could make a decision. Fear seemed to have zapped any ability to think for himself and he just followed the trio into the alley at the back of the building and to the waiting car.

"I want to come with you," Giorgio insisted of Gabe and Vinnie. This was something he had to do and they were not going to usurp him on this.

Gabe looked at Giorgio and realised the same. He nodded. "I'll follow in your car. I've always wanted to drive your Porsche!" He smiled in spite of the seriousness of the circumstances as Giorgio threw his keys to him. "I'm sure you still have some questions for Ray." He turned and hurried out of the alley and down the street to where Giorgio had earlier parked his car as Ray was bundled into the car that Sal waited in.

Ray sat in the back with Giorgio on one side and Vinnie on his other. Blood was seeping into the upholstery from Ray's bullet wound but nobody was worried; the car would later be erased in any one of a hundred different ways.

"So how long have you known who your family are?" Giorgio asked him.

"What does it matter?" Ray replied, his voice thick with misery.

"If you answer all my questions, I may take it easy on you."

Ray considered this for a moment. He knew he was going to die, that much was a given the moment he had smashed Marco's brains in. He had never considered that he might be dispatched in the same way however, just that he would be shot with a single bullet to the head. He wasn't afraid of dying now that he had achieved his main aim in life for he believed he had nothing left to live for. But he was more than a little afraid about being tortured beforehand – he had not considered that until now but he had watched a lot of mob movies since discovering his parentage and knew what could happen. He decided to put his life in Giorgio's hands and play along with his cousin's game.

"I guess I found out when I was about ten. I knew my mother wasn't my birth mother, she threw that at me plenty of times. She would never say who my father was, I guessed he was paying her to keep her mouth shut. She just said he was an important man who didn't want me. One of her many girlfriends told me his name. She also told me my real mother was a drug addict."

"Well, that's not true. She was just a scared kid that your father took advantage of. No doubt he wanted to train you and be a good dealer for him, make him a load more money." Giorgio sneered.

"We'll never know. I dug around, found out who she was, rich little Mexican bitch living it up with her new family down Mexico way. I wanted her dead, she was next." Ray spat out his hate towards his mother. "I searched for stuff on Joe and found out that he had been murdered too and it didn't take a genius to work out that it was all a cover up, just that there was no proof. I'm surprised that you didn't know, Gio, you being the son and heir and all that. Anyway, it's a long story that I'm not getting into now so I guess you'll never hear it, but I got in with some people who knew your lot back then and they told me the rumours."

"People? What people?" Vinnie asked. It was not going to be for Ray to decide what he was or wasn't going to go into.

"Dominic Russell. I was seeing his daughter and then he gave me a job. He's a good guy and I like him a lot – we have a lot in common. He doesn't like you Delvecchios too much either but would never go into why."

Vinnie knew who Dominic Russell was and was curious that he would have held a grudge for all of these years. He had been in love with a friend of Sarah's who had turned out to be an FBI plant so she had to go. They had made it look like a robbery gone wrong. Dominic had always had his suspicions but the Delvecchios were very good at covering their tracks. Vinnie was going to track down Dominic and have a word or two with him. It seemed he had a lot to answer for. Vinnie had suggested to his brother many years ago that something should be done about Dominic Russell but Marco had vetoed any action. Now it seemed that Marco's decision had literally been the death of him.

"Anyway," Ray continued. "I know Marco had Joe killed and it seemed only fair to kill the man who killed my father." He looked at Giorgio. "You get me, right, Gio?"

Giorgio said nothing but turned away from Ray. Of course he understood what Ray meant and how he was feeling but he was not going to show him the slightest bit of compassion. Giorgio had been told that many people had suffered at Joe's hands and if Marco had ordered the hit on him, well then, he would have deserved it. His father had taken the decision, one which wouldn't have been taken lightly given that it was his brother, his flesh and blood. Giorgio was not going to do an autopsy of a piece of business from twenty years ago. It was done. He had plenty of questions that he needed to ask Gabe and Vinnie but now was not the time, not in front of Ray. There would be time for his questions after. Now, he still had questions for Ray and his time was running out.

"How did you get my dad to trust you? He always had trust issues."

Ray shrugged. "I just told him the truth. I told him I was his nephew. That seemed enough for him and he just came running to meet me. We met up twice before… " he faltered.

" …you killed him." Giorgio finished the sentence for him. "What happened that night?"

"We had already arranged to meet up, providing he could slip away. He didn't want anyone to know who he was meeting, not yet. He had some strange notion that it was all going to work out real nice, that we would all end up playing happy families or some such shit. I think he wanted to ease his guilt over killing his own brother. You know, Joe is dead but at least he can give the prodigal nephew a home, a job, family, whatever it was that he thought I needed. So the last time we met up, I just decided he had to die. You say my dad had caused people pain but that was nothing to what your father did for many years. He had the life and death decisions over a lot of people and I decided that it was going to end then and there. I was going to be the judge, jury and executioner just this one time.

"As he got out of his car, I shot him in the leg to slow him down, but you already know that." Ray clutched his still bleeding leg. "When he went down, I wanted to just shoot him in the head but, more than that, I wanted him to suffer. He'd made so many people suffer that I felt he deserved it. I had my lucky baseball bat from home in my car so I used it. I tried out for the Texas Rangers a few years back – did you even know that -but it didn't work out for me so I used it for some other good. I was so angry with him that once I started hitting him, I couldn't stop. He looked up at me, as though he was daring me to kill him so I just carried on. After maybe ten hits, the anger started to fade and I stopped. He was just about breathing. I wanted to shoot him again, to put him out of his misery but I knew that he was going to die and this would make him die in pain and alone."

Giorgio reached over and punched Ray in the knee, making him scream out in agony. He wanted Ray to know pain and he would, before much longer. When Ray had got his breath back a little, he continued, unaware of Giorgio's change of heart.

"I watched Marco as he somehow managed to get onto his knees and crawl back to his car. I don't know how he found the strength or reserve to do it, but he was a determined son of a bitch. He got his mobile phone and I knew then that he might survive and I couldn't allow that. So I picked up the bat again and hit him one last time around the back of his head. He slumped forward and I watched as he took his last breath. I waited and waited to make sure. Then I left."

The other passengers in the car were silent. No-one knew how to react to the story, or even if it was true. They each had their own images of Marco being battered to death, images that would not leave their consciousness for a long time. They each just wanted to get to wherever Sal was driving them to, so they could watch Ray die. Giorgio had a lot of anger he needed to expunge. He, maybe more than his companions, was going to enjoy seeing Ray die. More so, he was going to enjoy inflicting pain and killing him.

They drove for the next fifty minutes in near silence. Ray was beginning to slip in and out of consciousness from pain and blood loss but every time he dared close his eyes, Giorgio would punch him in the head just enough to bring him back around. He was thinking hard about how to make it as painful as possible for Ray in light of what he had just revealed.

Ray on the other hand, was hoping that his frank confession would make his cousin go easy on him, just a little. If not, he would at least die in the knowledge that Giorgio knew how painful his father's death had been and Ray could take comfort in the fact that his cousin would be suffering, regardless of how it ended for him.

They pulled off the US-21 and slowed down as they drove down a deserted dirt track. The wheels of the car crunched on the dirt and gravel below and Giorgio turned to look behind him – he didn't want his car on this road but Gabe had had the sense to stop off the main road and was going to double back to a rest stop a little further back wait for them. They wouldn't want anyone seeing a black Porsche near here and connect the events that may lead the authorities back to the Delvecchios. It was just easier. About a further mile in, Sal drew up and cut the engine. He turned around to look at Ray in the back seat. He was sweating heavy now from fear and blood loss. He knew it was time.

Giorgio bounded out of the car with enthusiasm. He had been waiting for this moment and just hoped that Vinnie and Sal would let him do it his way. He was relishing the thought of making Ray Boulter suffer. Laughing, he helped Sal drag Ray out of the back of the car and off away down a grassy path towards a waterway. Vinnie opened up the back of the car and pulled something out. He slapped the baseball bat into his hands, the noise terrifying Ray all the more as it echoed around the empty landscape.

Ray simpered and looked up at Giorgio. "Gio, you said you'd take it easy if I told you." He was trying to hold back sobs now and close to wetting himself, desperate to hold back and avoid further humiliation.

Vinnie handed his nephew the bat.

"I never said I would, only that I might." Giorgio looked down at the green bat. "How appropriate. A Marlins bat – my dad's favourite team." Quick as a flash, he wound himself up as though he were playing ball as he so often had with his dad and brother but this time, Ray was the target. The bat found its mark and hit Ray square between the shoulder blades, sending him sprawling to the ground, howling with pain.

"You are fucking scum and your father was scum." Ray screamed at his attacker.

This just served to anger Giorgio more and he took another swing at him. This time, he aimed for his chest, to push the air from his lungs and maybe break a rib or two. Ray was now reduced to just moans as Giorgio rained blow after blow onto the fallen man. He aimed for anywhere other than his head as he didn't want Ray unconscious. Not yet.

Vinnie walked away unneeded, seeing that Giorgio had the stomach and ability for the job and stood next to Sal and they watched Giorgio, knowing that Marco would have been so proud of the way he had stepped up. His mother, well, she would most likely have heart failure if she found out about this but it would have to be one more secret that they kept from her. He watched as Giorgio kept up the barrage of hits on Ray now lying foetus-like on the ground, moaning quieter and quieter as each blow hit him. Twice, the cry of pain got louder as the bat broke another bone but as he had vowed, Ray did not once plead for mercy or beg for his life.

All of a sudden Giorgio just stopped the beating and looked down at his victim. "How many times did you hit my father before you killed him?" He was breathless from the exertion the act of beating Ray caused him. A thin film of sweat covered his face and neck but he felt good from the adrenalin that was coursing through his veins.

Ray managed to raise his head up and smile at Giorgio. "You can carry on hitting me if it makes you feel better. I don't care."

"No. Do you know what? I'm bored now." He aimed the bat at Ray's head, swinging it to line up the shot as though teeing up his best golf putt. He coiled to strike but something stopped him. He laughed as he saw Ray flinch. Instead, Giorgio took out the gun that had been given to him earlier that afternoon by Jimmy Caruso's man and aimed it at the back of Ray's head, execution style. Giorgio looked to Vinnie as though for approval, which was given at the slight nod of his uncle's head and Giorgio fired a single bullet into Ray's brain. Ray jerked once in a death throe as the bullet rattled into his brain, spinning around in there and turning everything to mush. Then there was absolute stillness and silence. Giorgio watched as blood seeped out of the black sticky hole and mixed with the sand and gravel around him. He smiled in satisfaction.

Vinnie walked to his nephew and slapped him on the back, congratulating him without saying a word. He approved whole-heartedly of the way Giorgio had dealt with Ray. He squatted down beside the corpse and watched a moment to be sure Ray was dead and then took something out of his jacket pocket that Giorgio couldn't see and after a moment, straightened up with a smile of his face. Then Giorgio saw the syringe.

Vinnie realised Giorgio was waiting for an explanation. "This just makes it look like a drug deal gone wrong." He explained as he put the empty syringe into a brown paper bag. "You okay?"

Giorgio shrugged and began to walk away. "My dad is still dead," he shouted over his shoulder.

Vinnie walked behind him, hurrying to catch up. A clean car would be waiting for them a mile up the road. Sal remained behind so he could put Ray's corpse back into the car that had bought them here and after a thorough dousing of inflammable liquid, the vehicle would be set alight when Giorgio and Vinnie were a safe distance away. Sal would be the fall guy if there should be any witnesses to the explosion.

"Your dad would be proud of you, Gio. You showed real balls back there and a lot of restraint. You did a good job. I know how hard it is sometimes to keep your mind on the job and do it as it should be done and not just go in like some street punk."

Giorgio said nothing. He didn't feel the elation that he hoped he would when his father's killer was dead. He felt no peace, no closure. His mother was still a widow. He still had no guarantee that he would be named successor. Giorgio was a brawn man, proven, but was he a thinking man? Even though Vinnie had said he'd done a good job today, he still lacked experience. He was still too young to many people.

"Let's go," he said, still walking at a steady pace. About ten minutes later, just as they got to the second car they heard the explosion that Sal had set. Minutes later, he came running around the corner, hot, bothered and dusty and jumped into the back of the car. Vinnie floored it and kicking up dust and stones, they headed off to meet Gabe at the rest stop.

Giorgio was given his car back and told to take a steady drive home and to keep to the limits. No-one was to draw any attention to themselves and the remit was to pretend everything was normal.

"How did you know I was in South Beach?" he asked Gabe as he turned the ignition.

"Katey said you'd rushed off to South Beach and was worried about you. I was about half an hour away when Caruso called me. He was concerned you were calling in personal favours like the procurement of a weapon. His guys stayed on you until they saw where you were going and then called it in."

Giorgio nodded.

"How did you know where to find him?"

"Katey knew him."

Gabe raised an eyebrow. Alarm bells began to ring. "Do we need to worry about Katey?"

Giorgio gave him a sharp look knowing just what Gabe meant by that question. "No, we do not. You leave her alone, Gabe, I'm telling you!" He warned.

Gabe held his hands up in submission, calming the younger man. He had no intention of winding Giorgio up, he needed him on his side. "Okay, but maybe we need to check her out if she is going to be a part of your life. You know how this works."

Giorgio nodded his reluctant acquiescence and although he didn't like it very much, he knew that it was necessary. He just wanted to go home and shower. He put the car into gear and squealed away from the rest area.

En-route back home, he called Katey. When she answered, her voice was terse. She was not impressed with Giorgio's prolonged absence.

"I'm sorry I've been gone so long, I will make it up to you later tonight," he promised, knowing he was in trouble. All of his hard work with her was likely to be slipping away.

"Don't hurry back. Rosa has just called a cab for me, one that you are paying for," she replied.

"Hey, come on, there's no need to leave. Give me an hour and I'll be back in Palm Beach. You and I will go out tonight and I'll show you some great bars and clubs and it's all on me."

The silent pause on the line meant that she was thinking it over and Giorgio knew she was going to concede. He knew that she was falling for him and was just playing hard to get to keep him interested. If only she knew, Giorgio thought, that she didn't need to play games, that she had won and he was hers. He knew there was the trust issue and his going AWOL like he had today wouldn't do anything to diminish that lack of trust. He would just have to keep up with the game she was playing.

"Okay Gio but it's champagne all the way. You have much to make up for," she teased with good nature back in her voice.

"I know and I will. I'll see you soon."

It was just gone six o'clock when Giorgio arrived back home. As he pulled his car up he could see the others weren't back yet but he knew they had some housekeeping to do before they could clock off. He knew what they were going to do with the car they had travelled in and also the gun he had used and guessed they wouldn't be home til much later tonight. He thought perhaps that he should delay his evening out with Katey, to go and help the guys out with the disposal, but he had also been instructed by Gabe to go straight home so that was what he had done. He needed this night out; surely no-one would begrudge him? Besides, if he turned up at a bar or a club, no-one would suspect his actions of earlier that day.

As he walked through the front door, he was annoyed to be confronted by his mother. She had her arms folded across her chest and she looked pale and bedraggled.

"What's been going on, Gio?" she demanded.

Giorgio sighed. He knew that only the truth would suffice so he gave it to her. "We got him. Ray's dead."

Sarah looked stunned and for a moment, couldn't say anything. She unfolded her arms and paced the hallway for a minute or two, thinking, taking it in. She stopped and looked at her son again. "Are you sure it was him? Do you know for sure that he killed Marco?"

Giorgio nodded.

Sarah choked back a sob.

"Ray confessed to all of us. He did it as revenge for Joe and because he felt we all had somehow wronged him. He just had a chip on his shoulder and this was his way to purge that. He needed to get stuff off his chest before he died and said some strange things. Things like Joe wasn't killed by some random junkie, but that Dad had ordered the hit on his own brother and sweet Jesus! You tried to carry it out! Is that true?"

Sarah nodded. "In a round about way, yes, it is true."

Giorgio swore loudly. The word hypocrite threatened to leave his lips.

Sarah continued regardless. "Your Uncle Joe had been causing us all trouble for a few months. Your dad had him down as a liability as a user and a dealer and the fact that he hated your dad so much. He hated the fact that I was back in Palm Beach and that you had been born and Adam was on the way. Joe had a chip on his shoulder that maybe he passed down to Ray, I don't know. But the consensus was that Joe was too much of a threat to everything your dad had worked for and built up. Joe was a ticking time bomb that the wrong drug could have exploded. Long story short, Joe tried to kill me, and you and Grace were threatened by him on more than one occasion so the decision was taken. It was sanctioned in the usual way and Joe was taken out."

"By you?"

Sarah laughed bitterly. "No, although God knows I wanted to be the one to pull the trigger on him. I hated Joe with a passion. He had just killed two of my best friends so yes, I wanted him dead. Deader than I have ever wanted anyone before and believe me, there have been a few of those over the years. But at that moment, Joe was at the top of my 'want dead' list. I drove to the restaurant ahead of time to where the hit was arranged and just hoped that I would be early enough and have enough time." Sarah paused for a moment as she searched her memory from all of the years previous. It had been a defining moment in her marriage and she knew it could have gone any number of ways instead of the almost perfect way it had. "Vinnie was supposed to kill Joe, and he got there not long after I had. Vinnie tried to talk me down and although I shot at Joe, it was Vinnie's bullet that killed him. I will always regret that. Perhaps it was just as well though, as your father went ballistic when he discovered that I had been in the restaurant. He was going to leave me to deal with the police myself but realised he had too much to lose from such a risky conversation. It still took him a number of weeks to forgive me that little episode." Sarah laughed at the memory of her often scowling angry husband at that time. She had always managed to calm him down and see things from her side of things. His scowling and short temper had always been a turn on for her and she always relished finding an activity to calm him down. It had always worked.

Giorgio turned and walked away from his mother. The confession of her actions had shocked him to the core and he was unable to talk to her. He needed distance between them. Her words were hypocritical considering all of the haranguing she had given Marco about their son being indoctrinated into the family business. He had grown tired of her repeating that she did not want Giorgio or Adam doing what Marco did but that had not stopped her from doing that very same thing and doing some unofficial contracting for Marco. What else had she done that he did not know about? He ran up the stairs, leaving her staring up at him and she was saddened that he knew her biggest secret.

"Gio, I need to know more about Ray!" she called up at him. "Tell me what happened!"

The young man ignored Sarah calling after him and raced up the stairs two at a time. He had other things that his attention required.

He paused for a moment at the guest room door where Katey was ensconced just long enough to catch his breath. He knocked and walked in without waiting for a response.

She turned around and squealed in surprise as Giorgio caught her in a state of undress, having just stepped out of the shower. Giorgio couldn't help but smile in spite of himself but at least had the courtesy to act embarrassed.

"I'm sorry, I had no idea you were naked!" He laughed.

"You are supposed to wait for an answer before barging into someone's room, Gio!" She grabbed a sheet from the bed and wrapped it around her voluptuous body but not before Giorgio had got a good eyeful.

He walked slowly over towards her as she began backing away towards the bathroom. "You do know that it was just a matter of time before I saw you naked?" He reached for her and pulled her to him, wrapping his arms about her. He kissed her gently on the lips. He kissed her again, a little harder this time and parted her lips with his tongue. But as soon as he felt her respond, he pulled away. "I have to get ready to take you out, you sexy minx. Give me a half hour and I will come back for you," he winked at her and walked out of the room.

Katey groaned with a growing frustration and threw the sheet to the floor. She was finding it more and more difficult to say no to Giorgio.

What she was unaware of was the state she had left Giorgio in. It had been the seventh level of torture for him to walk away from her, knowing that she was naked under the almost see-through sheet. He had seen her, albeit a very quick peek as nature intended and he now knew exactly what he was missing out on. It was killing him. A cold shower would help cool the fires but he knew it was just a matter of time before she gave in to him and he was finding the agony sweet.

Sarah watched her eldest son disappear up the stairs away from her and turned her back on him. She had so much to explain to him and yet he wouldn't listen to her. She would track him down tomorrow and make him sit while they talked it through. She was so angry that Giorgio had found out about her ridiculous attempt on her brother-in-law's life and she was desperate to piece it all together. How had he found out? Vinnie and Gabe were the only living people who knew the truth that she knew of and they had been sworn to secrecy. They wouldn't betray her now, would they? Even with Marco gone? But had that night so many years ago led her to this heartache now? She found it almost impossible to believe that Marco had been killed by the nephew that no-one knew had existed until now. Ray Boulter must have plotted and schemed for years to track down his real parents, their family history and background. Why he hadn't just tried to blackmail both Calliope and Marco was beyond her – both were rich and could pay out any sum of cash that he demanded. Could but were unlikely to, not if she had known her husband. He would never be open to blackmail but Ray wouldn't have known that. So perhaps retribution was Ray's real motivation. That just left the question of why he would seek revenge for a man he had never met and who had abandoned him at a young age. The question to which she would never get an answer now that Ray was dead. She would just have to believe her son and her brother-in-law.

She realised with a jolt that she had not heard Vinnie's side of the story so she made her mind up to seek him out. She walked into the kitchen just as Vinnie and Gabe came in the side door. Vinnie was seeking out Marco's whiskey. They both looked at her as she entered the room. Both had guilty looks on their faces.

"Gio told me that you got him," she said, her tone quiet.

"Well, actually, Gio tracked him down. We just got a tip off and followed him to assist if he needed it. Which he didn't," Gabe told her. "Marco would have been proud."

Sarah nodded. "So I'm led to believe. So what? You just stood and watched while my child killed a man?"

Vinnie took a step towards her and reached for her hand. "This is what Gio does now Sarah. He is not a child any longer. This is what he wants to do and always has. Marco has been mentoring him for a good long while now and dare I say that he is good at it. Avenging his father's death was Gio's idea, we didn't tell him to do what he did, we were there just to help out. As Gabe said, in all honesty, we weren't needed today. You know what goes on Sarah, this isn't news; you have known this for a long time and I know that Marco kept very little from you. This was what they both wanted."

Sarah had nothing to say to either of them and walked out of the kitchen, disgusted with the events and Vinnie's dose of the truth. It was what she had always feared but had hoped deep down that Giorgio would wise up to what his father's business was all about, the legal and not-so legal side, go back to school and get a proper job. Perhaps she was a hypocrite but she had wanted more for her sons.

She realised that Vinnie was following her and she stopped. She was so tired and didn't have an ounce of fight left in her anymore. She did not want to argue with Vinnie and didn't want to talk to him very much either. He came up behind her and his strong arms encircled her waist. She stiffened up, not knowing who might be around to witness the scene. She wanted to just sink into his hold and be swallowed up by him. But it was too soon.

"I know it's difficult," he spoke very softly. "But Gio has his head in the right place. Granted, he still has a lot to learn and I want to stay here and support him, pick up where Marco left off – with him, not you!" he added before she got the ridiculous idea that he was trying to fill Marco's shoes with the whole family. "Gio cannot do this on his own, not yet and I think he could benefit from my help. And so could you." Vinnie nibbled her earlobe gently, reawakening her tired heart just a little.

"I seem to have no say in anything in my life anymore. My kids have all grown up and have their own opinions on just about everything. My husband, well, we all know what happened there.

His businesses have been taken over unofficially by people who shouldn't have any say in the matter and I know there will be a lot of fighting before this is over. I don't know what to do and I don't know who to turn to."

Vinnie sighed. "You know you can always rely on me, that will never change. I have told you many times over the years and now is no different. In fact, now it is more important than ever for you to lean on me and I hope Gio knows that too. Have you talked to him?"

Sarah pulled away from Vinnie's embrace and turned to face him. "No. He has found out what happened to Joe and how I was involved and now he won't talk to me. I think he hates me," her face was etched in pain as she said this.

"I'm sure that is not the case. He is too much of a mama's boy to hate you, especially now he knows you are a deadly assassin!" His words were light hearted and bought an enervated smile to Sarah's pale face. "He'll be okay. He just needs a little time to adjust. From what I hear, he has a new focus in his life now. Scott tells me he has fallen in love proper for the first time."

"Well that's news to me, Vinnie. Not long ago Gio would have come to me with this. It just proves me right, my son hates me." Sarah moved into the lounge and collapsed onto the sofa. She was so weary so she closed her eyes and allowed her head to fall backwards onto the cushions. For the first time in over a week, a tear slipped out and slid down her face, followed by another and then another. Pulling a cushion to her chest and hugging it tight as if to hold her heart within her, Sarah cried until the cushion was soaked by her tears. She knew Vinnie was just outside the door and was leaving her to grieve physically for her husband and after about half an hour, she felt some kind of relief. The heavy weight that had been lying on her chest had lifted just a little. She grabbed a box of tissues and wiped her puffy red eyes and blew her nose. Exhaustion had gripped her and she curled up onto the sofa where she sat and within seconds, was sound asleep.

The loud music was pumping and Giorgio and Katey could hear it even before they pulled up at the valet station. As Giorgio parked his car and left it idling, he looked over at Katey and smiled. He felt an incredible urge to reach over and kiss her but he just about resisted. Slowly, slowly, he thought.

The valet drove off in the Porsche and Giorgio took Katey's hand and together, they walked towards the entrance of the club. Katey had expressed an interest in '49' on their way into town and Giorgio had promised her he would take her there. She had doubted that even *he* would be able to get them in; it was usually by invitation only and very prestigious.

As Katey went to join the end of the long queue which didn't ever appear to move along, Giorgio carried on walking, pulling her along with him. Her face frowned in confusion but Giorgio just grinned at her bewilderment. As they neared the front of the queue, the doorman looked up at the pair and, immediately recognising Giorgio Delvecchio, parted the barrier rope and let the pair in. They were waived on through, bypassing the cashier and the entrance fee and the double doors were opened for them as they entered the clubs interior.

There Katey stopped and drank the room in. It was almost a fable to her, all of her friends had gushed about this place although none of them had ever managed to get inside and yet here she was. She had misjudged Giorgio's reach and wondered what else she may have misjudged about him.

She looked around the dark room lit by blue and white wall lights all around the edge. A small dance floor at the back of the room was lit up by red lights and the DJ was bellowing into the microphone from a platform above the dance-floor. He was announcing the next song as a tribute to some girl called Stephanie who was celebrating her 25th birthday today.

The room was packed and as people walked by the couple they would jostle Giorgio and Katey into each other, a contact that they both enjoyed. Giorgio laughed while Katey pretended to be embarrassed.

"Come on, let's get a drink," Giorgio suggested.

Katey nodded in agreement and wondered if he would get served. No-one had questioned either of them but Giorgio wasn't of legal drinking age yet. Regardless, Giorgio strolled up to the oval-shaped bar as though this wasn't an issue and joined the throng of people three deep waiting for drinks. Giorgio waited patiently to be served while holding up a hundred dollar bill in an effort to attract the barman's attention. It served his purpose. A barman Giorgio didn't know made a bee-line for him and asked him what he wanted.

"A cold beer from the back of the cooler and a bottle of Kristal with one glass and an ice bucket."

"Sorry. No champagne." The barman shouted back at him above the noise.

Giorgio felt his body tense with anger. He didn't want to be shown up in front of Katey. Perhaps, he thought, I didn't hear him correctly.

"No champagne?" he repeated.

The barman shook his head.

"At all? No bottles of anything?" Giorgio was incredulous.

The barman didn't say anything more and turned away to serve someone else when Giorgio demanded to see Billy.

"Billy? The manager?"

"No. Billy the fucking kid, moron! Yes, Billy the manager." Giorgio felt Katey tug his hand – she didn't want a scene and she didn't want him to get angry. She could have a cold beer too. It wasn't worth them getting kicked out of here now that she had finally made it inside.

"Hey! Gio!" A loud voice was heard above the music. "Everything okay?"

Giorgio turned around and saw the manager standing behind Katey.

"No Billy, everything is *not* okay! What sort of shit-hole are you running here?"

Surprised and shock registered on Billy's face and he knew that immediate and drastic measures were needed. "Okay, let's sit you both down and tell me what you need." he started to usher them away to a booth that a bouncer was clearing of its current occupants.

"We need a fucking drink, Billy and you have no champagne!"

Billy sat them down at the now vacant booth and motioned for a cocktail waitress to join them. He instructed her to get a cold beer for Giorgio and a very cold white wine for Katey. Once she was on her way, Billy turned back to Giorgio.

"Our champagne delivery was late. It's not chilled, that's all. By the time you finish this drink, I guarantee the champagne will be on your table."

"Late deliveries? You need me to talk to people?" Giorgio offered.

Billy thought about this for just a second but then he shook his head, saying he could deal with it. He had to show Giorgio he was up to the job of club manager.

Giorgio nodded, dismissing Billy and turned his attention back to Katey. She was looking worried. He took her hand in his and caressed it with tenderness.

"What's up?" he asked. His lips were close to her ear so she could hear him over the loud thumping music.

She shrugged. "I just don't like confrontational scenes. It makes me feel uncomfortable. What would happen if we were to get thrown out of here?"

Giorgio laughed despite Katey's discomfort. "That would never happen!" he looked around the packed club, surprised that it was so busy on a Monday night.

The waitress bought their drinks over and moved away. Katey took a slug of her wine and looked back at her companion. "How can you be sure we wouldn't get kicked out?"

He just sat there and grinned at her. "Because I own the bloody place!"

Katey laughed nervously, not entirely sure if Giorgio was being truthful. However, when she thought back over the evening, the queue bypassing, not paying to get in and the preferential treatment by the manager, it all made perfect sense.

Giorgio further clarified. "I own forty-nine per cent. Dad was going to sign the other fifty-one per cent over to me when I hit twenty-five. Something to do with licensing laws."

"Wow!" Katey was now impressed. "So this will all be yours?"

He nodded. "Soon. That may change now… " He broke off not wanting to think about whether he may have inherited this club sooner than was intended after the unexpected demise of his father. Giorgio knew he wasn't even old enough to buy a drink here, let alone own and licence it but he still hoped Marco had willed it to him.

The champagne was bought over as well as another bottle of cold beer for Giorgio. Katey giggled as Giorgio popped the cork and it gushed over and onto the table. He poured some of the liquid into the glass and she accepted it gratefully, guzzling down the first lot almost in one go. As he poured her another, she took his hand.

"Gio, despite me saying that I wanted champagne tonight, your money, this club doesn't impress me, you know." The bubbles were going to her head.

Giorgio shrugged. "It doesn't matter if it does or it doesn't. I still want to treat you and spoil you. I think you are worth spoiling and it's nice to have a beautiful and unimpressed girl to indulge."

Katey felt her face flame at his words. She had never thought herself beautiful. She knew she was attractive and could always have her pick of men but she was struggling to understand why someone such as Giorgio Delvecchio, who was without doubt a major catch, had any interest in her. That was the reason why, despite every fibre in her body wanting to be touched by him, she refused to sleep with him. She liked him very much and didn't relish the thought of being discarded by him the morning after. Staying just friends would be much less painful in the long run.

She switched the subject. "So how did it go today? Did you catch up with Steve?"

Giorgio was not comfortable discussing this with her so he just shrugged without commitment. "It was fine. Did you buy anything shopping?" He too, changed tack.

She laughed. "Just several coffees while I waited around for you to get back," she teased.

"I know and I really didn't want to leave you. We were getting along so well." He bought her hand to his mouth and brushed his lips across her palm. It set shivers of ecstasy down her spine and she let him continue to prolong the intense pleasure.

"We get along great, Gio and that's the problem. I don't want to ruin that by sleeping with you. I don't want to wake up tomorrow and find that you have had what you want from me and have moved on to the next girl."

He smiled wryly. "I only have myself to blame for you thinking that. You have only lived around here for a short while but I expect you have heard all sorts of stories about me, most of which are maybe true. But now that I've met you, I don't want to be like that anymore. I just want you." He reached over and kissed her gently on the lips, a movement so soft, it made Katey want so much more but then he pulled away. "But I will wait for you, however long it takes because I believe you will be worth the wait. And I will speak to you the following morning, and all the mornings after that."

Katey said nothing for a while as she caught her breath and tried to hide the effect that this young playboy had had on her. She laughed nervously as her heart raced. "You do, at least, talk a good talk and I want to believe you. Mostly, I want to spend the night with you," she smiled seductively at him. She was tired of playing games now.

Giorgio smiled inside because he knew he had won. He still refused to make it easy for her; she had made him wait and he could hold on a bit longer. Now it was his turn to play the game that he was already the victor and an expert in.

Tuesday

Giorgio had called Peter to come and pick them both up and now the family chauffeur was trying to help a very drunken Katey out of the back of the car while Giorgio pushed her out from inside. She had got far too drunk again, blaming her inability to cope with expensive champagne. She laughed uncontrollably as Peter handed her over to Giorgio to deal with and he walked her through the front door. Giorgio was hoping the family were all in bed by now; it was late and he didn't want to have to explain Katey's predicament to anyone, least of all his mother. She would not be impressed.

Giorgio's luck held out as he managed to get Katey up the stairs and almost through her bedroom door when his brother poked his head out of his own bedroom door, wondering what the ruckus was.

"Don't let mum hear or see you, Gio. She was in a pretty bad way tonight and she wouldn't appreciate this little scene," he warned.

Giorgio smiled a little nervously at Adam. "I know Adam. Katey just had a little too much to drink tonight, that's all."

"I'll be fine Adam. I am sorry I'm in such a state Gio, I just wanted to have a good time with you tonight," she slurred her words as she smiled at him.

Giorgio got her inside the room and closed the door quietly. Katey flopped onto the bed and lay there as the room spun around her. Giorgio slipped off her shoes."

He looked at her closely. "You're not going to be sick, are you? Clarice will go mad!" Giorgio couldn't help but be amused by Katey's drunken state.

"I won't be sick," she promised like a fool and stood up slowly. She began to undress. "Are you going to make love to me tonight?"

He laughed. "No, Katey, I am not. You are going to get undressed, get into that bed alone and sleep it off." Despite his words, he still couldn't help but watch her as she finished undressing and then naked, slipped under the covers.

As she settled, she realised he was still watching her. "Are you sure you don't want to get in with me?"

He laughed again. "Goodnight Katey!" He left the room and went to his own bed. He was going to enjoy himself when he eventually got his hands on that girl!

As he walked down the hallway, he bumped into Sarah who was heading to her own room after falling asleep earlier in the evening on the sofa. She threw a sly and knowing smile at her eldest son. He chuckled.

"Nothing gets passed you, mum but nothing is going on between us. Not yet. She just had too much champagne."

"And you didn't take advantage of that? You are growing up, Gio."

Giorgio just shrugged. "I don't want to be the stupid kid anymore. Too much has happened and I need to grow up. This terrible event in our lives has shaken me and all of us up and it's about time I became the man dad wanted and expected me to be."

"I don't think people think you're a kid, Gio. Events such as this can change a person and perhaps you are a testament to that fact," she paused. "Do you want to talk about, well, what we started talking about earlier tonight? About your Uncle Joe?"

Giorgio looked at his mother for a moment. He shook his head slowly. "Not right now, but it is something that I need to know more about. There can't be anymore secrets between us. It's been a long day though and I just need to sleep. We'll talk tomorrow?"

Sarah nodded and turned towards her bedroom.

Giorgio was awakened by movement in his room and lay still, not daring to move. He had heard his bedroom door close quietly and wondered where his baseball bat was. Then he remembered he had thrown it through the window last week and hadn't retrieved it yet; that could be his downfall.

He felt the sheet being pulled away from his body and the tension in his body gave way to surprise; he sat up with a start. His eyes flew open and he saw the smiling face of Katey standing at the end of his bed, dressed just in her underwear. She was staring at his nakedness and the state of arousal he almost always found himself in first thing in the morning.

"What time is it?" he asked sleepily. It felt like he had only been asleep for an hour or so.

"Just after nine," she replied, still grinning.

"Do you like what you see?" he asked her.

She nodded. "It's only fair to peep. You have seen me in the buff twice now and I expect you took advantage of me last night."

"How many times! I will not take advantage of you, I want you to be a willing and consenting participant." He lay back down and put his arms behind his head and let her stare at him. He relished the attention he was getting from her.

Full of purpose, she crawled slowly onto the bed and straddled him, meeting no resistance whatsoever.

"If I say no?" he asked, grinning

She laughed, knowing it wouldn't happen. "It seems to me that I have the upper hand here and that you are in no position to say no to me. I have locked the bedroom door so no-one is going to come in and rescue you." She leant down and kissed Giorgio, long and hard, the denied passion in both of them building up in the kiss and stoking the fires further. Giorgio put his arms around Katey and pulled her body flat onto his, his hands moving up and down her body, delighting in the feel of her flesh in his hands. Katey moved down and took each of his nipples in turn into her mouth, rolling her tongue over them and feeling the hardness of them. Giorgio moaned in delight as she nipped them gently and he closed his eyes. Much to his further delight, she moved further down his body, kissing each inch until she got to the control centre of his body and she giggled again as she toyed with him using her tongue.

"I wouldn't do that, if I were you," he murmured.

Her head shot up in surprise. "Don't you like it?" she asked.

"Oh yes. I just like it too much really."

"Oh. I see," she turned back to her task realising that if she carried on for too long, their first time together might end too premature. She didn't want that. She had waited for too long to be here with Giorgio and wanted to make the most of it. Katey wanted to stay here with him all day.

Suddenly, Giorgio pulled her off him and spun her on her back. "I think that's enough of that for now!" He was grinning and he kissed her mouth, tasting her all over again. His hands roamed over her luscious body as he kissed her neck, exploring her for the first time. His fingers encircled her nipples, standing hard and aroused by each titillating touch. Katey felt like she was being electrified every time his fingers found a new spot and she was trying hard to keep her moans of ecstasy under control, knowing that they weren't alone in the house but it was proving an almost impossible task and this just intensified the feelings. She squirmed under Giorgio's touch and reached down for him. She was ready and didn't want to wait any longer. Giorgio moved to kiss her while reaching over to his bedside drawer.

"What are you doing?" Katey asked breathless.

He turned back to face her, grinning like a fool as he held up a square of foiled wrap. "Gotta be careful, babe!" With a deftness brought on by much practice, Giorgio opened the packet with barely a missed heartbeat and slipped the condom on with expertise. He looked at Katey again and kissed her as he moved on top of her. She guided him in.

She laughed in utter delight as he moved, thrusting slow and deep, wanting to prolong the moment with her.

"I think I love you, Katey. Will you marry me?"

"Not a chance! Ask me another time when your balls aren't making your decisions for you."

He laughed and kissed her neck as she clutched him to her, digging her nails into his back as her breath became raspy. She could feel the tension building up in her and wanted to cry out but held on. When the release came, she bit into Giorgio's shoulder, muffling her cries as the waves of ecstasy hit her. This in turn built up the excitement in Giorgio until he finished just moments behind her with a loud groan.

He buried his head in Katey's hair as the moment passed and he lay motionless on top of her, catching his breath. He wanted to prolong the moment and didn't want to let her go. He laughed out loud as he realised that normally at this juncture, he was always eager to get gone.

"What's so funny?" Katey asked. Concern was evident in her voice.

"Nothing babe. Just a silly thought that went through my head. I was just thinking how wonderful that was and how great it is to just lie here with you. I just don't want to move."

"Well, you'll have to soon as you are a dead weight on me." She smiled at him and kissed his nose. As Giorgio moved to lie beside her and curl her up in his arms, she thought about how content she was right then. She played with the hair on the nape of his neck, damp with sweat from their exertions and thought about what he had said during their lovemaking. Could he want to marry her already? That seemed a little far-fetched and she wondered what his agenda could be. She was due to leave and go home in a few weeks and she knew there wasn't much chance of a lasting long-distance relationship for them; there would be too many temptations for someone such as Giorgio Delvecchio. Her heart felt heavy with a sudden uncertainty about the future and a life away from Giorgio. She berated herself for allowing herself to have got into this situation, of being here in bed with him and sighed heavily.

"You okay?" Giorgio asked her sleepily.

"Sure. Why wouldn't I be?"

"You were just frowning. No regrets?"

She shook her head. It wouldn't do to voice her thoughts and fears now, it would make him back off.

Giorgio kissed her on the lips. "Good. Let's grab a shower."

Katey just nodded and followed him into the bathroom that adjoined his room.

Sarah had woken up in her empty bed, again feeling such a sense of loneliness that it defied belief. She had yet again cried herself to sleep last night and it had served to lessen the heaviness in her heart enough that she might be able to make it through the day without shedding a tear. Then she could retire to her room again that night to do the same thing over again. It seemed like this was the only way to get through the days and the idea that this was how she would spend the rest of her life frightened her. She would miss Marco every day until she breathed her last breath but she hoped the acute pain she was currently experiencing would, at some point dissipate.

Sarah sat up in bed and looked out of the window. It was another beautiful morning in Palm Beach County and it promised to be a hot one. She decided to go and see Andrea as she needed to talk to someone about the conflicting emotions and who would not hate or judge her for what she needed to say.

So after breakfast, she called her friend and they arranged to meet in the coffee shop they favoured. Andrea said she could be there in half an hour which was fine as she had to be at the funeral home at one o'clock for the start of the visitation of Marco. Sarah was dreading this, maybe more so than the funeral itself. She would have to sit for hours on end in the same room as her dead husband while hundreds of people came up to her, offering false condolences and sobbing false tears. Most of them had never met Marco and wouldn't have given him the time of day if they had. Hangers on, her mother would have said. Sycophants, Sarah thought. But either way, it was part of the process that Sarah would have to deal with before the funeral on Thursday.

Sarah left a note on the kitchen table for her family to let them know where she was. Not that anyone seemed to care; they were all doing their own thing at the moment. She knew that next week, she would have to take control and get things onto a new reality or the rip in the family would become greater and maybe even irreparable.

At the coffee shop, Sarah ordered herself a drink and Andrea's usual and settled down to wait on the squishy armchair in the corner. She tried to organise in her mind what she was going to say to Andrea but her thoughts were so jumbled that it was almost impossible to order them. Sarah just knew that it had to be said.

She was just about to order another drink when her friend arrived looking smart and demure. Andrea had a good secure life without the trials and tribulations Sarah seemed to have endured over the years and it showed. The two women looked classes apart as they sat together.

"So, how are you doing?" Andrea asked as she politely drank her cold coffee.

"I slept with Vinnie." Sarah just blurted it out. It was the easiest way.

Andrea almost choked on her drink and then looked at Sarah in stunned disbelief. She had always known that there was history between Sarah and Vinnie and it had occurred to her very briefly, that with Marco no longer around, at some point in the distant future they might have another pop at a relationship, but hells bells! Marco hadn't even been buried yet!

"Say something." Sarah pleaded to break the now fallen silence.

"I-I don't know what to say, Sarah. I'm just shocked."

Sarah nodded in understanding. It had shocked her too. "Just don't hate me," she said quietly.

Andrea reached for her friend's hand. "I don't hate you Sarah and I never will. I just don't understand why."

Sarah shrugged, having no real answers herself. "We were in Dallas. Andrea, I miss Marco so much that it's killing me and Vinnie just takes the edge off it. I never meant for it to happen, it just did and I didn't want to stop it. I needed the closeness, the intimacy and to feel something other than this pain in my chest," Sarah's voice broke a little and she paused to regain control. "You know, the worse thing is that I want it to happen again. I look to the future and I don't want to be on my own and Vinnie is a good way out of that."

"Okay." Andrea didn't know how to handle this revelation. She took a sip of her coffee and tried to think of something to say. "Is it just that Vinnie is 'handy' or do you have feelings for him?"

Sarah thought about the question for a moment. "A little bit of both, if I am honest. I have always had some sort of feelings for him but I have never had to address it before now. I chose to be with Marco because I loved him so much more and I don't regret that for a single second. I wouldn't even look at Vinnie if Marco was still here. But he's not. He's gone and I will never see him again and that tortures me more than you can imagine. I have to think about the future; a future without Marco."

"Don't you think that taking up with Vinnie now is too soon?" Andrea asked without wanting to upset her friend. Her tone was gentle.

Sarah nodded. "Yes, it is. I have mixed feelings about what happened in Dallas but it has happened and I can't undo it. I don't want Vinnie to walk away from me, from us, thinking I don't want him."

"If he is the man you think and hope he is, he will wait for you until you are ready. Let's face it; he has just lost his brother. He is grieving too."

"He said he would wait. Why do I want him so much?"

Andrea shrugged. "Because you miss Marco, I would think. There is a void in your life that you are desperate to fill and Vinnie is willing to step into that void. Also, he is forbidden fruit and we all want what we can't have. You know you shouldn't want him but you do and that makes the wanting of him more acute."

Sarah smiled at her friend. "You are right, as always. You should have been a marriage counsellor or something. Vinnie and I will wait until the time is right and then see how things go. He wants to hang around anyway for Gio, in case he needs him."

"Is Gio taking over?"

"It's not as simple as that, unfortunately. Gio has to have backing from the others and I don't think he'll get it. He's too young but it will all be decided after the funeral. I know Vinnie is happy to back him but I don't think that can be said about anyone else. They all think he's too young and inexperienced and hasn't proved himself enough at the moment. To be honest, that's what I'm hoping is decided as I'm not sure I want my boy getting too deep into this."

"Sarah, from what Cliff tells me, he is already deep into this. I only get to overhear slivers of information but from what I know, Gio has been helping his dad out since he was about fifteen."

"I had figured as much but I was still hoping to be wrong. Gio is his own man now and I have to accept that but as far as I'm concerned, he is still too young to be involved in this without Marco to guide him and it frightens me. He's not yet twenty-one. What if he is too young for this responsibility? What if inexperience gets him or others hurt, or worse? I couldn't cope with losing Gio as well."

"Gio has some good people around him, Sarah. Whenever he does eventually take over, he'll be fine. Vinnie, Gabe, Scott – they will all steer him in the right direction. Besides, as you say, Gio might not get the vote on Thursday."

Sarah smiled. "Let's hope not, Andrea, however awful and unsupportive that may make me sound. So, what time will you be there this afternoon?"

They fell into conversation about more mundane things before both women got up, paid their bill and left the coffee shop.

Thursday

Vinnie gently touched Sarah's forearm, startling her and she turned to look into his worried face, his green eyes showing concern for her as well as being full of grief for his own loss. He looked dazed but he was trying to hold it together for the sake of those around him whom he cared about deeply. He could have his time later but for now, he was needed.

"The cars are here," he said to his sister-in-law.

Sarah nodded once in acknowledgment of what this would mean and her heart lurched. The very moment she had dreaded through all of her married life was now upon her and she felt nauseous. Her throat went very dry and she gulped back the brandy she had just poured for herself. It burned down her throat and warmed her stomach and seemed to galvanise her so she took a deep breath and left the dining room. She saw her family gathered by the front door as they waited for her; Grace and Scott, Giorgio and Katey, and Adam, all dressed in black and looking defeated yet united in grief.

"Okay?" Sarah asked everyone, her voice just above a whisper and received curt nods in response. No-one had the fortitude to speak as it might lead to tears already. Sarah walked past them and they fell into step behind her as they all went outside and into the bright sunshine.

As Sarah walked out she was stopped in her tracks as she stared at the car that carried her husband's coffin. It was bedecked in a multitude of colourful flowers; so many that they almost hid the casket within. Her awe was interpreted by hesitation by Vinnie so he guided her into the limousine behind the hearse. She was glad of his assistance as her legs were threatening to give way. Vinnie continued to prop her up regardless of outward appearances – his main consideration was helping Sarah to get through this event.

Grace, Scott and Adam climbed into the limo with Sarah but Giorgio directed Katey into the car behind that his aunt, uncle and cousins were just getting into. Giorgio couldn't bear to be in the same car with his mother and her oh! so public lover. It was the funeral of his father for god's sake!

The family cortege moved off slowly down the driveway, Marco's last journey from the house he had called home for all of his life while his beloved wife stared out of the car window, seeing nothing as her heart broke afresh.

Sarah didn't register any of the passing scenery as they made their way through the streets to the church. People stopped to stare at the passing vehicles. Some would know whose funeral it was while others wouldn't care. It wasn't their tragedy. They had enough to deal with in their own lives without taking on other people's sadness.

All too soon, they arrived at the little church that had been the Delvecchio's place of worship for many years. Giorgio Senior and Graziella had been married there, their children had all been christened there and Sarah and Marco had had their wedding blessing there. Marco would soon be reunited with his mother, father and brother, all of which were buried in the small cemetery at the back of the Catholic Church.

As the family emerged from the two vehicles, Sarah was astonished and overwhelmed by the sheer number of people who had turned up at the church for the service. Many of the faces she recalled seeing on Tuesday but could remember just a handful of names. She saw Nathan Dando, her old friend from San Francisco here to pay his respects and that of the Miotto Family from Marin County. She made eye contact with him and he smiled in encouragement for her, his face full of sadness for her loss.

As they entered the church behind Marco, the organ music assailed her ears and she gripped her daughter around the waist for support for them both. The two women fell into the front pew as friends and family filled up the seats around them.

Sarah took in none of the service, not even Giorgio's emotional eulogy for his father and was only aware things had come to an end when the priest gently touched her shoulder to lead her outside and into the cemetery. She found a modicum of courage that had eluded her for days and she walked out with her head held high as she followed her husband on his very last journey, a picture of demure suffering and a faint trace of tears in her eyes. The sun was getting so hot now that she began to perspire; the sun was attracted to her black mourning clothes. She began to feel a little lightheaded and dizzy. Sarah wished this was all over so she could go home and be alone.

She knew Vinnie and Giorgio stood behind her as she settled onto one of the chairs by the graveside and the priest began his final words of goodbye.

Marco's coffin was being lowered down into the cold, dark earth when Sarah felt all semblance of control slip away. All of a sudden she couldn't bear the thought of her beautiful, wonderful husband dead and cold, buried under all of that soil, forever in the pitch black. She couldn't help but still see him alive and laughing, or hearing his temper as he exploded when one of his men had messed up, or when he was loving and tender with her. She just wasn't ready to say goodbye yet.

"No!" she cried out.

A comforting hand from behind was placed on her shoulder and Grace, already sobbing freely, took her mother's hand and squeezed it hard. It wasn't comfort enough. Sarah shook them both off.

"No!" she stood up. "Please don't." Tears were free falling down her face and she couldn't see for them. "Please don't put Marco in there."

Already fractured hearts around the graveside broke in two as they witnessed this desperate outpouring of grief. Giorgio walked around to his anguished mother's side in an effort to try and calm her and get her through this ordeal but she was so stricken that she tore herself away from even his touch.

"*I can't bear it!*" She screamed aloud.

"Sarah…" Vinnie called out to her and reached for her.

Without warning, Sarah's legs gave way and she collapsed by the grave, caught by her dejected son before she hit the ground. Vinnie was there immediately to help Giorgio carry her away from the distressing scene, telling the priest to continue as they left. They looked for somewhere a little more private and found a bench under a tree and laid her down on this, fanning her with a service booklet until she opened her eyes again.

Sarah looked from her son to her brother-in-law and back again as realisation hit her. She sat up in a bit of a daze and took the bottle of water that Vinnie offered her. She took a sip.

"I'm sorry," she whispered as the tears began to fall again. "I just…"

Vinnie softly shushed her as he took Sarah into his arms and rocked her back and forth. She sobbed in his arms and no longer cared who was watching.

Giorgio watched the two of them, taking a step back and unsure what to say or how to feel. Since meeting Katey, he had discovered real love and couldn't even think about losing her so he had only a small understanding of how his mother must be feeling now in losing her soul mate and husband of almost thirty years. He knew then that he had no right to judge her or her actions and that she must get through it any way she could. Giorgio looked towards to the graveside and saw the group of mourners begin to break up and move away. Katey stood with Adam and Grace, all three of them looking over towards him with concern for Sarah. They all wanted to help but had no idea what to do and they didn't want to crowd her and make things worse.

"I'll be right back," he said quietly to his uncle and walked back over to be with his siblings and assure them that their mother was okay.

"Is she alright?" Adam was the first to speak as Giorgio approached, his face pale with the strain of the day.

Giorgio shrugged. "She is just devastated and I think it all got too much. It's too bloody hot and that was the final straw. I'm calling the doctor out to her when we get home." He took hold of

Katey's hand. "Come on, let's get back." And he led them back to the car that was waiting to take them all home.

When Sarah realised they were quite alone in the cemetery, she stood up and still feeling woozy, she reached for Vinnie for support. As the earth swayed and then became motionless once more, she started to walk back towards the grave.

"I need to go and say goodbye," she smiled weakly, as though apologising to Vinnie.

"Maybe another day?" Vinnie suggested, sure that Sarah had had enough emotional upset for one day.

Sarah shook her head in a typical display of defiance. "Now."

She made her way back over, taking great care as she picked her way past other flower covered graves until she reached the new one. Marco's. She gazed down at the bronzed coffin in the damp earth and tried not to think of him lying within. It would set her off again and she struggled to keep her tears in check.

"I always thought we would have much longer together, much more time to do the things we never seemed to have got around to doing. I wanted to travel the world with him if and when he ever retired. We wanted to cruise the Caribbean and wake up on a different island every day. He always wanted to go to Asia, to Hong Kong especially and we had planned a grand tour in our heads, taking in Thailand, Hong Kong and Japan." She smiled at the imagery that played through her mind as she saw them trying to climb Mount Fuji, eating Thai green curries alongside a fabulous beach in Thailand and taking the Star Ferry across Hong Kong bay. It would never happen now. She took a deep breath. "We were supposed to see Adam graduate Med school and be a top doctor, meet a girl, get married, all of that. Gio has now fallen in love and Marco didn't even know. He'll never see Connor grow up, never meet his other grandchildren and I am struck with the unfairness of all of that." She paused and picked up a lone flower that had fallen out of a posy and threw it down onto the coffin. "Perhaps Ray did get the right person after all because the two people that helped kill his father are the ones that are hurting the most at the moment." She sighed. "Having said that, I am grateful, and it has to be said, somewhat surprised that Marco lived to be fifty-seven. He made lots of people unhappy through the decisions that he made, probably made a lot of widows, a lot of angry sons. It's just ironic that what ultimately killed him was not of his doing. It should have been you or me that Ray killed, not Marco. Not this time. It's like Joe has risen from the grave to strike again and wreak his final act of revenge. Will it ever end?" She looked across the grass pathway to where Joe Delvecchio lay, close to where Graziella and Giorgio lay, but not next to. Marco had wanted it that way. He felt his brother did not deserve the honour. Now Marco filled the space next to his father.

Vinnie followed her gaze but said nothing for he agreed with everything she had said.

With a heavy sigh, she blew a kiss towards her husband and with a heart threatening to break all over again, she began to walk back to the car.

Giorgio watched from a distance, trying not to notice as one by one, Scott, Vinnie and Cliff all disappeared. He tried to fade into the wall and took the last sip of his now warm beer as he seethed. He knew they were going into his father's office for discussions, most likely about him and to decide on whether he was ready. He fought the urge to just go in there and demand they all leave, that he was in charge now but he also knew that that wasn't how it worked.

Giorgio knew that Nathan Dando from San Francisco was already in the 'privy council' along with several other important high-ups he knew by reputation, two from New York and one from Philadelphia, the East Coast mob. He wanted to know why he hadn't received his invite to this meeting. He had right to be there, whatever the outcome.

Katey appeared at his side with a cold beer for him and he took it with gratitude, smiling his thanks at her before his mind turned once again to the meeting taking place without him. In his agitation, he swigged down over half the beer in one go as his anger raised to the surface once more.

They stood in silence for a while each lost in their own thoughts while looking around at all the 'guests' getting drunk around them.

Grace soon found them and put her arm around her brother, wanting to comfort him but not having the words. Nothing she could say would make this situation any better and she knew what Giorgio was waiting on. Grace glanced round at the visitors who were acting as though this were a grand garden party and not the funeral of her father.

"Mum's asleep." She settled on a safe subject after a few moments of awkward silence. "The doctor gave her a shot to knock her out and help her rest. She hasn't slept well since... since it happened." She still struggled to say the words.

Giorgio nodded but said nothing as his attention was suddenly back on his uncle as he emerged from the house looking around for someone.

For him.

Giorgio stood up from the wall he had been sitting on and headed over to where Sal stood.

"Do you want me?" he asked him, his voice full of hope. He was weary of waiting around to be summoned.

Sal nodded and turned to go back into the quiet house without saying a word. Giorgio followed him back through the lounge and down the hallway into the office.

Giorgio was confronted by all of Marco's top men and his brother-in-law. Most were standing or leaning against the wall or the window. It was not a huge room and there were a dozen or so people in there. Gabe and Vinnie were the only two who were sitting and Marco's chair was unoccupied. Giorgio's heart began to race with anticipation as he imaged some big show of him being seated in that black leather chair in front of all of these people. It would be like a coronation and what a gesture of faith that would be for him! People would have to sit up and take notice of him, that's for sure.

"What's going on, Gabe?" he asked his father's best friend and the man he had trusted most throughout his life, looking him directly in the eye. But Gabe's face was deadpan and he gave nothing away.

"We need to talk to you, Gio." It was Vinnie who spoke. Vinnie felt he owed his nephew the explanation he knew he would be needing. He knew of Giorgio's quick temper, the flashes of rage he was apt to show, so much like Marco, and Vinnie was prepared for that. He still hoped that Giorgio would control his feelings and understand the reasons behind the decision that had been made, especially in front of these important guests.

Hoped but wasn't convinced.

"I'm not going to like this, am I?" Giorgio asked. A sick feeling of dread had appeared in the pit of his stomach.

Vinnie shrugged. "Knowing you, I doubt it but you have to hear me out, Gio. I am hoping that you will understand the decision that has been made and why." Vinnie had earlier voted for Giorgio to take the top spot but he was the only one that had. He had pushed for the conditions that had been set on his nephew's behalf and now he hoped Giorgio would accept them.

Giorgio knew then that he was not going to be taking over from Marco. The business he was in did not allow for the provision of wills; the decision as to who was next in line was decided by the survivors and depended on the strength of the people who put themselves forward for the job and who they had to back them up. Giorgio always knew that his age would count against him, and although he had been his father's protégé for six years now, he knew he still had a lot to learn. This knowledge didn't stop the bitter resentment, disappointment and some degree of hatred from welling up inside him. He could only direct his feelings towards one person.

"So who then, Vinnie? You?" he asked, his anger rising once more.

Vinnie nodded but said nothing.

Giorgio wanted to punch the life out of Vinnie then but he knew it wouldn't help him in the slightest so he kept his fists clenched by his sides. "You have now taken everything from him, haven't you? First his wife, and then his business. Are you sure you didn't put Ray up to killing him?"

Vinnie gave him a long, icy stare. "I will ignore that remark this time because I know you are grieving and upset," Vinnie took a deep breath. "But if you ever say anything like that again... " His voice trailed off leaving nobody in any doubt that he would not be taking insubordination from anyone, least of all Giorgio.

"This situation, it will only be in place for five years and then it will be reviewed, we hope, to a more satisfying conclusion for you, Gio." Vinnie continued. "It has been decided that you are too young and still too inexperienced to lead this Family. You will be directly below me and will take on more responsibility so you can earn your own way from now on. In these five years, you will gain the experience in leadership that will make it possible for you to command the Delvecchio Family in the way that Marco wanted you to."

Giorgio was not to be placated. "Fuck the lot of you!" He could no longer control his rage and turned to leave.

Sal placed a hand on Giorgio's arm as he tried to storm out. "Gio, it's the only way and it's a good option. Five years is nothing," he said, trying to calm his nephew.

Giorgio scowled at his uncle and shook him off. He pushed past him and slammed the door as he left.

"Well, that went well." Gabe snickered to the silent room. Gabe knew that Giorgio would soon calm down and see the situation for what it really was, that they were in effect holding everything in trust for him until he was ready for the role. Vinnie was the obvious solution for temporary leadership, being Marco's sole surviving brother but even Gabe knew it wasn't the perfect solution. The rumours were flying about the relationship between Vinnie and Sarah but it wasn't Gabe's concern as long as it didn't affect Vinnie's business decisions. He would always be around to look after the Delvecchios and would never let Vinnie take over permanently. Giorgio was destined to lead. Giorgio was like a nephew to Gabe and he would make sure Marco's son would inherit his birth right in due course. He'd give Giorgio a few days to calm down and then they would talk again.

Giorgio needed to vent. He raced upstairs to Sarah's room to rage at her for bringing this situation on them all and especially him but she was in a deep drugged state and would not rouse for a good few hours yet. He was not ready for Katey to see this side of him yet, she would probably run a mile and no-one else would really understand his frustration, not Adam, not Grace and unlikely his best friend.

He slunk out of the side gate and headed to the beach for some alone time. He felt like he had been mugged of everything he had ever wanted and worked for. His whole world had collapsed in on him and now, even the ruins had crashed down on his head. The man who had always wanted to be Marco Delvecchio had taken just one more step to getting his own way and Giorgio felt helpless to stop him. In his blind rage, he couldn't help but wonder if Vinnie had had something to do with Marco's death.

Giorgio walked along the waters' edge, his fast pace matching his rage. He allowed the cool waters of the Atlantic Ocean to lap over his shoes as the Florida sun began to disappear behind the horizon, leaving behind a hue of citrus and plum colours streaking across the oncoming night sky. His shirt had become untucked and his black tie was askew and he looked like an emotional wreck. For once, Giorgio didn't care about his appearance, didn't care that his eight hundred dollar Armani shoes were being ruined by the salt water and sand mixture at his feet. He didn't even care that Katey might be getting frantic as she began to search for him, unaware he had slipped out. He just carried on walking, wanting his anger to burn out before he did something too destructive when he stumbled across the beach bar that was about a mile from the house. It was a place he had spent many a drunken night in with Jesse and he ambled up the sand toward Shady's Shack, deciding his anger was a little more under control. He sat on the stool and was relieved to see that the owner was on duty tonight. He wanted a cheerful face and one that wasn't falling over itself to be sympathetic. He'd had enough of that today.

"Hey Shades, how are you doing?" Giorgio knew Shady quite well and he was one of his better customers.

Shady turned to face Giorgio and he smiled at him. He reached down into the fridge and pulled a cold beer out. He opened it and placed it in front of Giorgio.

"Thanks buddy but I've come out without any cash. I was in a bit of a hurry to get away."

"I reckon you're good for it, Gio and besides, I'd say you need it. I heard about your dad. I'm really sorry, he was a decent guy."

Giorgio nodded. "Yep, he was. We buried him today and it's been a real shit few days and I could do with a good line of credit here. Do you mind if I sit here and get stinking drunk and come by with the money tomorrow?"

"You need just beer?" Shady smiled at him.

Giorgio nodded. "Thanks man, but I don't touch that shit. I have enough vices and problems without drugs to add to it all and I'm pretty sure my girlfriend wouldn't hang about if I did drugs."

"Girlfriend? Gio, I've never heard that word applied to you before! She must be a very special lady," Shady teased. "What will the women of Palm Beach do now that their object of desire is unavailable?"

Giorgio laughed. "I have a good looking brother they can start on. He's a nicer guy than me anyway, when he's not got his nose in his books. I should bring him by before he goes back to college. And Katey, you should meet her."

Friday

It was still early, not quite eight o'clock and most of the family were still sleeping. Sarah knew that Vinnie would be asleep still but she needed to talk to him and she strode across the lawn towards the pool house with a new sense of purpose. Vinnie had been up late last night to begin to organise things and she knew this even though she had been out for the count, thanks to the sleeping pills the doctor had given her. Her head felt clearer than it had it weeks and she felt ready now to take on the world. She once again noticed the fresh morning air, the birds singing in the trees and the gentle hum of the pool heater as she passed the pool. She had flashes of memory of that hot Sunday afternoon nearly two weeks ago. Their last one as a complete family.

Sarah knocked on the door and listened intently for an answer or an indication of wakefulness from within. She received neither but pushed the door open and entered anyway.

Jamie was asleep on his back in the bed in the corner and furthest from the door. He snored but looked peaceful and untroubled as he slept and Sarah envied him. He didn't need any drugs to help him sleep and she wished her own children were as untouched as their cousin was at the moment.

But she had chosen Marco all those years ago and not his brother and as a consequence, her children were all suffering now. She was determined to make life as durable as possible for them at the moment and ease their heartache as much as she could. She felt strong enough to deal with this now.

Sarah looked over at Vinnie and her resolve crumbled just a little. He had so few similarities to Marco but those that resembled him took her breath away. The long dark eyelashes that rested on his sun kissed face and the strong prominent nose. Their eye and hair colour were so different that you could be forgiven for not seeing a family resemblance but it was there if you looked for it.

She stood for a moment and admired his sleeping form. Sarah could tell he was naked with just a sheet pulled up and partially covering his middle. His naked chest with thick curls of pale hair further bleached by the sun of the past few days made her heart race a little. She could make out his solid legs under the sheet and remembered the feel of them solid and muscular entwined in her own. His blond hair was ruffled from sleep and he looked so desirable to her that she wanted to crawl into bed beside him, wake him up and make love to him.

However, she sat down beside him on the bed and he didn't stir. She put a hand on his shoulder and shook him very gently until Vinnie opened one eye and smiled when he saw who had woken him from his deep sleep.

"Hey. Good morning. What time is it?" he asked in a sleep laden voice.

"Just after eight. I know it's early but I need to talk to you before anyone else wakes up and ruins the moment. Can you get dressed and meet me outside? I have coffee waiting."

He nodded. "Give me two minutes to throw some clothes on."

Sarah just smiled and left the pool house to wait outside. Vinnie had joined her before she had taken her first sip of coffee. She poured Vinnie a cup as he sat down and took the coffee from her. He was glad of the wake-up juice.

"So I'm guessing that this is a serious talk?" He asked, gulping his morning drink.

Sarah nodded. "It is and I'm not sure where to start."

"Just speak from the heart Sarah. I'm a big boy and I can take it."

Sarah couldn't help but smile at his words. That was half of the problem. She took a deep breath and got her mind away from the contents of his underwear. "I think we rushed into things, Vinnie. Don't get me wrong, I needed and enjoyed the night we had together and I hope we have many more. It's just that now is not the right time. I'm still grieving for Marco and I imagine I will for a long time. He was the love of my life and I don't know if I will ever get over losing him but I hope that when I am ready to move on, that you will be there for me."

Vinnie couldn't help but smile. "You said 'when' you are ready, not 'if'. I like that, it gives me hope. And you know I will wait. I have waited twenty-five years. A few more won't make much difference."

"My kids need me to be focused on them at the moment and not a new man in my life. They won't thank me for that. And if you get a better offer meantime, I expect you to take it. I won't cling on to you. You are a good man, Vinnie and you deserve to be happy, so if some blond floozy comes along before I am ready, well then, I expect you to take up with her."

"And maybe I will. Just to pass the time before until we can be together. And not hiding in the shadows, we must be open and up front with everyone. I'm sure Gio knows something, he was really pissed off with me yesterday."

"I haven't seen him since the cemetery yesterday. What happened at the meeting?"

Vinnie shrugged not wanting to divulge the details. It went against everything he believed in to tell anyone about what went on. He also knew though, that Marco had kept very little from her and it wouldn't do for him to begin by keeping secrets from her. Sarah would never put up with it.

Sarah sensed his hesitation. "You know Vinnie, I always found out everything in the end. Marco couldn't keep anything from me, I made his life too difficult and eventually, he stopped trying to hide things. Well, apart from this business with Ray, it would seem," she added rather bitterly.

Vinnie reached over the table for her hand and with tenderness, he squeezed it to encourage her. "I have been put in charge for five years. Gio was deemed too young and too inexperienced to take over just yet and he isn't at all happy about it. I don't know if he is most unhappy about me taking over or because he has to work under me. I just know that he is not my biggest fan at the moment and I can't say I blame him. From his point of view, I have stepped into his father's shoes and his side of the bed. I think I would feel the same if I was him."

"Everything seems to be such a mess at the moment. It's Gio's twenty-first birthday next week and we had this big thing planned for him. I don't suppose for one minute he will feel like celebrating, especially in light of what you just said."

"Maybe if you asked him, he might surprise you. Maybe he will just want something low key."

Sarah stood up and smiled at Vinnie. "You're right. I will ask him over breakfast. I need to get in and make a start on the day. I guess you have to think about moving to Florida again, huh?"

Vinnie nodded. He wanted to move into the house. He just wasn't sure how to ask her. It would have to come up in conversation soon but maybe not today. Giorgio would probably end up killing him unless he calmed down.

Sarah did not see her eldest son at breakfast and Katey told her that he hadn't come home last night. Katey looked incredibly downcast as she relayed this to Sarah and the older woman felt sorry for her. Sarah wasn't worried about Giorgio, he often stayed out all night, usually in the bed of some unsuspecting girl. But that had been the old Giorgio. She had hoped that the new Giorgio, the one who was supposed to be in love with Katey was better than that and would have been home in his own bed. Perhaps yesterday had made him sink back to his old ways and she fervently hoped that Katey was not going to put up with his behaviour. Sarah had grown to like Katey over the last few days and was pleased with the change she had bought about in Giorgio.

But it was no longer Sarah's business and she left the kitchen to go and take a shower and as the warm water drenched her, she thought about Giorgio and how he had been passed over, for five years anyway, in favour of Vinnie. She couldn't and wouldn't pretend that she was not pleased as it meant that Giorgio would be kept safe for at least that time. She had always known with some degree of certainty that while Marco had been around, Giorgio was assured his safety but if he had made top spot, Giorgio would then become a target. She had been worried that there would have been no-one to take care of her boy but that seemed to have been taken care of as well. She knew Vinnie would see him right and in five years, well, Giorgio would be on his own then but he would with luck, be better equipped to handle it.

When Sarah later walked downstairs to begin her day, the front door banged open and Giorgio staggered in. He was manhandled upstairs by his mother to her room and away before Katey could see him. He reeked of stale alcohol and looked like he had been sleeping rough for days. Giorgio's eyes, usually sparkling with life were blood shot and there were heavy black circles beneath them. He had a red welt across his cheek that appeared as though he had been in a fight and his hair was tumbled and sandy.

"What the hell happened to you?" she demanded, unable to keep the simmering rage from her voice.

"Just a drink too many. I slept on the beach last night and I feel rough as anything. I need a shower. Is Katey still here?" His breath was putrid and Sarah recoiled from him.

Sarah pushed him into her own bathroom and slammed the door shut. "Yes, she is," she called out through the door. "But if you keep messing her around like this, she won't hang around if she has any sense. I'll go and get you some clean clothes."

"Okay. Okay! I don't want a lecture," he said, not being in the mood.

"Maybe you don't want one but you sure seem to need one, Gio. This is why you... " she stopped, knowing she had already said too much.

Giorgio opened the bathroom door. "This is why what?" His gaze bored into his mother's eyes. "This is why Vinnie is taking over? Because I am a drunken waste of space?"

"You said it son, not me!" Sarah was so angry with her son and very confused by her feelings. She wanted him to run the business but wanted him to stay alive and the two didn't always go hand in hand. Giorgio was never going to amount to anything as long as he kept playing at being a playboy and not master of the family.

Giorgio stared at his mother, hurt beyond belief. Her words had too much truth in them but for as long as he could remember, she always supported him. Even when he had spent a couple of nights in jail, she had been there to bail him out, still on his side laughing at him, saying it was what all teenage boys went through, a rite of passage. Now though, she was openly disapproving and clearly disappointed.

"I can't win with you, can I? When I behave like this, it's wrong. I do what Dad wants me to do and you don't like that either. Well tell me, what *do* you want me to do? Tell me how you want me to behave and I'll try my best!" Giorgio was shouting at the top of his voice and had attracted his brother's attention.

Adam had appeared at the door to their mother's room and was listening with horror at the row that was that going on before his eyes. "Hey, come on! Don't fall out with each other. We are all upset and nobody wants to say something that can't be unsaid," Adam said, trying to placate the two.

Giorgio and his mother were still staring at each other, not wanting to back down. "Adam, maybe you want to play the peacemaker but I'm not sure I want to. Whatever I do is wrong and I don't think I even want to try to get it right anymore." Giorgio ranted. "You seem to be the blue-eyed boy now and you are welcome to the role, brother. I have had enough of trying to be what Dad wanted to me be when it is in direct competition with how *you* want me to behave." Giorgio was now directing his rant back at his mother. "Maybe I want to do my own thing and if that is getting drunk and spending the night on a sunbed on the beach than maybe that is up to me. I don't need this shit anymore!" He turned and stormed to his own bedroom, slamming the door behind him when he got there.

Adam walked to his mother's side to comfort her. "You okay?" he asked.

Sarah was struggling to hold back tears of sadness and frustration. She shook her head. "I don't know what you kids want from me anymore. You may all have grown up in your own minds and body but you are still kids to me. I just don't know how to help any of you right now but it seems as though you don't want my help."

Adam put his arm around her shoulder. "Hey come on. We will always need you, you're our mother," he said softly. "We are all just trying to deal with this in our own way, you included and Giorgio's way is to blame someone else. He has always been that way, you know that. I'll talk to him later when he has had a chance to calm down a bit and taken a shower. He's stinks!" he laughed.

Sarah smiled and hugged her youngest son. "When did you get to be so grown up and sensible? I seem to have blinked and you are all adults with your own thoughts and opinions."

"You and Dad made us the independent people we have become, you deserve all the credit," he paused. "If you don't mind, I'm gonna spend a few days with a friend in Atlanta before heading back to school. I just feel the need to have a break from here. The memories and now the rows; it's all too raw."

Sarah felt a stab to her heart but she also understood. If she had a choice, she would have loved to disappear for a few days as well. Graciously, she kissed Adam on the cheek. "Of course I don't mind, my darling. Just call me at least once a week so I know you're okay. When are you leaving?"

Adam looked down at his feet. "After lunch," he muttered.

Sarah sighed. "Okay. We'll have a happy farewell lunch then. I'll go and sort something out for us all." She wasn't convinced that many of the Delvecchio family would be around to see Adam off.

"Come on Katey. Let's get out of here!" Giorgio called out as he came out of the shower feeling something near to human again. He had, he thought, managed to convince Katey of the truth, that he had just got drunk alone at the beach bar and then passed out as he started to walk back home. She had not been happy that Giorgio had got in such a state and hadn't taken his phone out with him so he might have been able to call her. Katey knew that Giorgio liked a drink as much as she did as the first time she had met him at that party, he had been in a drunken state but now was not the time for either of them to clean up their acts. Both had too much on their minds right now.

Katey smiled at him as she picked up her bag with her overnight essentials in and said she would load up his car as he dressed. Giorgio winked at her with a promise of things to come as she left the room. He was desperate to make love to her when he got home but he had been in too much of a repulsive state and she hadn't wanted him to go near her. Now, after a shower and some strong fresh coffee he was ready but they were getting out of here and he didn't want to delay that for any reason. It would make later so much more fun!

Katey was walking down the silent hall towards the stairs, listening for sounds of people as she went and trying not to draw attention to herself. She didn't want to run into anyone at all. She tiptoed down each stair and once at the bottom, she hesitated and listened once more, looking directly at the door to the office that had belonged to Marco Delvecchio. Her curiosity was getting the better of her and she made a move towards the door. Her heart was pounding rapidly as her hand reached for the door handle although she feared the door would be locked. Then she heard a chair scrape on the floor inside and she bolted back toward the front door, breathing hard as she caught her breath and her nerve.

Katey picked up Giorgio's keys from the hall table and went out into the sunshine. Her breathing returned to normal as she put her bag in the back of the Porsche and then leant against the car to wait for Giorgio. She could just about see through the window to the office, the blinds not being completely closed against the sunshine and she saw Giorgio's uncle Vinnie sat behind the desk. He looked like he was alone and was busy and hassled. He had a frown on his face as he looked through some paperwork. Giorgio had told her this morning the reason for his disappearance last night was that he was pissed off that he was not taking over the family business, and Vinnie was going to instead. That was why he felt he needed to get away for a few days and think about what he was going to do. He thought a few days in South Beach or the Keys with

Katey would do him the power of good. Katey was not going to deny him, despite her deadlines: she wanted to spend as much time with him as possible and get to know him so much better.

Her lack of patience soon got the better of her and Katey wandered back inside to chivvy Giorgio along. Even he shouldn't take this long to throw some clothes in a bag. As she entered through the door, Vinnie came out of the office. He smiled at her.

"Have you seen Sarah this morning?" she asked him a little nervously. He was a very foreboding man, tall and muscular and Giorgio had told her stories about him. He was not a man to anger.

He shook his head. "Have you tried the patio?"

"No. It's just that Gio and I are taking off for a few days and I don't know if he has any intention of letting anyone know. I just wanted to let someone know as I'm sure he would be fretted over if he disappeared."

Vinnie wondered how much longer his nephew was going to keep playing the spoiled kid but he realised that Giorgio had always been like that when he couldn't get his own way. It became apparent to Vinnie then just why the people who knew Giorgio best had decided he wasn't ready for position of Boss. He would want to kill anyone who got on the wrong side of him. Who knew what would happen to the business if that happened? Marco had been irresponsible when he took over at twenty-eight and the power had gone to his head. All sorts of bad decisions had been made that had many repercussions. The decision had now been made to avoid that happening again and now it would appear that Giorgio was proving everyone right.

Vinnie aired none of these thoughts to Katey but promised her he would tell Sarah when he saw her. Maybe it was what everyone needed right now, some time away from each other before the strain of grief took its toll. He left Katey standing by the door and headed into the kitchen.

Katey took a brief look at the open office door before deciding now was not the time.

Vinnie found Sarah in the lounge, in silence just staring out of the window but not seeing anything. She had a cold cup of tea in her hands and Vinnie took it from her grasp.

"Would you like me to make you a fresh one?" He asked her.

She smiled her thanks at him even though his tea making left a lot to be desired. "Adam wants to go back to school ahead of time and stay with a friend en-route. He says he needs to get away and I don't blame him."

Vinnie took a deep breath. "Gio is the same. I have just seen Katey and the two of them are taking off soon."

Sarah snickered. "My kids can't bear to be around me. Do you think they blame me for Marco's death?"

Vinnie put his arms around her despite the fact that she had warned him off just that morning. She didn't resist and he felt her relax in his embrace. "Of course not," he assured her. "Why would they blame you? If it wasn't for you and your perseverance, we might not even have got Ray yet. Now that we have, Marco can rest in peace and we can all grieve for him knowing that his killer is rotting in hell."

"As may Marco be."

Vinnie squeezed her tighter. "Don't think like that. My brother may have had his faults and he may have done a lot of things that perhaps he shouldn't have, but he also did some great things. He did a lot for charities, drug rehabilitation, children's homes, all sorts of good things. He was a great father and he loved you very much. You know all that, Sarah, so please don't think ill of him."

Sarah nodded. "You're right, as always. I just wish I didn't have to be on my own. Maybe I should have had that fourth baby that Marco always wanted. It would still be in high school and wouldn't be able to leave me." She turned and smiled at Vinnie. "I am so glad that you are here though. Perhaps we should get you and Jamie a room within the house and make it all a bit more permanent."

"That would be nice but it would just be for me. Jamie and I have decided that he should return to Chicago and take over the running of our interests there for the time being. My place here is just for five years so I don't want to cut all my ties back home. It may be that we decide for Jamie to take over permanently up there and then I may retire when I'm done here. I'll be sixty one by then and might decide on a nice house on the beach further down the coast to live out my years."

"It must be nice to have a plan for the future. Losing Marco has made me realise how fragile everything is. All of our plans have come to nothing now and I seem unable to look past the end of one day."

"It's still early days yet and time will make things better. One day, you will look further into the future and who knows? Maybe we can find a quiet place down the coast together?"

Sarah kissed his cheek. "I'll go and sort out a room for you with Clarice."

As Giorgio sped through the streets in his Porsche in the late afternoon, Katey felt care free once again as she sat beside him. The wind blew through her dark hair and she felt the sun beating down on her head and she couldn't help but smile. She knew the next few days were going to be fabulous as she thought of all the alone time she was going to have with the gorgeous man sitting next to her, concentrating hard on driving and weaving in and out of traffic as he hurried to get to their destination. Katey knew Giorgio was not concerned with traffic cops and didn't slow down for anything. She laughed in a childlike way as he floored the pedal to beat a red light. It was the beginning of a new Katey, worry-free and happy.

She had one thing to worry about and that was her assignment which was becoming overdue. She would have to put some serious work in when they returned from their little break.

They hit South Beach a while later and headed to Katey's house. The plan was to stay there for tonight before heading south to the Keys in the morning and finding a hotel with room service to hole up in. Katey knew her flatmates would still be at work for at least another hour so she and Giorgio would have the place to themselves for a while and she was feeling the need for that. She leaned across and put her hand in his lap, massaging him as a grin played across his face. He couldn't wait to get Katey inside.

Katey had never known anyone like Giorgio Delvecchio. Without doubt, he was extremely handsome and rich and the confidence that those two assets brought were not in reserve. He was a marvellous lover, teaching her things that even Katey had not been aware of and she was no blushing virgin. He made her feel like she was the most important person in his life, something that no-one except perhaps her father had ever managed to do. She had spent her life with her father after her mother had left not long after she had given birth to Katey, but her father had always seemed sad, as though something or someone was missing from his life. Katey knew from quite a young age that her parent's relationship had never been a good one and they were wrong for each other but it would cost her dad too much to divorce her mother so she knew the missing link in her father's life was not her mother. It wasn't until quite recent that her father had opened up to Katey and turned her life upside down.

She wanted to open up to Giorgio about the important parts of her life but the opportunity had not yet arisen. Now, they were having too much fun to add a black cloud to their lives and, she reasoned with herself, Giorgio had enough going on and wouldn't want to hear it. Soon was soon enough.

Despite her initial hesitation and misgivings about Giorgio, she had got him totally wrong to start with and was now so glad he had pursued her and not given up the chase regardless of her frequent knock backs. She was determined that she was going to make him forget all the other girls and women he had known before and make him happy. She couldn't bear the thought of him with anyone else, neither the thought of her being with anyone else; it made her feel physically sick.

Much as she had predicted to herself, they just about got inside the house when he was pulling her clothes off, knowing they had the place to themselves for just a short time. Giorgio pulled Katey into her bedroom with very little reticence and after unbuttoning her shorts, threw her back on the bed. Grinning, he took off his own trousers in a hurry and kicked them off into the corner and then stripped off his shirt, flinging that into another corner. Giorgio buried his face into Katey's ample breasts, loving the softness and growing familiarity of them. His tongue found her hardened nipples and he toyed with her. She squealed in utter delight and wriggled beneath him as she reached down for him, knowing her was hard and eager for her. He flinched at her touch, unable to stand the exquisite heat of her hands around him. He didn't wait to take her underwear off, it would waste too much time. He just pulled them aside and plunged into her, gasping as he did so.

"No condom?" She was just able to register that he had not gone in prepared but somehow didn't care – she just wanted him thrusting deep inside her.

"Maybe if I get you pregnant, you would have to marry me," he grinned at her as he began to build momentum. He knew he wouldn't be long and hoped she was there or there abouts with him.

"Maybe we should get married in the Keys. On the beach, at sunset. Just you and me," she purred.

"Really?" He stopped moving and stared down at her.

"Don't stop!" She groaned. "Or the engagement is off!" She pulled him down and kissed him passionately as they moved together.

When Giorgio woke up a few hours later, he was alone. He reached over to where he had last seen his new fiancé before exhaustion had taken him and instead of her soft black hair, he found a sheet of paper. With a start, he sat up and read it slowly, his heart pounding as he read the few lines she had scribbled on it.

'Have gone out to tidy some loose ends and get some food in – be back soon – I love you!'

It was signed off with several kisses and Giorgio lay back on the pillows and breathed a sigh of relief. When he had first seen the note, he had thought it was a *'Dear John'* note and for a second, his world threatened to cave in.

Giorgio decided to get up and wait for Katey in the lounge. He felt around beneath the bed, looking for his discarded clothes. He found his trousers quick enough and dragged them out and then ducked his head under the bed to look for everything else. He was surprised at how messy it was under the bed; Katey had piles of paper and books, for her coursework, Giorgio assumed.

Wanting to know more about the woman he was about to marry, he pulled a small pile of papers from underneath and placed them on his lap. Giorgio was eager to know more about her college course that she was completing, she was always so vague about it. Hurricanes, was all she had ever said and it occurred to him how strange it was that she never mentioned what school she went to or what she hoped to achieve once the course was complete.

As he flicked through the paper work, he sat up sharply, shocked by what he was seeing. He leafed through page after page but on pretty much every one was a detailed description of one member of his family or another; Marco, Sarah, Gabe, himself, even the beginnings of a 'dossier' on his uncle Vinnie. There were newspaper clippings pertaining to various antics of his family and more recent columns of news about his father's death and the theories surrounding it. The consensus of the hacks was that Marco had been killed by a mugger. This theory had not been corrected by any member of the family especially as it now suited them for the public to believe this.

Giorgio delved deeper under the bed and found notebooks full of Katey's scribblings that he speed read through and what he read chilled him to the bone. She even had a crudely drawn Delvecchio Family tree, using words such as Captain, Soldier and Boss, words that she shouldn't know and more to the point she should not know who to apply such words to. There were dates of major events going back as far as five years ago and details of trips Marco had made to New York, Chicago and San Francisco. Giorgio knew that his father had made frequent visits to those cities; he had accompanied him several times to meet other heads of families and begin to forge relationships and lay foundations for the future.

But here, now, Giorgio next found a file on himself and that scared him. There were details of his disastrous school grades as well as pictures taken of him from various ages from around fourteen upwards. There were distance pictures of him playing tennis at the Palm Beach club that he had gone to with his mother on many occasions – mainly from his point of view for the rich women that might want younger flesh and he hadn't been wrong on that score. There were references to the few times he had been arrested, for the most part for drunken behaviour and it had never amounted to anything, no permanent record of it as far as he was aware but Katey had it all here in her notes.

Giorgio could feel anger and confusion and no small amount of hurt rising in him that she had such detailed information on his family and he couldn't understand why she just hadn't asked him. Was he such a monster that she was too scared to ask? From the amount of information she had, it was obvious she had been compiling it for many years and he was starting to think that she was with him to spy on him and the Family. That begged the question as to who she might be working for. His feelings of betrayal were tremendous.

Giorgio got out of the messed up bed and walked over to Katey's wardrobe. He felt it necessary to find out more about who this girl really was and tentatively began to route through her clothes and other belongings stashed away. He didn't know what he was looking for but knew there must be something. Part of him deep down didn't want to find anything at all to cast a shadow over his happiness and to doubt Katey - he wasn't sure his battered heart could cope with it. He was angry with himself for finding what he already had and wished he hadn't nosed around. He was about to marry this girl, why would he have any doubt as to her integrity?

He found nothing untoward in the wardrobe and began to feel a little better. Maybe she had always had a crush on him –who could blame her – and she just wanted to know a little bit about what she might get herself into. She was no different in that respect than when he found a serious girlfriend and Gabe was required to look into their background. Still, he wasn't one hundred per cent happy with not finding anything at all so he walked over to Katey's bedside table and began to search through the drawers. He wanted to prove himself and his suspicions wrong now and wouldn't stop in his endeavours until he had exhausted all possibilities of finding Katey to be what he hoped she was - honest, loyal and not about to cleave his heart into more shattered pieces.

Giorgio rummaged through the bottom drawer and at the back, and he found a brown paper bag hidden right underneath other innocent looking paperwork. He peered inside and found a dark blue passport with gold lettering on the cover. With a sick feeling of dread, he opened the passport up to the photo page and saw that it belonged to Katey Russell and the face staring back at him in the photo beneath the American eagle was the same Katey that he had just betrothed himself to.

"Fuck!" His mind went straight back to the words Gabe had uttered when he asked if they needed to worry about Katey. He had told Gabe in no uncertain terms that she was good, he would vouch for her and that they had nothing to worry about with her. Why would he think anything else? He had fallen in love with her and it would now appear that she was not what she seemed and to make matters worse, Giorgio didn't even know who she was, what she wanted or why she had lied. It chilled him.

He sat on the bed staring at the passport in his hands, slumped in defeat and wondered if he should confront her. But what would he say? He wanted to know the truth but he didn't know how deep and with whom she was in with. He wanted to call Gabe but was afraid of what his instant fix would be. There would be no second chances for Katey and Giorgio wanted to avoid that. He may be mistaken. There could be a thousand innocent excuses for Katey's investigation of him and his family.

But he couldn't think of a one.

He fumbled around in his jeans pocket for his phone and launched the internet browser, knowing he had to start somewhere. He Googled the name 'Katey Russell' and came up with far too many hits for him to be bothered with right then. He sighed in frustration and then tried to recall their many conversations to see if she might have given herself away. If she wasn't what she seemed, she was good at covering her tracks as Giorgio couldn't think of one tiny slip up.

But he also couldn't remember her saying very much about herself at all. She had never said where in England she had been born or went to school. The more he thought about it, Giorgio realised she had always been vague about herself and he knew squat about her. He had broken his father's cardinal number one rule – never get involved in anyone unless you really know who they were. This rule had been created after his mother had become friends with a woman who had wormed her way into the affections of the Family many years before and had turned out to be an FBI collaborator. Marco had dealt with the problem then and now, it seemed that Giorgio had another problem to deal with.

The front door slammed, making Giorgio jump as he did not want to be caught with the mystery passport in his hand. He needed time to think and work out what, if anything, he needed to do. He would have to wait a while to investigate further and make an informed decision, he owed Katey that much at least. In a hurry, he placed the passport back in the bag, taking care to fold the paper down the same folds just as he had found it and put it back at the bottom of the drawer. He closed the drawer just as Katey walked through the door. He looked up at her with a fixed smile on his face.

"Still in bed?" she laughed.

He shrugged. "You have worn me out, what can I say?" He lumbered out of the bed and walked over to her to kiss her passionately. "Are you sure you don't want your folks to be at our wedding?"

She stiffened a little and turned away from him, busying herself with taking her shoes off. "It's a long way from England for them to come. Maybe we could visit them after? We're not that close, to be honest."

He nodded, accepting her excuse. "Are they English? Or just Americans living in England?" He tried to keep the tone in his voice casual. He was still hoping there was some small and honest detail that she had just forgotten to tell him that would easily explain his doubts away. American parents living in England would be the perfect reason and they could carry on without her ever knowing his current thoughts.

She laughed. "What a funny question! They are English, of course. Can't you tell by my accent that I'm all English?"

"Sure. I was just thinking that I don't know too much about you and seeing as we are about to get married, I thought I should find out. What are your parents' names?" he pushed, still desperate for clarity.

"Mum is called Ellie and Dad is Simon. They live just outside Oxford and have done all of their lives. What's this about?"

"Well, when we get married, we'll be asked questions about one another, you know, so they don't think it's a marriage of convenience so you can get your green card or whatever. Katey, I don't even know your birthday!"

Katey smiled tolerantly at him and sat down on the bed. "I'm Katey Elizabeth Riley, October twelfth, born and raised in Oxford, England. I went to a local comprehensive school and left with the minimum high school qualifications to get me into university. After leaving college, I came here to Florida as I have a fascination with hurricanes, which you know. I had lots of rows with my parents, which I don't think I have mentioned at all. I have one brother, older, called Freddie and a dog called Barney. Happy?"

Giorgio smiled. It was not a happy smile as the little dialogue that Katey had just delivered had given her away. Before this morning, he wouldn't have thought anything at all about what she had just said or how she had said it but now his mind was open to doubts and looking for errors. Now he knew beyond all doubt that she was not who she said she was and he needed to find out who she really was. He had lived a life time with a mother who was a perfect English woman in every way, never wishing to adopt an American accent or their 'dreadful way of speaking' as she often put it and Giorgio knew how they spoke and he could tell a mile off that Katey was as American as he was.

He nodded. "Get dressed, let's go."

"Now?" She looked confused.

"Yeh, you want dinner, don't you?"

Saturday

Gabe was troubled and tired. He had received a call from Giorgio late last night while the younger man was hiding out in the mens toilets in a bar in South Beach. It had been just past 1 a.m. and Gabe had been just about to turn in for the night. Since the call, Gabe had been calling in favours from all over the state as they tried to find out just who Giorgio's new girlfriend was. A low-level employee, who was able to hack into most law enforcement database systems, had called Gabe around 4 a.m. with some bad news. Katey Riley didn't exist, despite the existence of a British Passport. Katey Russell, however, was born in Miami, in West Palm Beach actually, but had moved away to Dallas at the age of five. Her parents had spilt up and she had lived with her dad for most of her life. Her father was Dominic Russell and Gabe knew him from before.

He had been a friend of Marco and Sarah's and had fallen in love with a mutual friend of theirs. This friend, a woman by the name of Beth Rogers had been an FBI collaborator and had been dispatched in the only way such people can be. The Family had made it look like a robbery gone wrong and had even staged the robbery for when Sarah was with Beth for good measure, causing Sarah to become inadvertent collateral damage. Dominic Russell had always had his doubts as to the reality of the robbery and Beth's subsequent death and swore that he would be watching the Delvecchios and would eventually discover the truth. This had all been so many years ago that even Gabe was doubtful if he would have been waiting this long for revenge. Gabe didn't know how Dominic Russell fitted in to all of this, but he would find out and he could be dealt with at any point.

Gabe's more pressing problem was Katey's dossier on the Family that Giorgio had discovered and who else might know about it. If she was as clever as she should have been, there would be a copy of it somewhere and this copy should fall into Law Enforcement's hands if Katey was to suddenly disappear. It was becoming apparent that Katey would need to be dispatched but whatever happened needed to look like an accident and the best way Gabe could think of would put Giorgio in danger too. That was what was troubling him.

But he had to think of the bigger picture and there were too many people who could suffer as a result of what damage this girl might do to the Family, and to himself especially. He had stayed out of prison for the most part and wasn't about to spend his retirement waiting for a date with a lethal injection. Gabe had too much to lose to let this one go and just hope for the best.

With his mind made up, he knew he would have to call Jimmy Caruso which was somewhat regrettable. He didn't want to be indebted to the Carusos but Gabe couldn't take this to a Family member. They wouldn't want their Prince of Palm Beach getting caught up in this so close and they would insist he find another way. There was no other way if they were all to get through this and he just had to pray it would work out in Giorgio's favour. First, he called Giorgio.

"Hey Gio, sorry to wake you so early. Go to the Keys, get married, have a great time. Just don't tell your mother that I knew you were planning on tying the knot as she'll have my balls for breakfast."

"It's all good?"

Gabe could hear the hope in Giorgio's voice and smiled, thinking it would be a harsh lesson learnt. "No, it's not at all good but you have to act like everything is fine – she cannot know. Just expect it," he said and put the phone down. He didn't think Giorgio needed to know who she was, not just yet. It had to look convincing and the less Giorgio knew, the better, for the moment at least and if he came through it, Gabe would tell him everything. It was enough to know something was going to happen to give the boy a fighting chance. He owed that to Marco's son.

Gabe then called Jimmy Caruso and got him out of bed.

"I thought you wanted to be in Key Largo?" Katey shouted above the roar of the traffic as they left town and headed south on the US-1. The wind blew her hair around her face and she kept pushing it away, smiling over at Giorgio as she struggled with the task.

"I'm getting married and going on honeymoon. I don't want to share that with half of Florida. I've heard of a quiet place a bit further on and we can find a man to marry us there. We'll be having our dream wedding on the beach at sunset tomorrow." He smiled across at her and Katey responded by placing her hand between his legs and squeezing him until it threatened his resolve. He had been having a silent argument with himself since before he called Gabe that perhaps he owed her the benefit of the doubt rather than a bullet to her brain. But his gut was telling him that she had betrayed him in some form or another. He wanted to give her the right to reply and defend herself even though she'd had the opportunity to come clean several times since his chance discovery. He was almost reconciled to the fact that Katey Riley, or whatever the hell her name really was, had to go.

But first he had to know.

Giorgio pulled off the main road and drove away from the highway until he reached a small wooded area. It was quiet here and they could talk without interruption. Katey looked across at him and smiled, opening the door as she did so. She raced round to the other side of the car and grabbed his hand pulling him into the trees.

"You are insatiable, Delvecchio!" She grinned at him as she pulled him along.

"Katey, wait... "

But she would not wait. She pushed him against a tree and kissed him hard, tugging at his belt as she did so. Giorgio tried to push her away; he wanted to talk to her but as her hands slipped into his waistband, he relented. He'd had plenty of goodbye screws before. This was just one more. He just couldn't refuse her frantic pulling of his clothes.

He spun her around so Katey was against the tree and lifted her up, sliding into her as he did so. She hung onto him, panting heavy as she looked into his beautiful eyes, not noticing the change in him. Giorgio methodically pumped. He didn't take his eyes off her face, trying to read her, trying to understand her.

"Why did you lie to me?" he asked without stopping.

Her eyes grew large in shock. "What?"

"You are not Katey Riley and you are not English. Who are you and why do you have a file on me?"

She tried to push him off her but he was too strong for her. He was going to do this his way and she was going to tell him the truth.

"Gio, please stop. I can't talk while… " She stopped talking. He had closed down on her and she could tell from the look in his eyes that the Giorgio she had fallen in love with was gone. "I love you," she tried weakly. Her words fell on deaf ears and she stood against the tree, one leg over his hip while he roughly bored into her, scraping her buttocks against the coarse bark of the tree and just waited for him to finish.

As he was doing up his trousers afterwards, she glared accusingly at him. "Do you mind telling me what that was all about?" She glanced around acutely aware that they were alone and in the middle of nowhere.

"I'll tell if you will! Who the fuck are you and don't you dare lie to me!" he shouted.

Katey took a deep breath and sat down on the grass. He stood, pacing in agitation. He was supposed to have kept on driving and not deviate off the route to Key West. This was not part of the plan and he knew they would have to get going soon.

"What do you know?" she asked.

"I know you are Katey Russell because I saw your passport. Your real one, hidden away. When you delivered your little discourse on your Englishness, you gave yourself away too many times in one sentence. Why was that? Everything before then was in prefect English. Too perfect really, if I think about it. Did you want me to find out?"

She shrugged. "Maybe I did, I don't know. But I do love you Giorgio, whatever I started out to do."

He sat next to her. "And what was that?"

"My father is Dominic Russell and he knew your mother and father from years ago, about the time you were born. My parents were together but not happy and I was apparently just a drunken mistake. So imagine how that makes me feel. My father was actually in love with a friend of your mothers, Beth Rogers. My dad told me this story about five years ago, after another event and… "

"What story?"

"Beth was killed by your father, or at least he had her killed. Dad said he was always too much of a coward to kill anyone himself."

"You'd be surprised," Giorgio muttered and let Katey continue.

"Dad always knew the truth but could never prove it. Beth had told him that she was working with the FBI to help them bring down your Family in exchange for a leaner sentence she was serving. I don't know what for, before you ask. Dad never felt it important and I didn't ask him. Anyway, after Beth died, we moved to Dallas. I was about five, I guess but I don't remember."

Katey's sudden American accent felt strange to Giorgio's ears but he said nothing, just let her tell her tale.

"So, the parents split up, I live with Dad, Shelley, my ex-mother moves to California never to be heard of again. Life is okay. I grow up, go to university, meet a guy and fall in love," she paused and looked at Giorgio's impassive face. "I'm being truthful with you, Gio. I want us to have a clean slate, that's why I am telling you this."

He looked at her but hid his disgust. She was only telling him because she had been found out and not because she had had some attack of conscience.

"Anyway," she continued. "The guy I fell in love with, I think you know him – or I should say, knew him. It was Ray Boulter."

Giorgio felt his rage and he stood up to walk away. None of this made any sense to him. He was about to marry the ex-girlfriend of the man who had killed his father? His long-lost cousin?

"I had no idea that Ray knew any of you or was related to any of you. He was having a few beers with my Dad one evening while waiting for me to get home and Dad let it slip that we used to live in Palm Beach and Ray asked if we knew of you. The connection was soon found and both men had a real or imaginary grudge against your family and your dad in particular. They shared it and all the information each other had on you all and over time a plan was hatched to bring you all down."

"And you were part of this? Whoring yourself to me?" Giorgio wanted to hit Katey and it took self-control to step further away from her.

"No, it was never supposed to go that far. Why do you think I turned you down so many times? I just wanted to get close to you and see what I might find out. But then I fell in love with you," she said quietly.

"Hah! Don't make me laugh, Katey! You and Ray hatched up this plan together and…. wait a minute! You are the one who told me where to find him. You must have realised what would happen to him?"

She nodded. "Ray began to get… I don't know, frightening, scary perhaps. He was starting to freak me out. His desire for revenge was eating him up and he changed so much for the worse. I knew he had killed Marco and… "

"You *knew*?" Giorgio punched the tree he had just had Katey up against. His knuckles began to bleed. "You knew that fucker killed my dad and yet you said nothing? You agreed to marry me, knowing what you knew? Did you think I would never find out? Do you know anything about me or my Family and what happens to people who betray us?"

Katey sat in silence, her head bowed in regret. "Yes, I do. That was why I lead you to Ray. I wanted him gone and out of my life and I knew that was one way to do it. To be honest I don't know if I would ever have told you any of this if you hadn't found me out, Gio, I really don't. I just know that I want to marry you."

"And this file you have? Who else knows about it?" He sat beside her, his calm veneer restored.

"No-one. That was just for my own amusement. I was always interested in you and your family; it seems so exciting and romantic almost. The power, the wealth and the respect! When I marry you, no-one will piss me off again!"

Giorgio laughed a little. Katey seemed to have it all worked out.

Now though, Giorgio was unsure what to do. He had a feeling, a gut instinct that she was finally being honest with him and as he looked sideways at her beautiful face he wondered if he could still marry her. Wasn't there some law stopping wives being forced to testify against their husbands? Giorgio was unsure if he had told her anything illegal and Katey hadn't been told who had killed Ray although she knew the group of people who were complicit in his murder. If he married her quick enough, it might be okay.

He stood up. "Come on," he ordered.

Confused, Katey just stared up at him. "Where are we going?"

"You still want to marry me, don't you? Let's get to Key West before it's dark."

They hit the main highway again and Katey relaxed. She had weathered the storm and realised how foolish she had been. She had come far too close to losing Giorgio and much worse, her own life. She would have to tread very carefully in the future to avoid such a situation again and she would do just that. She looked into her future and knew she would never want for anything again, materially, at least but wasn't fool enough to believe that she would always have Giorgio's affections to herself, wife or not – he was and always would be a player.

Giorgio glanced across at her and smiled. He would make her happy every day for the rest of her life. He really did care for her and she was good for him and would keep him in check. As they headed up over another bridge, Giorgio peeked into his rear-view mirror just in time to see the old Cadillac speed up and head for his rear. His reactions weren't quite quick enough to put his foot down and the heap rammed into the back of the Porsche.

"Son of a bitch!" Giorgio shouted and looked for somewhere to pull over but there was nowhere. He realised that the driver of the car behind him had no such thought and was instead speeding up to ram him again.

"Baby, put your seat belt on!" Giorgio shouted to Katey who was now looking scared but she speedily did as she was commanded.

As the two cars collided once more, Giorgio put his foot on the gas pedal in an effort to get away, a simple task in the car he was driving. He would inspect the damage later and someone would be made to pay. As his attention was diverted, he jerked the steering wheel over to get out of the busy lane he was in, but overcompensated at the speed he was now travelling. The barrier at the side of the bridge was torn through as though it was inconsequential material and the car and its two occupants plummeted over the side. The bridge was not a very high one but Giorgio knew the water beneath was deep and as Katey's terrified screams ripped through his mind he wondered if either of them would survive the impact. He heard Katey scream out for him but he couldn't look over at her, unable to respond.

As the deep blue water came up to meet them, Giorgio took a deep breath. He did not have his seat belt on and when the vehicle hit the water, he was thrown clear. The force of the downward maelstrom pulled him under and he seemed to be plummeting right to the gates of hell and for far too long. His lungs began to burn with the effort of not breathing in and he wasn't sure how much longer he might be able to hold his breath for. Seconds later, all of his kicking and his survival instincts began to work and he realised he was heading back to the sunlight and more important, to air. As Giorgio broke the surface, he gasped and sucked in the sweet air. His lungs ached as he looked around for

Katey. He gagged and coughed up salty sea water, trying to take deep breaths as he did so.

Giorgio could see a whirlpool of water and bubbles breaking through where his car and his fiancée had disappeared. He swam over to it and looked up onto the bridge to where he could see a crowd gathering. He shouted as loud as he was able for someone to help him but he knew that no-one would be brave enough to jump.

At least he hoped they wouldn't.

Knowing he had to make this look good, he called out Katey's name and taking another deep breath, he dived back down under the water. He swam down as far as he could. He saw his treasured car bounce off the bottom as its front end hit the sandy ocean floor and in the car, still strapped in was the woman he was about to marry. She was still struggling to get her seatbelt off and she looked over at Giorgio in panic. He did not swim any closer to her but stayed where he was just watching.

Katey realised then that this was it. This 'accident' had been planned and she was meant to die. She only hoped that someone would find the file she had made on the Delvecchios and put two and two together. She looked at Giorgio one last time and breathed in a lungful of salt water.

Giorgio could feel the air in his lungs begin to run out so he kicked for the surface once more.

"Help me!" he shouted up to the crowd on the bridge. He had to make it look good but knew no-one high up on the bridge would be coming to his rescue and even if they did, they would never reach Katey in time. Not now.

He dived once more, a little for appearances but also to make sure that Katey was not going to resurface. As he got to the bottom he could see her motionless body, her eyes staring lifeless at him. He stayed there for as long as his lungs would allow before he swam heavenward one final time.

A boat had appeared on the scene and he was thrown a lifeline. He began to shout in what he hoped was a panicky way.

"My girlfriend – she is still down there!" he gibbered as he was helped on board the little pleasure craft.

A middle aged man in shorts and sunglasses sat Giorgio down on the boat and put a blanket around his shoulders. "She's been down there way too long, son. I'm sorry, but she ain't gonna make it back up here now." The man said this with more sorrow than Giorgio could muster. He was numb. Those sons of bitches could have killed him too!

As they headed for the shore, he was given a shot of whiskey for the shock and by the time they had reached land, the police were waiting and a helicopter had arrived with police divers in board. Giorgio heard a distant splash and he realised that one of the divers had jumped in the water to search, rescue or recover. He knew that they wouldn't find Katey alive now. He had seen her drowned body himself but he looked over the water at the scene where the diver had plummeted into the deep water. Anyone watching Giorgio would think he was just hoping for a miracle, that his girlfriend was going to be pulled from the water alive and that was just the impression Giorgio was trying to give out.

His shoulders slumped as the police walked towards him, knowing he would have to give a brief initial statement. He watched the police change their attitude as he gave his name and he wasn't sure if they were on his side or not, but it didn't matter. He hadn't done anything wrong. Some stranger had rammed his car from behind and his girlfriend had died. He had plenty of witnesses up on the bridge that would validate his story and these two policemen could believe him or they didn't. He didn't care. His shock was genuine. He couldn't believe Gabe would put him in the line of fire, regardless of who Katey was and what she may have done.

"Do you know who may have wanted to harm you or your girlfriend?" The younger of the two policemen asked.

Giorgio couldn't help but laugh. "You know who I am. You know that my father has just been murdered. You must also know that a lot of people want me dead just because of my surname so you figure it out. The Caddy that rammed me – there was an altercation at the stop light before Islamorada, just engine revving and the like. I paid no attention to it or the driver because when you drive a Porsche, you get that a lot. I guess I just pissed the wrong guy off," he shrugged. It was the best he could come up with and the police seemed to be satisfied with his explanation, at least for the time being. Giorgio hoped that the Caddy was clean away and he hadn't dropped someone in it. Tough, after what they had just put him through.

It was suggested that Giorgio go to the local hospital to be checked out but he refused, saying he wanted to stay here until Katey was found. He played the part of grieving boyfriend very well and sat at the water's edge, watching as a police boat was manoeuvred into position at the site and soon after, Giorgio was aware that they had freed Katey and were bringing her up. There was a flurry of activity on and around the police boat before it sped off taking Katey away and Giorgio knew he ought to find out where they were taking her. He still needed to play the grieving boyfriend for a while longer yet. Some of his grief was genuine.

He meandered back and forth along the shoreline just looking out across the water. Everything had happened so fast he hadn't had time to come to terms with the events and to adjust to life without Katey. He almost wished he had never found those newspaper clippings yesterday that were under her bed and maybe everything would be fine. He would still have that gorgeous, incredibly sexy woman in his life. She had said she loved him, that they were still to get married so surely they could have moved past this? If only he hadn't called Gabe and got him involved so damn fast!

"Hey." Gabe's familiar voice called out to him.

Giorgio turned and saw the man who, apart from his father, was always there to tidy up after him, whatever the mess and whatever the consequences. Giorgio knew then that there had been no alternative to what had happened.

Gabe walked down the small beach to meet Giorgio and put his arm around his shoulders. "You okay?" He seemed genuinely concerned and also relieved that Giorgio was okay, on the outside at least.

Giorgio shrugged. "I'm not sure how I found myself at the bottom of the ocean," he said to let Gabe know he was not impressed with the termination order.

Gabe looked around surreptitiously and shrugged. "We don't know what Katey knew and had to make it look good."

"Katey knew a little but she told no-one else. Her little file was just for her eyes and nobody else has a copy and no-one else is going to."

"Ah-huh. And you know this how?"

"We had a nice little chat and she told me everything. I have no reason not to believe what she told me was the truth. The file was in my bag in the back seat of my car. I doubt it will readable if anyone should care enough to try once the sea water has done its thing down there. It would probably just look like a college project."

Gabe looked long and hard at Giorgio. "Are you having regrets?"

Giorgio shook his head. He knew that this was the only way. He knew that once a trust had been broken, it was extremely hard although not impossible to get it back. This way, the Family would live to fight another day.

"So I guess this is going to prove everyone right about me?" he asked.

"In what way?" Gabe asked in a faraway tone. He was looking for a police officer to ask if he could take Giorgio away and back home. The boy had been through enough and they needed to talk away from prying eyes and wrong ears.

"Stupid kid gets into trouble yet again. Grown-ups have to wade in and sort out the mess." Giorgio sounded angry and Gabe assumed the anger was aimed inwards.

Gabe laughed. "You're a kid, Gio and you still have a lot to learn regardless of what you believe," he paused in thought. "Can I be honest with you? I don't understand why you are getting so uptight about this Vinnie thing. No-one, and I mean no-one takes over this business at the age that you are now. Your dad was twenty-eight and he would be the first to admit he made a lot of mistakes because he was too young and inexperienced. He tried to kill your mother, for Christsakes! That was the pinnacle of his idiocy and inexperience."

"But… "

"There are no buts, Gio. Your uncle has offered to take up your apprenticeship in order for your education to continue and when you are twenty-five, a decision will be made to see if you are ready to take over. As long as you stay out of trouble, and I mean kid-trouble, and you carry on learning as you have been, I can foresee no reason why you can't be head of this Family. It is all in your hands, Gio and only you can fuck it up."

They both went silent as a policeman came over to say they could leave now that Giorgio's statement had been taken but that they would stay in touch. Giorgio and Gabe headed for Gabe's car parked up on a side road. Gabe started for home and they drove in silence for a while.

"Vinnie wants everything my father ever had."

Gabe smiled. "No. He just wants your mother and nothing anyone says or does will stop that if it's what she wants too. He won't be head of this Family forever, it's not what Marco wanted, and it sure as hell isn't what I want," he looked across at Giorgio to see if he understood. "You get me, Gio?"

The younger man nodded. "I think so."

"You get to make decisions, but Vinnie has to sanction them, that's all. If he deems it the right thing to do, it will be done. He will want to please you as pleasing you will make Sarah happy. Someone will always be covering your back, Gio."

"Do you have my back, Gabe?"

He laughed. "Always have done. Why do you think I am here today, helping you out?"

"I've behaved pretty dumb over this whole Vinnie thing, haven't I? My dad always relied on you and I guess I can too."

"Of course you can and don't ever forget that. In five years time, I'll still have your back. It's pretty much a done deal but you have to trust me too."

Giorgio smiled and sat back in the seat. He looked out of the window as the Keys flashed by him, not seeing anything but his future.

And in an instant, it seemed okay.

Printed in Poland
by Amazon Fulfillment
Poland Sp. z o.o., Wrocław

62644252R00136